ALSO BY LEILA SALES

Mostly Good Girls

past PERFECT

LEILA SALES

Simon Pulse

New York London Toronto Sydney New Delhi

SIMON PULSE
An imprint of Simon & Schuster Children's Publishing Division
1230 Avenue of the Americas, New York, NY 10020
First Simon Pulse paperback edition May 2012
Copyright © 2011 by Leila Sales

For information about special discounts for bulk purchases, please contact
Simon & Schuster Special Sales at 1-866-506-1949 or business@simonandschuster.com.
The Simon & Schuster Speakers Bureau can bring authors to your live event. For more
information or to book an event contact the Simon & Schuster Speakers Bureau
at 1-866-248-3049 or visit our website at www.simonspeakers.com.
Designed by Mike Rosamilia
The text of this book was set in ITC Baskerville.
Manufactured in the United States of America
2 4 6 8 10 9 7 5 3 1
The Library of Congress has cataloged the hardcover edition as follows:
Sales, Leila
Past perfect / Leila Sales.— 1st Simon Pulse hardcover ed.
p. cm.
Summary: Sixteen-year-old Chelsea knows what to expect when she returns for a summer of historical
reenactment at Colonial Essex Village until she learns that her ex-boyfriend is working there, too, and then
meets the very attractive Dan who works at a rival historical village.
ISBN 978-1-4424-0682-7 (hc)
[1. Interpersonal relations—Fiction. 2. Dating (Social customs)—Fiction. 3. Historical reenactments—Fiction.
4. Summer employment—Fiction. 5. New England—Fiction.] I. Title.
PZ7.S15215 Pas 2011
[Fic]—dc23
2011025811
ISBN 978-1-4424-0683-4 (pbk)
ISBN 978-1-4424-0684-1 (eBook)

*Dedicated to my parents,
with all my love*

past **PERFECT**

And I've been standing on the same spot now since it's been over.

—Shout Out Louds

A dreaded sunny day, so I meet you at the cemetery gates.

—The Smiths

CONTENTS

Chapter 1
THE SUMMER

There are only three types of kids who get summer jobs at Colonial Essex Village instead of just working at the mall, like the normal people do.

Type one: history nerds. People who memorized all the battles of the Revolutionary War by age ten; who can, and will, tell you how many casualties were sustained at Bunker Hill; who hotly debate the virtues of bayonets over pistols. They are mostly pale-skinned, reedy, acne-scarred boys in glasses (unless they can't find a pair of historically accurate glasses and are forced to get contacts). I don't know if they were born so unappealing, and turned to history for companionship because they realized they were too grotesque to attract real-life friends, *or* if their love of history came first, and maybe they could have turned out hot, but instead they invested all their energy in watching twelve-hour documentaries about battleships. It's a chicken-or-the-egg type of question.

The second type are the drama kids. The drama kids are not so interested in authentic battle techniques, but they are *super* interested in dressing up like minutemen. And they are interested in staging chilling scenes in which they get fake-shot and fall to the ground, bellowing, "Hark! I'm wounded! Oh, what cruelty is this?" even when the history nerds grouch because that is not how it happened at all, and, in fact, no soldiers were wounded during the Battle of Blah Blah Blah.

The third reason for a teenager to work at Essex would be if her parents work there. Which is why I do it. Because my dad is the Essex Village silversmith, and my mom is the silversmith's wife, and I am the silversmith's daughter.

The silversmith is the guy who makes silverware and jewelry, and also sometimes he does dental work like fillings. Paul Revere was a silversmith, too, as my dad likes to remind me, when he's trying to make me value his profession. Silversmiths play an important role in society, or at least they did in the 1700s.

Thanks to my dad's career, I've worked at Essex since I was six years old. Well, I wasn't technically employed for the first few years, since I did it for free. It was more like Take Your Child to Work Day every day, except that I had to wear a historically accurate costume of tiny boots, petticoats, a pinafore, and a bonnet.

When I turned twelve, I started getting paid—not a whole lot, but nothing to turn up my nose at either, especially since the only other jobs available to twelve-year-olds in my town are being a mother's helper or trying to sell baked goods on street corners. And the baked goods market is really saturated. So historical reenactment was a solid gig for a while, and I had more independent income than anyone else in my middle school. I used it to buy a trampoline.

But now that it's nearly the end of junior year, I'm sixteen years old, which means I'm legally employable. I can finally get a real job at a real place. A place where my coworkers won't spend their lunch breaks debating who would have won the Revolutionary War if the French never got involved; where I can wear shorts instead of floor-length skirts; where might even be *air conditioning*. Also and most importantly: a place where my parents don't work.

Don't get me wrong, I love my parents and all. But my father and I have the sort of loving relationship in which, whenever he says more than one sentence in a row to me, I want to stab myself in the heart with a recently formed silver knife.

"So obviously what we want to do this summer," I said to my best friend, Fiona, "is work at the mall."

"Yeah . . ." Fiona said in a tone that meant *No*. We were having this conversation over ice cream in her kitchen, a few weeks before school let out for the year. Fiona and I had recently decided to devote the summer to becoming ice cream connoisseurs. Which essentially meant that we were going to eat as much ice cream as possible, and then discuss it intelligently and rate it on qualities such as "flavor" and "texture."

"We *could* work at the mall," Fiona said. "Or, instead of that, here's another idea: We could work at Essex."

I sighed. "Fi—"

"*Think* about it," she said.

"Trust me, I've thought about it for the past ten years. Working at Essex is not really that fun," I tried to explain to her. "It's like going to family camp, only you have to be in character all the time, and strangers watch you and ask questions."

"I actually love being in character," Fiona reminded me. "And I love having strangers watch me."

Fiona is a drama kid, and she's *good.* She can belt out songs, and she emanates this confidence that just commands attention when she's onstage. You can't help but watch her. To top it off, she's tall and willowy with waist-length chestnut-brown hair and catlike green eyes. I will be surprised if Fiona *doesn't* grow up to be a famous actress.

Fiona and I have never spent a summer together because she's gone to the Catskills for theater camp every year since we were little. But this past fall Ms. Warren lost her job, which meant some corners had to be cut. And theater camp was corner number one.

"How about we work at The Limited?" I suggested. "If you want, we could pretend to be characters who work at The Limited. And strangers will watch us fold shirts and stuff."

Over her bowl of mint chocolate chip, Fiona argued, "But if we work at Essex, I can have some romantic historical name, like Prudence or Chastity."

"Your name is already *Fiona*," I said.

"Chastity Adams," she continued dreamily.

"Your name is already *Fiona Warren*." Fiona's ancestors legitimately moved from England to the Colonies back in the days when there were Colonies. She doesn't have to *pretend* that's her story—it *is* her story. Plus, she is not particularly prudent or chaste.

"It'll be like living in *Pride and Prejudice*!" she said.

"Wrong century."

"Really? When's *Pride and Prejudice*?"

"Eighteen hundreds."

"Isn't that when Essex is set?"

"No. Really, Fi? I've worked there for the entire time you've known me—*you* want to work there—and you don't even know when it takes place?"

"Just tell me?" Fiona widened her eyes and pouted a little.

"I'll give you a hint: *Colonial* Essex Village."

She hazarded a guess. "Seventeen hundreds?"

"1774. Two years before the Declaration of Independence. Immediately before the First Continental Congress."

"You sound like a history nerd! Anyway, what does it matter? The past is the past. It's all kind of the same."

Fiona is not dumb, by the way. She's just an *actress*. Stories, emotions, people: that stuff interests her. Dates and facts leave her cold.

"Look, Chelsea," she said. "I promise this year won't be like every other summer. It will be two months of you and me running around together in beautiful old-fashioned dresses. You won't have to spend the whole time locked in the silversmith's studio with your parents. We can ask for a station together! Like at the stables or something! Nat says all the cool kids work at the stables."

It was obvious that Fiona had never been gainfully employed before, since she seemed to envision it as a constant *Gone with the Wind* experience, minus the death and destruction.

"We're not allowed to work at the stables," I explained. "We're girls. Girls didn't muck out horse stalls in 1774. Also, is this really just about Nat Dillon? Is that why you're so into this Essex job?"

Nat Dillon always plays Romeo to Fiona's Juliet, Hamlet to Fiona's Ophelia, the Beast to Fiona's Beauty. Occasionally they hook up in real life. The rest of the time they only stage-kiss. My theory is that Fiona wants to take things to the next level—like, the level where Nat is her boyfriend—but she's in denial about that. She shook her head and said, "I want to work at Essex because it will be good for my *acting career*, and because we can do it together. And, fine, the presence of cute boys doesn't hurt."

"There are no cute boys at Essex," I said. "With the possible exception of Nat Dillon, and that's only if you're into long hair." Nat wears his hair in a ponytail. He's always lovingly combing his fingers through it. Don't ask. "Everyone else there is ineligible. Trust me. I've grown up with most of them."

"Your problem is that you hate true love," Fiona said, clearing our bowls. "And I give this mint chocolate chip a six. The chocolate chips are strong, but the mint part should be mintier. Dyeing ice cream green does not actually make it taste any more like mint."

"Five point five," I said. "The mint part is the important part, and any ice cream manufacturer who doesn't under-stand that is a sociopath." As ice cream connoisseurs, we are extremely discerning. "And it's not that I *hate* true love. It's just that I don't believe it exists. Especially not at Essex. I can't see hating something that isn't even real. That's like hating centaurs or natural blondes."

"How many times do we have to go over this?" Fiona heaved a sigh. "Just because Ezra Gorman turned out not to be the love of your life doesn't mean there *is* no love of your life. It just means it wasn't *him*."

Fiona has been coaching me through my breakup with

Ezra for weeks. She was really good at it for about three days. Then she got bored and now mostly just says things like, "Are you still not over that?"

"If you work with me at Essex this summer, I promise you that I will find you true love." Fiona took my hands in hers and stared earnestly into my eyes.

I snorted.

"You will learn to love again," Fiona continued, sounding like a movie trailer voice-over.

And at that, I totally lost it. "Okay, fine, Crazy Girl," I said through giggles. "Let's do it."

But I want it to go on record that I didn't say yes because of the true love thing. I said yes because there was no point to working at The Limited if Fiona wouldn't be there with me.

Chapter 2
THE MODERNERS

To help her adjust to life at Colonial Essex Village, I made Fiona a list of the questions that visitors were most likely to ask her. I am, after all, an expert.

This was my list:

1. "Where's the bathroom?"

This is far and away the most common question. You don't actually need any sort of historical knowledge to work at Essex. You just have to know where the nearest toilet is.

What you are *supposed* to do, when moderners ask for the bathroom, is feign confusion. "A room for a bath?" you're supposed to say. "We don't have one of those! Why, we take only a couple baths each year! We have a wash basin, if you would like to use that."

Eventually, if they look like they're going to pee their pants, you can say, "Oh, do you by any chance mean the privy?"

And they, crossing their legs, are like, "Yes! Oh my God, the privy, please!"

And then you say, "It's in the visitors' center in Merchants Square." And then they run off as fast as possible.

I go through that whole charade when I'm in a bad mood, or when my parents are listening. The rest of the time I just give them directions right off the bat. It's not their fault that they're moderners.

2. "Don't you get hot in those clothes?"

True answer: yes. Of course you get freaking hot. It's the middle of a sunshiny day in summertime in Virginia, and you are decked out in lace-up boots, floor-length petticoats, a skirt over the petticoats, a long-sleeved gown over the skirt, and a mobcap. You can't go swimming or eat ice cream or even carry around a modern water bottle. *Of course you are hot.*

But what you have to say is, "No! This is just how we dress. There is no way to be any cooler in the summertime without exposing your legs, which a lady would *never* do." You have to say that, because that is historically accurate.

3. "What's your name? Are you Abigail Adams?"

No. There is only one Abigail Adams at Essex, and she's been Abigail Adams for the past twenty years, and she takes her role *very* seriously. She got special speech coaching so she even talks like they did in Colonial times—or what we think they talked like, since they did not (surprise!) have tape recorders then. If you ever told a moderner that you were, indeed, John Adams's wife, then you can be sure that the real Abigail Adams would get you fired, possibly after first breaking both your kneecaps.

My real name is Chelsea Glaser, but no one was named Chelsea Glaser in the Colonies. My Colonial name is Elizabeth Connelly, and, since I've gone by that every summer for most of my life, I respond to it just as if it were real. I chose "Elizabeth Connelly" because it's Irish sounding, and, with my dark hair and blue eyes and freckles, I could pass for Black Irish. It's all a lie, though. My actual ancestors were Ukrainian Jews, and I have never been to Ireland at all. I don't even like St. Patrick's Day.

4. "Is that real?" (Asked while pointing at anything at all.)

Of course, everything in Essex is *real*, but what the moderners are actually asking is, "Is that really preserved from Colonial times?"

A handy guide:

Things that are real: all the buildings, the furniture inside the buildings, the gravestones, the weapons, the portraits in the Governor's Palace.

Things that aren't real but look like they are: our clothes, the items sold in the gift shop, the materials that my dad or the blacksmith or the basketmaker uses, all of us employees.

Things that aren't real and don't look it: the parking lot.

If a moderner asks you whether something is "real" and you're not sure, err on the safe side and say yes. Even if the item in question isn't from 1774, it's still probably from 1997 or something, which means that it was still made in the past.

5. Most people just want to know your name, whether you're overheated, and where they can find the nearest toilet. But some people also want you to know that they are really, really good at Colonial history. They blindside you with questions like, "I'm looking for the grave of Jebediah Winthrop. What? You don't know who Jebediah Winthrop is? The man who modified quill pens so they could write at a forty-five-degree angle? He's buried here, in Essex! How do you not know where his grave is?"

You're never going to be able to answer these people's questions, and that is okay, since they don't actually want answers. They just want to impress you with how unbelievably smart they are. And they want a fresh audience for their stories, since everyone they know is, for some reason, sick of hearing them babble on about Jebediah Winthrop.

Those are pretty much the only questions people ask Colonials. If they want you to tell them anything else, just make it up. They will believe you, because you are wearing a costume.

Chapter 3
THE EX-BOYFRIEND

*E*ssex does not waste a goddamn minute. The last day of school was Friday, June 25th, and then I had all of three hours to rejoice in my newfound freedom before it was time for Fiona to pick me up for Summer Staff Orientation.

"We're seniors now!" Fiona shouted over the blaring loud-speakers in her car. "Helloooo, world!" She took both her hands off the steering wheel and waved them in the air.

Like I said, when Ms. Warren lost her job, some corners had to be cut. But those corners did not include the cherry-red convertible that was Fiona's sixteenth birthday present.

"I already feel different," Fiona said as we cruised down the wide, tree-lined drive toward Essex. "More capable, more mature. I have a *job*, for example. I am a wage earner."

"I'm just glad this year's over," I said, sticking my arm out the window, letting my fingers drag through the wind as it rushed past. "I couldn't be readier for summer."

Junior year had been hard. Well, not all of it. During the winter, I had been dating Ezra, and that was easy. Dating Ezra was so easy. But he broke up with me on April 17th, and everything since then had been hard. Choosing what to wear every day, knowing he might see me, was hard. Taking notes in Latin class, knowing he was sitting three rows behind me, was hard. Walking into the cafeteria, knowing I wasn't going to sit with him, was hard. I went to this school before dating Ezra, and I stayed in this school after dating Ezra, but somehow, in those five months that we were together, everything in that place became infused with a little bit of Ezra-ness. There was nothing I could do there, nowhere I could go without being reminded of him, and of us.

Ezra had nothing to do with Colonial Essex Village, and for that I was glad. It's hard to get over someone when you still have to see him every day.

Fiona parked in the lot just as my parents were walking to their car. It was six o'clock, so they had finished work for the day. They had only partially changed out of their Colonial costumes, so my dad was wearing buckle shoes, breeches, and a Washington Nationals T-shirt.

"Hi, Mr. and Mrs. Glaser!" Fiona chirped.

"Hi, girls!" Mom gave me a big hug. "How was the last day of school?"

I shrugged. Fiona and I go to a charter school, which maybe sounds fancy, but it's just school, like any other place. All it takes to get in are halfway-involved parents and halfway-decent grades. It just has a higher college acceptance rate than my town's public high school, that's all.

"Well, *I* had an excellent day," Dad informed us. "I had a long conversation with a professor from Stanford who's writing a comparative paper on the gravesites of all the signers of the Declaration. Fascinating!"

Dad loves talking to professors because he used to want to be one himself. He grew up in Wisconsin, a state wholly unconnected to the American Revolution, before moving east to get his degree in history. There he discovered the irresistible appeal of Colonial reenactment, and boom, that was the end of his career in academia.

"Are you excited for orientation?" Mom asked Fiona and me.

Fiona nodded, but I just shrugged again. Orientation is always a long-winded speech by Mr. Zelinsky, Essex's director, and then a whole brunch of dos and don'ts. Like, *do* greet moderners with a smile. *Don't* tell them that, in Colonial times, parents used to whip their children, and so now all young visitors to Essex are whipped in a historically accurate fashion. That's what the apothecary a couple years ago used to tell kids, before he got fired for drinking on the job, and for keeping actual laudanum in his fake laudanum bottles.

"Well, *I'm* excited to have our junior interpreters back," Mom said. "It's been lonely without all of you. Just a bunch of us old fogies."

"Denise," Dad called, jingling his car keys. "It's getting near dinnertime. Let the girls go to their meeting." My father does not have a lot of patience for small talk, unless he is the one small-talking.

"All right, all right." Mom hugged us both again. "What time will you be home tonight?"

"Oh," I said. Fiona and I exchanged a glance. "We might go out after orientation. You know, with some friends or whatever."

"Just call if you'll be out past eleven," Mom said.

"It's summertime!" I objected.

"Okay, call if you'll be out past midnight."

Then Dad yelled "Denise!" again, and they left us.

"Do they really not know?" Fiona asked in a low voice as she and I walked through the main gate.

"All the grown-ups here act like they don't know. They must have some idea, though. They can't be *that* clueless."

"I'm so ready for it," Fiona said, getting a skip in her step. "I've never been in a *war* before. I've had to listen to you talk about how awesome this War is for years, and now I *finally* get to play."

"Shut up," I muttered. "There's Mr. Zelinsky."

Fiona's mouth formed an O before she snapped her lips shut.

The director stood greeting new employees as they filed into the church. The church is a big, white clapboard building filled with pews, perfect for staff meetings.

"Elizabeth Connelly!" Mr. Zelinsky boomed, crunching my body in a hug. He's a tiny man with an oversized voice and an oversized attitude. "So charmed to have you join us again for yet another tremendous summer. Your mother tells me you considered deserting us this year! For the 'mall'?" He also has this way of saying modern words like they're some crazy slang that he's never heard before.

"Oh, well . . ." I shrugged.

"Miss Connelly, Miss Connelly." He took me by the shoulders and slowly swayed me back and forth. "Simply put, we could not do it without you. No one knows this place like you do, I daresay not even myself."

"Glad to be back, Mr. Z," I told him, which actually, now that I was there, felt true. The air at Essex smells fresher than the air anywhere else. There's something about it that just feels like home.

"And, prithee, miss, remind me your name."

Mr. Zelinsky gave a small bow to Fiona, who didn't miss a beat. "Fiona," she said, dropping only a mini-curtsy, since her jean skirt had about as much fabric as a headband. "Fiona Warren. But I want to go by Temperance."

I snorted. Fiona has no sense of temperance.

"Of course," Mr. Zelinsky said smoothly. "Welcome to Essex!" And he ushered us into the church.

It took my eyes a moment to adjust to the dim interior lighting. The first few rows of pews were filled with junior interpreters, mostly middle- and high-schoolers. I knew a lot of them from previous summers at Essex, or even a couple of them from school, but there were some new faces too.

"Hi, Chelsea!" a bunch of people greeted me when we walked in.

"Let's go sit with Nat." Fiona steered me toward Nat Dillon, who was instantly recognizable, even from behind, by his long, flaxen ponytail. I don't know what my best friend sees in him. I guess he's nice and smart and they have similar interests and whatever. But, I don't know, ponytails are just a deal breaker for me.

"Hey, Chelsea. Hey, Fi." Nat and his friend, Bryan Denton, scooched down the bench so we could sit. "Happy summer!"

"I know, right? Best day ever." Fiona scraped her long, thick hair off her back and piled it on top of her head. Nat did the same. Honestly, those two.

"We were just discussing tactics for the War," Bryan told me.

I loathe everything about Bryan. For one, he is the sort of person who not even kidding uses the word "tactics" in casual conversation. He was the youngest person ever to get a job at Essex without his parents already working there. The summer after fourth grade, his parents went to Mr. Zelinsky and were like, "We're sick of buying season passes to this historical village every single year. Will you please just let our son work here. We will pay you." Bryan is clingy and toadlike, and also his teeth are crooked because he refuses to get braces because they would be anachronistic. For some reason, Bryan harbors an enormous crush on me, even though I have never done anything to encourage this. In fact, whenever possible, I act to *discourage* it.

For example, now I said, "You know the rules. No talking about the War where the bosses can hear."

"But I had a really great idea! For a tactic!" Bryan persisted, bouncing a little in the pew. "I was reading in *Essex: An Extended History* that there's a woman buried in the graveyard here who gave birth to *twenty-two* children. Only three of them were stillborns. Medical scientists theorize that her uterine lining was twice as thick as the average woman's. She died of smallpox, ultimately, in 1748 . . ." Bryan is also the sort of person who unabashedly remarks on dead women's uterine linings.

Now, how this information was going to help us win a War, I could not imagine, in part because I had stopped paying attention. I saw someone on the other side of the church who looked like Ezra, and I can't pay attention to anything when a person who looks like Ezra pops up.

Whenever I see a guy who resembles my ex-boyfriend, here is what happens:

1. I stop listening to whoever is talking to me.
   Or, if I'm the one talking, I just fade into silence
   without even noticing. Maybe I will keep nodding
   and smiling, but I'm not really there.
2. I develop this intense tunnel vision where all I can
   see is the Ezra look-alike, in stark relief, and everything else blurs off to the sides.
3. I stop breathing, which, in turn, means that
4. I get dizzy.
5. I start sweating.
6. My neck and chest turn all red and blotchy.
7. Then, once I realize that the guy in question is
   not actually Ezra, I start breathing again, and I get
   this huge rush of adrenaline that almost makes me
   vomit. And then I try to get back into whatever
   conversation I was in, before I briefly disappeared
   into psycho-freak-ex-girlfriend land.

My problem is that Ezra is of average height and average
build, he has brown hair, and he likes to wear jeans. So I
have one of these panic attacks pretty much every time I see
a boy, unless he is really tall or really short or obviously my
dad or something.

When I saw this Ezra look-alike in the church as Mr. Zelinsky
took the pulpit to begin orientation, I went through steps
one through six. But I couldn't quite get to the final step

(the one where I notice the guy is not Ezra and almost throw up), because it really seemed like . . . I mean, this guy really *could* be . . .

"Fiona," I whispered, trying to breathe like a human being. "That guy over there. In the second row. Is that . . . Um . . ." Deep inhalation. "Is that Ezra?"

Fiona flicked me with her hair as she looked over, then flicked me again as she turned back to me. "Yes," she said.

I clutched the pew and sunk down low so that he wouldn't see me. "What is he doing here?" I whispered.

"Uh, working here, probably," Fiona answered with a shrug. "Unless he likes to hang out at staff orientation meetings for fun. Chelsea, you know you have, like, red things all over your neck right now, right?"

"You know you're, like, the worst best friend in the world right now, right?" I snapped back.

Fiona arched her eyebrows in surprise. "Whoa there, killer. What's wrong? It's been ages. You see him every day at school. You never act like it's a big deal then."

"Of course it's not a big deal. It is a very small deal. It's just different," I said, shielding my eyes and turning my head to look in the opposite direction from him. "It's different when I'm not . . . prepared for it."

"You guys talking about Gorman?" Nat asked, jutting his chin toward Ezra.

"No," I answered, at the same time that Fiona said, "Yes,"

in part because she is the worst best friend in the world, but mostly because she will say yes to anything Nat Dillon asks her.

"I do not respect that guy," Bryan said fiercely.

"You don't respect that guy because he got to date Chelsea and you didn't," Fiona pointed out in a brief moment of wisdom.

Bryan opened his mouth to make what I'm sure would have been an appalling retort, but, thankfully, Mr. Zelinsky began his remarks at that moment.

"Young ladies and gentlemen!" he said. "Welcome to the forty-ninth summer of Colonial Essex Village. Though time has passed in the outside world since Essex was first added to the National Register of Historic Places, here it remains always and forever the summer of 1774. Unrest is brewing— King George has recently passed the Intolerable Acts, and it will not be long before war breaks out."

There was some rustling throughout the room at the word "war," and Fiona and Bryan both elbowed me at the same time, jostling my body between them. Mr. Zelinsky didn't notice.

"Indeed, this is a difficult time to be a Patriot, but it is a difficult time to be a Loyalist, as well. Difficult, yet thrilling! We stand upon a precipice from which we dare not fall. And it is in that milieu that we all will live for the next ten weeks. I am pleased to see so many returning faces, as well as many new ones. But for all of you, new and old, I want to be clear that your primary responsibility this summer is to make all of our guests feel that they have truly stepped back in time. Make them believe that the past is, in fact, their present.

"Who would care to explain to all of us just *why* the study of history is so important?"

A lot of hands shot into the air—Bryan's first, of course.

"History is important because it's all events that really happened and if we don't study it then we won't know what really happened," Bryan announced.

Sometimes—let me say *most* times—Bryan does not have anything wise to contribute. He just can't pass up the opportunity to talk.

Mr. Zelinsky slid his gaze over to me. "Anything to add, Miss Connelly?"

I am Mr. Zelinsky's plant in the audience. After so many years, there is no part of his orientation speech that I don't know by heart. I rattled off, "It's important to study history because those who do not learn from the past are doomed to repeat it."

Mr. Zelinsky nodded at me, and Bryan mumbled, "That's what I said." Then orientation continued with instructions for what time we had to report to work every day, and where we could eat lunch, and when to pick up our costumes, and on and on, but I didn't bother to pay attention. Ezra was sitting a few rows away. *Why was he here? How* dare *he be here?*

At last, Mr. Zelinsky concluded his speech. "I look forward

to seeing you in costume and ready to go on Monday!" A couple other administrators handed out thick handbooks of Essex policies and historical facts. We all streamed out of the church before Mr. Zelinsky had even left the pulpit. Why would you take thirty kids who *just* finished school for the year and then make them sit still and listen to a lecture? I ask you.

We all headed "to the parking lot, to get our cars." That was our cover story, if anyone asked us, which no one would, since Essex is deserted by Friday night. Of course, all of us junior interpreters knew we weren't really going to our cars.

Really we were going to War.

Chapter 4
THE ENEMY

$\mathcal{L}$ ike anyone else, we have our enemies. Of course, we have our enemies.

My father once explained it to me like this: If you're going to open a new restaurant, you might think you'd want to open that restaurant on a block where there are no other dining options. But, actually, the savvy business strategy is to open your restaurant in a neighborhood with *lots* of other restaurants. Then this area will become an eating-out *destination*, and your restaurant will get more traffic. This is why clothing stores are in malls, where there are lots of other clothing stores. This is why there are three ice cream shops on High Street, and none anywhere else in my town. This is why Universal

Studios theme park is a few miles away from Disneyland. And this is why Civil War Reenactmentland is across the street from Colonial Essex Village.

Yes, I am serious. There is a Civil War living history village. *Directly across the street from my living history village.*

We hate them, obviously. We hate them and their more technologically advanced rifles and their non-tricornered hats. My dad hates them most of all, although sometimes he will concede, as he stands at the edge of Colonial Essex and stares across the road at Civil War Reenactmentland, "Well, it was an inspired business plan. I have to give them that. Inspired." Then he will keep watching it for a while, tapping his silver-tipped cane on the ground, before eventually muttering, "Assholes," and retreating to his silversmith workshop.

My dad, much as he hates Civil War Reenactmentland, does not actively fight back. But we do. This is the War that has been raging between the Colonial Essex junior interpreters and the Civil War junior interpreters, summer after summer, for as many years as I've worked here. There's a ceasefire every Labor Day, and then it restarts with a vengeance the following June. Unlike the Revolutionary War or the Civil War, ours is a War that will never end.

Virginia played a major role in early American history, so it makes sense that there would be a number of different living history museums in my state. But there is no reason why they have to be in the same very small *town*.

After we left the staff orientation meeting and walked to the parking lot, and after we'd made sure that Mr. Zelinsky and all the other administrators were nowhere to be seen, everyone scurried through the trees and down toward the brook. It was a dark, clear night, with countless stars overhead. Some people built a campfire, and others produced marshmallows, graham crackers, and chocolate from their purses, and we all crowded around to roast s'mores.

Fiona offered me a stick, but I shook my head. My stomach felt tight, and it got worse every time I looked at Ezra, who was sitting across the fire from me, not looking at me. Not like he *purposely* wasn't looking at me, because even that would have meant something, would have meant he thought or cared something about me. But this was like . . . he just didn't notice me.

Fiona's back was toward me as she faced the campfire, and I felt suddenly trapped on the outside of this circle of people. I tapped her on the shoulder. "I'm going to talk to him," I said.

"Who?" Fiona asked. "Oh, shoot." Her marshmallow had caught on fire.

"Who do you think?" I said.

She turned around, blowing on her charred marshmallow. "Really, Chelsea? Tell me, is it August seventh yet?"

I rolled my eyes at her.

"I'm sort of getting this vibe," Fiona went on, "like maybe it's not August seventh yet. But that might be just my opinion."

When Ezra broke up with me, Fiona told me that I was not allowed to talk to him again. I asked, *"Ever?"* and she said, "No. Just not for three and a half months." Then she marked the date in her phone.

Now she whipped her phone out of her skirt pocket, checked its calendar, and said, "It looks like, hmm, about forty-three days until you're allowed to talk to him."

"Fiona, August seventh is a completely arbitrary time constraint."

"Absolutely." She bobbed her head up and down. "It is an arbitrary time constraint. So what's your point?"

"I will talk to him for one minute," I promised. "Less than one minute. Just don't watch."

She bit into her marshmallow and its innards oozed down her chin. "Good luck."

I slowly walked around the campfire to where Ezra stood, and I placed myself directly in front of him, so he had to look at me. I refused to speak to him first, though. I have my pride. My pride is small and halting and bitter, but I have it.

"Hey, Chelsea." He gave me a polite smile, like we were *coworkers.*

The inside of my mouth felt cottony as I said, "What are you doing here, Ezra?"

The smile faded off his face. "I got a job here."

"I know that. I can *see* that. I mean . . . *why* did you get a job here? You knew that I work here."

He furrowed his eyebrows, looking puzzled in the light of the fire and the stars. "Last time we talked about it, you said you wanted to work at the mall this summer. You said you were through with Essex."

And is this sad, that my heart felt a little bigger, hearing him acknowledge that once we had talked, once he had listened to me say what I wanted to do over the summer? "But even if that were true, Ezra," I said, "Essex is *my* place. It's mine. You don't see me joining the boys' soccer team or the school paper, do you?"

"Well, I wouldn't stop you if you wanted to." He grinned at me. When I didn't grin back, he sighed. "Chelsea, I don't see what the big deal is. We'll probably run into each other even less here than we do at school. I'm not going to cramp your style. Promise. We're friends, right? We never stopped being friends."

This had been one of Ezra's big things when he broke up with me: how he still *liked* me, and liked spending time with me, and didn't want to lose our friendship, and whatever. Except that we had never been friends before we started dating, so I'm not sure what exactly he was talking about. Anyway, I had said fine, so then we became the sort of friends who never talk or hang out.

That was all I really remembered from our breakup

conversation. The rest of it, I just didn't like to think about.

"Look," he said, "I was working at a coffee shop on weekends—"

"I know," I said. "The Diamond Café. I *know*." It killed me to hear him act like this, like we were strangers.

"Right, but The Diamond Café closed down, and I needed a summer job, and Lenny said he could get me something here. So, I don't know, here I am. But if it really bothers you, Chelsea, I can quit. I don't want to make you unhappy. If this is making you unhappy, just say the word, and I'll take off."

I didn't know what to say to that. Ezra had *already* made me unhappy, and I guessed his working at Essex couldn't make that any better or worse. And I wasn't going to make him quit his job just because we broke up two months ago and I couldn't handle it. Because I should be over this. Obviously, I should be over this. So I shrugged and said, "It's fine. Just stay out of my way," and walked away. We are always drawing battle lines, between Patriots and Redcoats, between Civil War reenactors and Colonial reenactors, between Ezra and me.

"Everyone! Eyes front!" Tawny Nelson hollered, clambering up on a large rock.

Tawny is our General in the War this year. It was an obvious choice: she just finished her senior year, she's worked at Essex for ages, and she's clearly a warrior. I would not want to mess with Tawny Nelson. Last year she led a raid on Reenactmentland that successfully captured their Confederate flag. I don't know how she managed to do this without getting caught. That flag is always flying over there. Like, what did she do, scale their flagpole? In broad daylight?

Tawny is also one of the few African-Americans to work at Essex. They can't *not* employ interpreters of color, as that would be *discriminatory hiring practices.* But they also don't hire hundreds of people to play black slaves because, while that would be authentic, it would also probably be offensive. So Tawny portrays a middle-class girl in one of the historical houses, and everyone acts like, sure, there were all sorts of black middle-class girls in the Colonies in 1774.

"Yo!" Tawny shouted when we didn't immediately quiet down.

"Taw-ny! Taw-ny!" Nat started chanting, thrusting his fist in the air. The rest of us joined in. "Taw-ny! Taw-ny!" We raised our hands and marshmallow sticks up to her.

She stood atop her rock, hands on hips, chin raised into the breeze. "Soldiers!" she said once our cheers had died down. "I am proud to lead you into battle this summer. We will show those Civil Warriors no mercy. We will teach them that there is only one time in American history that matters, and that is the Colonial period. That is *us.*"

"Yeah!" a bunch of people shouted. "Get 'em!"

"And we are not afraid to fight dirty!" Tawny continued. "We will overrun their territory with historical anachronisms.

We will cut off their supply chains. We will do whatever must be done, anything at all, as long as the bosses don't find out about it. We will fight on the beaches, we will fight on the landing grounds, we will fight in the fields and in the streets, we will fight in the hills. We will never surrender!"

That last bit was definitely Winston Churchill, not Tawny Nelson, and it came about two hundred years too late. Nonetheless, the applause crescendoed, and Tawny had to wait another minute before she could go on.

"To get you all psyched for this year," she said, "I present to you the Essex Cheerleaders!"

Three theater kids bearing pom-poms pranced in front of Tawny's rock. They were two girls and a femme guy who had played the doo-wop girls in our community theater's spring production of *Little Shop of Horrors*. They were in Colonial Essex's dance program, which meant they spent the summer gallivanting around, demonstrating minuets. Last year, they had placed themselves in charge of leading fight songs against Reenactmentland. There was no question in my mind that Fiona would join them before this summer was out. She can't get enough of stuff like that.

Pom-poms aflutter, the Essex Cheerleaders chanted:

> *United we stand, divided we fall*
> *Just watch us as we beat y'all.*
> *You say "brother against brother"?*

Well, my brother screwed your mother
And she liked it!
We'll kick your shins and break your knee
'Cause all you got is Robert E. Lee.
Farbs!

They jumped up and down and kicked their legs and showed off some jazz hands, while everyone else hooted and hollered, "Farbs!"

Farb is a terrible thing to call a reenactor. My dad says it's shorthand for *Far be it from authentic*, but in the War, we just use it to mean that a reenactor is *sloppy* in his historical details. Or we use it when we just don't like someone.

The Essex Cheerleaders skipped back into the crowd to much applause, and Tawny resumed her speech. "As you know, soldiers, we are at a slight disadvantage this year. Because of the Barnes Prize."

We all booed. The Barnes Prize for Historical Interpretation is awarded by the National Register of Historic Places, very occasionally, to historic sites that are especially important, and that do an impeccable job of presenting the past.

Inexplicably, last summer the farbs at Reenactmentland won a Barnes. They found some letters or building specs or something proving that the Confederacy had built there a top-secret ironclad battleship, the CSS *South Carolina*, to send into the Battle of Hampton Roads. The boat sank before seeing any naval action, and it wasn't until Reenactmentland discovered this paperwork that historians could even confirm the existence of a CSS *South Carolina*. There were a million news articles about it, and suddenly photos of Reenactment-land's stupid battlefield were appearing on the covers of travel magazines. Even the Travel Channel filmed a show there, and they mentioned Essex at the very end, as an "additional attraction to visit if you have an extra day."

"Some might say we are at a disadvantage," Tawny continued. "But I say that just makes us the underdog. And no one ever expects how much damage the underdog can cause!"

Massive cheering.

"What I need now," she said, "is a second-in-command. Someone to keep track of our manpower and our resources. Someone who knows everyone and notices everything. A strategist, an ideas man. Someone who has Essex running through his veins. Who do I need?"

"Me!" Bryan shouted. He swung his hand in the air and jumped up and down a little, in case Tawny couldn't see him. "Pick me, pick me!"

But then Ezra shouted, "Chelsea!" and everyone turned to stare at me.

I gaped at him through the fire. What *was* this? Did he think he was doing me a favor? Was he trying to play a prank on me? And how was this his idea of *staying out of my way*?

Then Fiona piped up, "Chelsea would be great at it!" And

I would like to know what made my best friend and my ex-boyfriend, both of whom had *never worked here before*, suddenly feel that they were experts on what Essex needed in this War.

Everyone picked up the cry of "Chel-sea! Chel-sea!" with the exception of Bryan, standing near me with his lower lip stuck out, who kept mumbling, "Bry-an, Bry-an," like that was going to catch on.

"Chelsea?" Tawny looked down at me. "I would be thrilled to have you as my Lieutenant, and it seems that everyone here agrees."

"Yeah!" Loud cheering.

"What do you say?"

I locked eyes with Tawny and considered it for a moment. It would mean getting in more trouble than anyone else, if we got caught. But no one ever got caught. All the real employees at Essex and Reenactmentland turned a blind eye, just as long as no one got seriously hurt, which people barely ever did.

And it was such a high honor. The greatest honor anyone could have at Essex was to lead the War efforts. I felt overwhelmed that everyone here would trust me with that responsibility. These were my people. This was my community. And as I heard them all chanting my name, I wondered if I had ever seriously intended to trade this in for a retail job. There was nothing the mall could offer that would rival this moment.

So I said, "Yes. General Tawny, I accept."

Fiona shrieked and hugged me like I had just been crowned Miss Teen U.S.A. Then Bryan tried to hug me too, as if he were happy for me, even though he *obviously* was not and just wanted an excuse to touch me with his toadlike arms. Tawny reached a hand down toward me, I grabbed it tightly, and she pulled me up onto the rock with her.

Still holding my hand, Tawny hoisted our arms high, like we were already victors in this War. I gazed out over my cheering friends and coworkers and ex-boyfriend, and the fire and the fireflies and the brook and the trees and the summertime. And I felt happy, for a moment. For a moment, everything felt perfect.

And then it all disappeared as I was grabbed from behind, knocked over, pulled backward and down into nothing.

Chapter 5
THE KIDNAPPING

At first I could hear a lot of people screaming, but I couldn't distinguish any individual voices or words. I couldn't see at all because someone had hastily tied what felt like a strip of cloth over my eyes. And probably I would have been able to pull the cloth down, except that people were gripping my arms and legs, so I couldn't move at all. They were running with me, running fast, and I had no idea where. Soon my friends' screams faded away, so they must have carried me pretty far. Whoever "they" were.

I tried to kick my legs, but the people holding on to my ankles and knees were too strong. I twisted my head around as much as I could, hoping I could bite someone's hand, but I couldn't find anything. Then I realized that my mouth was unbound—no strips of cloth, no attackers' hands—so I started screaming. Loud.

"Help me!" I screamed. "Help! I'm being kidnapped! Help! Help!"

"Shut *up*," someone said. He didn't sound much older than me, and I couldn't decide which was worse, getting kidnapped by professional criminals, or getting kidnapped by a gang of underage amateurs. Either way, this was bad, so I kept screaming and thrashing, hoping that I could slow them down, or that someone would find me.

But instead they just kept running with me until, after some time—maybe five minutes, or maybe twenty—I was thrown down on top of something. A chair? My arms and legs were bound before I had the chance to figure it out, or to make a run for it.

Once they had ensured that I was firmly tied to whatever I was sitting on, my captors removed my blindfold.

It took my eyes a moment to adjust. When they did, I could see that I was in a grove of trees, not that different from the grove of trees where I'd been kidnapped. There were no lights other than the stars and the moon. And I was encircled by two girls and four guys around my age, all of them strangers to me.

"Who the *hell* are you?" I demanded.

"We're reenactors," said the shorter of the girls with a wicked smile. "And this is War."

I twisted in my chair, trying to loosen my hands. "Oh, *come on!* Are you kidding me? Work doesn't even start until Monday."

"Well, War starts today," replied a sandy-haired guy in Birkenstocks and cargo shorts.

"We were listening to you all," added the other girl. "With your 'we will overrun their territory' and your 'farbs.' That hurts, by the way." The rest of the Civil Warriors murmured their agreement. "That hurts. We earned our Barnes Prize fair and square. I'll have you know we are *extremely* conscientious about historical authenticity."

"Really?" I raised an eyebrow at their flip-flops and T-shirts. "You don't look it."

"Work doesn't start until Monday, remember, dumbass?" The shorter girl cuffed me on the arm. "Plus, you don't look it either, Miss Elizabeth Connelly."

I jerked my head toward her. "How do you know my name?"

"I visited Essex as a moderner last summer, to scope it out," the tallest of the boys volunteered. "You told me your name then. Congratulations on being selected as the Colonials' Lieutenant, by the way. What an honor. I hope that's living up to your expectations so far."

I glared at him. "You came all the way to Essex just to *spy* on us?"

"Yeah." He smirked. "I crossed the street. It was really rough."

"That's creepy," I said.

"War's creepy, darlin'," the short girl told me. Then, all business, she turned to her compatriots. "Okay, we have to go guard the entry points. Those Essex bitches are going to be swarming the place soon, trying to free the hostages, so we need all men at the front lines. Not you, Dan. Stay here and guard Elizabeth Connelly. Call my cell if there's any trouble."

The guy who had admitted to spying on me rolled his eyes. "I can't imagine what trouble *she* could cause."

"Just in case, don't let her out of your sight." The girl turned on her heel and disappeared into the trees, with the others following her, leaving only my guard and me.

He sat down on a tree stump and pulled a paperback book out of his back pocket, but he didn't open it. Instead he just watched in silence as I tried to wrestle free of my bonds. No luck. That's the thing about reenactors—they're into skills that no one learns anymore, like calligraphy and knots. Whoever had tied me up had probably been practicing these knots on his little brother ever since first reading a picture book on pirates.

And having this guy staring at me wasn't making my escape attempts any easier. He had this fascinated look on his face, and it was making me self-conscious. Also, he was kind of cute. Not *really*, of course, since he was the enemy, and the enemy cannot possibly be cute. He was only cute enough to make me wish I could free my hands so that I could fix my hair. I mean, fix my hair, then punch him in the face, and then run.

"You're not going to be able to get out of those," he said after I'd struggled for a few minutes.

"Wow, thanks for letting me know," I said. All that twisting around was making the rope cut into my skin. "I kind of figured that one out on my own."

"I'm just saying, you're not going to get out of here, so you might as well relax. Enjoy our quality time together. I'm Dan Malkin." He stretched out his hand as if to shake mine, then said, "Whoops, I forgot. You don't have any free hands right now." He pursed his lips. "Awk-ward."

"For some reason, Dan Malkin, I'm finding you incredibly annoying."

He looked offended. "You don't even know me, and you've already decided that I'm annoying?"

"I know you." I took in his cutoff jeans, threadbare Sex Pistols T-shirt, messy hair, and unopened copy of *The Sun Also Rises.* "You're a music and book snob. Which means you're probably no good at basketball, which further means that your height is a complete waste. You're important enough in the War to go on a kidnapping mission, but still unimportant enough that you're stuck guarding a hostage while everyone else is out fighting. You're annoying and you're a dumb Southern hick."

Dan didn't argue with my analysis. He just laughed. "Right

on. I couldn't have said that better myself. Only what makes you think that I'm a dumb Southern hick, my dear, cultured daughter of the silversmith?"

I shrugged. To be honest, I didn't really believe that he was. But I replied, "Your accent. *Ah'm a-fixin' to go catch me some Colonials.*"

"For sure." Dan nodded. "That is for sure what I sound like. Don't I feel put in my place now."

"Well," I said defensively. "You know what I mean. You have an accent."

"I did live in Georgia until I was ten," he said. "So I am, by definition, a slave-owning, Confederate flag-flying, coverall-wearing bumpkin."

"Hey," I said, "not my fault. If you don't like the stereotypes, you might want to get out of the Civil War reenacting business."

"Ah, but if I did that, I would miss out on scintillating conversations like this one." He flashed me a grin.

"Well, you'd better watch it this year. We're going to kick your ass."

"I like that spunk of yours, but, so far, it seems like *we* are the ones doing all the ass-kicking."

"Just wait. We have our own plans." This sounded like the sort of threatening, mysterious thing a Lieutenant would say, even though the only plans I'd heard referenced so far involved the phrase "uterine lining." Presumably, Tawny had some non-uterine plans, and I'd find out what they were. Just as soon as I wasn't kidnapped anymore.

"Really. What exactly are these 'plans' of yours, Elizabeth Connelly?" Dan asked. "Or, sorry, do you prefer to go by Chelsea?"

I caught my breath. It was one thing for this guy to know my Colonial name. That was part of the game. But my real name was different. "You *can't* know that from visiting Essex last summer," I said.

"We have superior War intelligence." Dan arched his eyebrows, seeming to enjoy my surprise. "We know everything."

"Oh, really? What else do you know?" I challenged him.

He ticked off on his fingers, "One, that you come from a family of reenactors; two, that you've worked at Essex for a million years; three, that you're sick of it; and four, that you don't know how to get out. So, is any of my intel wrong?"

I didn't say anything. That was more than pretty much anyone knew about me, except Fiona.

"It's cool," he said, "you're not the only one. My mom and both my sisters live and breathe the Civil War. So I know how these things go."

"I guess you're just the expert on me, then."

"I guess I am. Just like you already know that my basketball game sucks. So tell me." He leaned forward on the tree stump, resting his elbows on his knees. "Tell me one thing I don't already know about you, Chelsea."

I opened my mouth, but the only reply that occurred to me was *You don't already know that I think you're cute.* And that wasn't something I could say. That wasn't even something I should be *thinking.* He was a Civil War reenactor. He was the *enemy.*

"Really?" he teased after I'd been silent for a moment. "You're that two-dimensional?"

I shook my head, trying to clear my mind. Now that the phrase *you're cute* was on the tip of my tongue, I was having trouble thinking of anything else to say. "There's a lot you don't know about me. For example, I'm allergic to rope."

"Seriously?" Dan leapt to his feet, looking with concern at my bound arms. "What kind of allergic?"

I couldn't help it, I cracked up. "I'm kidding, Dan. But would you have let me go, if I'd been telling the truth?"

Dan shrugged and kicked at a stick, all apathy now. "Dunno. Probably not. It's War, baby. Allergic reactions are part of our game plan." He stared at me for a long moment, like he was trying to figure me out. "You Colonials," he said. "You're not how I thought you'd be."

I could feel my heart beat a little faster. "How did you think we'd be?"

"Huh." Dan half-grinned. "Good question. I guess I thought you'd all be . . . bratty. Stuck-up. Superior. Boring."

"Oh, then you were totally right, since I'm all of those things."

He rolled his eyes. "At least I know I was right about the bratty part."

I gave him my best angelic expression, all pouty lips and wide eyes. He just raised his eyebrows at me, one side of his mouth still curled up in a smile. There was a pause as we gazed into each other's eyes, me tied to the chair, him standing above me. A little too long of a pause. I cleared my throat. "So how *did* you know my real name's Chelsea? And don't give me any of that 'War intel' crap."

"Oh, that." Dan waved his hand. "We overheard all the Colonials chanting your name as we came through the woods. It didn't take any intel at all. Anyone in a two-mile radius would have heard you guys."

"Speaking of," I said. "Was I screaming, like, really loudly when you guys carried me over here?"

"It was almost unbelievable," he said, "how loud you were screaming."

"I figured. My throat hurts now."

"It was cute." Even in the moonlight, I could see Dan blush suddenly, like he hadn't meant to say that. "I mean cute like a wild animal is cute. That sort of thing. Like a lion cub, if you think that's cute."

"I *do* think lion cubs are cute."

"Okay, fine, maybe, but they can still tear you to pieces."

"*I* can't tear you to pieces. My hands are tied behind my back."

"Good point. Like a trussed lion cub, then." He gently punched my arm. "Hey. You have goose bumps."

I looked down at my arm. He was right. It was late, after all. It had gotten late and chilly. "Well, I *had* a sweater, but it's back at Essex. Along with the rest of my life."

Dan started to take off his hoodie.

"But then you'll just be cold," I objected.

"I don't mind. After all, you're the hostage."

"Right, but I think the hostage is supposed to suffer *more* than her captors."

"I'm not suffering," he told me. He leaned over me to drape the hoodie over my shoulders. It was sort of awkward, because of course I couldn't stick my arms through the sleeves, so I wound up wearing it more like a shawl.

I held still and watched him concentrate on arranging the hoodie, and I inhaled the night air and his boy smell. "Don't take this as a compliment, but you actually don't smell that bad."

Dan let out a burst of surprised laughter. "What did you expect me to smell like?"

"Well . . ." I wrinkled my nose. "I heard you guys soak your uniforms in urine."

"So you assumed I'd smell like pee."

"Yes," I said. "But you don't," I added kindly.

"Well, I'm wearing modern clothes right now. I'm wearing a T-shirt. I don't soak my T-shirts in pee."

"Of course not. Good point." Pause. "Wait, so you *do* soak your uniform in pee?"

"Not the *whole* uniform," Dan sounded offended. "Just the buttons."

"*Just* the buttons."

"Right."

"There is a garment which you wear on your body, after first bathing it in bodily fluids."

"Just the buttons! To give them an authentic patina."

"What the hell is an 'authentic patina'? Is that a thing?"

He started to laugh then. I did, too, and suddenly I felt something that I hadn't felt in months, something that I thought had disappeared with Ezra forever: I felt *into* this guy. I wanted to spend more time with him, I wanted to get to know him, I even maybe wanted to kiss him. And in that moment, I didn't care that he came from the wrong time and place.

Dan paused for a moment with his hands on either side of my shoulders, still holding on to the hoodie, and he opened his mouth as if to speak, and I thought maybe he would kiss me. Maybe it could be so easy.

Except then someone knocked him to the ground, and suddenly two other people were untying the ropes around my body, and I realized that this was it, I was being rescued.

"You goddamn cheating farb!" shouted Lenny, the Colonial who was pinning Dan to the ground.

My arms and legs were free, finally, and then I was being lifted off my feet again, because apparently that was the theme of tonight.

But it was different this time, because my rescuer was Ezra, and I just wrapped my arms around his neck. "We got her!" he shouted. "Let's go, let's go!" So Lenny jumped off of Dan, and the girl who was with them kicked the chair over, and Ezra tightened his hold on me, and we ran through the trees, out of Reenactmentland, and on to the street.

"Ezra," I said, once we were out of there, "I can walk. Put me down, for God's sake." So he did. He looked sweaty and flushed, but his eyes had a spark in them. If there's one thing Ezra likes more than competition, it's winning.

"What did they do to you?" Ezra demanded. "Are you okay?"

And I loved that he cared, but I also wanted to slap him. What, Ezra, *now* you care?

Somehow when Ezra had carried me away, he had brought Dan's hoodie with him. So now I put it on properly, sticking my arms through the sleeves.

I knew I wasn't supposed to talk to him until August 7th, because of Fiona's pointless, made-up, arbitrary time constraint, but I felt like I was allowed to say this, anyway: "You didn't have to rescue me, Ezra." And for some reason I felt like crying. "I didn't need you. I *don't* need you. I was doing fine." I flipped the hood up onto my head and walked away from him, down the road, to Essex.

Chapter 6
THE BURYING GROUND

I got in trouble, of course. I walked in my front door at 12:27 a.m., and my father was sitting in the dark at the kitchen table, waiting for me. He was wearing a bathrobe and slippers, and he looked terrible.

"Where have you been?" he growled.

This was a good question to which I had no good answer. "Reenactmentland" wasn't going to fly.

"What time were you supposed to be home tonight, Chelsea?"

"Well, you didn't set an actual *time*. Mom just said I was supposed to call—"

"And did you call?"

"No."

"Why not?"

I stood in the kitchen doorway, shifting my weight from foot to foot. All I wanted was to escape to my room, call Fiona, and go to bed. *Why didn't I call? Because I'd been kidnapped. Why do you* think *I didn't call, Dad?*

"Do I or do I not pay for you to have a cell phone *so that* you can call and tell me when you'll be home late?"

I shrugged.

"Have you been drinking?" Dad demanded.

"No."

"I hope you're not lying to me, Chelsea. Were your friends drinking? What have we always said about getting into cars with people after they've been drinking?"

"*Dad,* no one was drinking. Do you want to smell my breath? Here, smell my breath."

If I was in trouble for spearheading a War against a band of Civil War reenactors, I'd be like, *Okay, fair play, I guess I deserve that.* But it was just offensive to get in trouble for drinking, which I *wasn't even doing.*

"Your mother and I have been worried sick. Do you think we wanted to stay up all night, waiting for you?"

My dad is the master of rhetorical questions. I was tempted to answer, "Yes, I think you wanted to stay up all night, waiting for me." Or to point out that Mom was clearly asleep in bed, like a normal parent.

But my dad can be scary. He's a big, burly man with a big, burly voice, and he smiths silver for a living, plus he's a PhD in history. There is no point to arguing with him, and I know because I've tried.

"Don't just stand there and sulk, young lady. Answer me."

I sighed. "I'm sorry, Dad. I didn't mean to come home late, and I didn't mean to make you worry. I got tied up in things." Literally, tied up. "It won't happen again."

"You're damn right it won't. You're grounded."

"But Dad, it's *summertime*. This is so unfair! How long am I grounded for?"

He thought about it. "Until Monday."

"Wait, so I'm grounded for two days?"

"Yes," he said brutally. "You can spend the weekend boning up on your history."

"Oh. Okay. Can I go to bed now?"

He nodded, and we walked upstairs together. Before I went into my room, he kissed me on the forehead. "I'm glad you're home safe," he said.

I got into bed and tried to fall asleep, but there was a restless, buzzing energy throughout my body. It had been one hell of a long day. I had finished school for the year (good), found out my ex-boyfriend was working at my summer job with me (bad), been selected as the second-in-command for our War (mostly good), gotten kidnapped (bad), and met a guy who actually seemed promising (good) . . . except that he was a Civil War reenactor (very, very bad). I felt exhausted and wired, all at the same time.

My phone vibrated. Fiona. "I'm grounded," I whispered into the receiver.

"So are you not allowed to talk?"

"No, Dad didn't say anything about that." My father grounds me periodically, but he's not very good at it. He mostly just does it to prove that he has control. He doesn't care about the technical details, like whether I use the phone.

"Then listen, I just got off the phone with Nat."

"Did he declare his love for you?" I asked. I kicked my comforter off my bed and rolled over onto my side.

"Not yet. He was saying that in the future, whenever we have nighttime meetings at Essex, we need to post guards. We can't have any more kidnappings."

"No kidding," I agreed. "It sucked. More or less." I thought again of Dan saying *It was cute* about me. That part hadn't sucked.

"Nat was part of the rescue mission that found Tawny. But—get this—she had already managed to cut through the ropes they'd wrapped around her. Nat said she had a Swiss Army knife in her back pocket, and she got it out and sawed her way through without anyone even noticing."

This made me feel bad about myself. The only knives I used were butter knives, and I certainly never carried one around in my pocket. (Like, what, in case there was an emergency butter-spreading situation?) I wanted to be the girl who rescued herself, like Tawny. Instead I'd had to be rescued by stupid Ezra. Stupid Ezra whose body still felt exactly right when he picked me up and carried me away to safety.

"What was being kidnapped like?" Fiona asked, breathy with excitement.

"Boring. I just sat there. There was one kind of cute boy, though. One of the Civil War guys."

"Really? Tell me about him." Fiona can focus her attention like a laser when cute boys are involved. At all other times, she's really hit-or-miss.

"Well, *you* might not find him attractive since, you know, he doesn't have a long, flowing ponytail or anything. But his name's Dan, and he's tall and pretty skinny, and he dresses well, and he has this cute floppy hair. And he seems to be literate, or maybe he just likes to carry around books as props."

"I'd hit it," Fiona agreed. "Except that he's from the Civil War."

Quietly, I let out a long breath. "And we definitely can't date people from the Civil War," I said. "Right?"

"Of course right. Hello, *we are at War*. Dating someone from the Civil War would make you a traitor. Like Benedict Arnold."

"How the hell do you know who Benedict Arnold is? I'm very impressed, Fiona."

"I saw a movie about him once." She paused. "He was in

the American army for the Revolution but then he defected to the British, right?"

"Yes."

"Awesome, that's what I thought. Don't be Benedict Arnold, Chelsea! You're our Lieutenant. Can you even imagine what it would do to troop morale if you, of all people, hooked up with a Civil Warrior?"

"Calm down, Fi. All I said was that he's cute. It's an aesthetic judgment. I'm not actively planning to hook up with this guy. A lot of people are cute. That doesn't mean I'm trying to make out with all of their faces."

Fiona didn't accept this, since she usually *is* trying to make out with every cute person's face. She pressed on, "You two are from different times, and different worlds. It wouldn't work."

"Of course." I rolled onto my back and gazed up at the ceiling. "Of course you're right. It wouldn't work. I never thought it would."

As I put on my work clothes on Monday morning, I felt the past ten months slip away from me. It seemed like no time had passed since the last day I had worked at Essex, since the last time I'd put on this dress.

Every Essex employee gets one outfit. If you want more, you have to buy them yourself, and they are outlandishly expensive. Of course, *good* reenactors sew their own clothes, but personally I'd rather wallow in the same sweaty garments all summer long than figure out how to use a sewing machine. You have to thread a bobbin or something. It's very complicated. My father once tried to teach me, and we wound up screaming at each other. Not worth it.

My gown is forest green, fronted by a matching green stomacher with decorative stitching across it. I wear that over a navy blue petticoat, and under all of *that* I wear a plain white shift, which looks like an ill-fitting nightgown. Shoes are leather boots, made by the Essex shoemaker, Jonathan Shoemaker. (Colonial name. His real name is Jonathan Shulman. Close enough.) This whole outfit was assigned to me when I was thirteen, and I still haven't outgrown it.

My parents and I drove to Essex together. "Tell me, Chelsea, what have you learned from your grounding?" my father asked, glancing at me in the rearview mirror.

"Um . . ." Should I say, *Don't get kidnapped by hot Civil War boys*? Or should I say, *I've learned that my father is insane*? No, that doesn't count; I already knew that. So I didn't say anything except "Sorry," which was fine, since it turned out Dad wasn't actually looking for an answer.

We parked in the staff lot hidden behind the magazine, which is the building where the old weapons are kept. Ezra had been assigned to work in the magazine, so I planned to avoid it all summer long. Which actually would be the same as every other summer. I've never gotten especially jazzed about Revolutionary War cannons.

"Are you going to be all right today?" my mother asked, grabbing my forearm.

"Of course. Why?"

"Well, just that you've never worked anyplace other than with us, and I didn't know if you were nervous. . . . What if someone asks you a question that you don't know the answer to, and we're not there to help?"

"Mom," I said. "I will be literally down the road from you. If I scream loud enough, you will be able to hear me. And if there's a question I can't answer, I'm *sure* the boss at the graveyard will know."

This was the other thing I'd learned from my weekend of being grounded: that there was absolutely no way I would be able to survive ten weeks in the silversmith studio, day in and day out with my father, and his rhetorical questions, and his know-it-all attitude. I would snap. One or both of us would not live to see September.

Plus, Bryan Denton was going to be apprenticing at the silversmith's this summer. And the only thing that could be worse than Bryan relentlessly hitting on me from nine to five every day would be my parents witnessing every second of it.

My dad told me about Bryan's apprenticeship over brunch on Saturday, sounding very pleased. He has always been a Bryan Denton fan. "That boy has a good head on his shoulders," Dad said, to which I replied that if the only positive thing you can say about a person is that he has a "good head," then there is probably something malformed about the rest of him.

Dad just laughed at me and said, "You know what it means when a girl criticizes a boy, don't you?"

I tried ignoring him.

"You know what it means, right? When a girl protests that really she hates a boy? You know what that means?"

The "ignoring" plan never works. "Does it mean that she really hates him as much as she says she does?" I snapped.

He chuckled superiorly. "No. It means that she really has a *crush* on him."

I immediately left the kitchen and called Mr. Zelinsky.

"Elizabeth Connelly!" he cried into the phone, like the past sixteen hours of not speaking to me had been abject torture. "To what do I owe the pleasure of this call?"

"Mr. Zelinsky," I said, "I need to work somewhere that's not the silversmith's studio this summer. Anywhere. I don't care. Actually, I do care: If you could put Fiona and me together, that would be best. If that's not possible, fine, I will accept that, but just please, for the love of all that is holy and Colonial, get me away from the silversmith. I will make shoes, I will make barrels, I will make soap, but I cannot make silverware."

Mr. Zelinsky made some sympathetic murmuring noises. "Did you know, Miss Connelly," he said pensively, "that, unlike with iron, you cannot strike silver while it's hot? Should you strike silver while it's hot, it's likely to shatter."

"Sure," I said, because I found that out for myself years ago.

"Would you consider this *symbolic*?" Mr. Zelinsky asked.

"No? Wait, what would it symbolize?"

"The *heart*? If you strike it while you are hot—that is, *angry*—"

"Mr. Zelinsky, I can't handle metaphors today. I am begging you. I need to be reassigned."

So I got the burying ground. Fiona got assigned to the milliner's, which is where the cool girls work—though saying someone is "cool" by Essex standards is not saying much. Although I wished Fiona and I were placed together, I didn't need to spend every day sewing shifts and listening to Anne Whitcomb, Patience Algren, and Maggie Fairchild gossip about which Colonials are hooking up with one another and how far they've gone.

The only people assigned to the burying ground this summer are me and Linda Osborne, an adult interpreter. So there's no potential for drama, like the time last summer when the milliner girls cast Maggie out of their group for a few days (because she had made out with Patience's ex-boyfriend at a party). *That* was drama. But with only two of us in the burying ground, and one of us being a married woman in her thirties, probably no one was going to get cast out of anything. I suspected that Mr. Zelinsky assigned me to the burying ground because I am unfit for human company.

After I said good-bye to my parents and reported to the

burying ground, Linda explained to me that my job was to wander atmospherically amongst the gravestones and answer people's questions if they had any.

The morning got off to a brisk start with five different people asking me if I was hot in my costume. I said, "Who's wearing a costume?" and, "Certainly not!" I wasn't even totally lying, since it was early enough in the day that the temperature hadn't gone up to a hundred degrees, yet.

A little girl in a floor-length gown, bonnet, and sneakers approached me. "Are you . . ." she asked, then trailed off, looking toward her mother for support. Her mom nodded encouragingly and snapped a couple photos with her expensive-looking camera.

"Are you Felicity?" the girl finished bravely, squinting into the sunlight to see my face.

"Nay," I said. "My name is Elizabeth Connelly." I curtsied.

The girl looked confused. "I don't have that doll."

"I am not a doll," I said with a laugh. But this chick wasn't laughing.

"Mama, why don't I have an Elizabeth Connelly doll?" she demanded with a scowl.

"We'll get you one at the gift shop," her mother promised. "They do have those at Ye Olde Shoppe, right?" she asked me, pronouncing it like *Ye Oldie Shoppie*.

I cleared my throat. "Well, Elizabeth Connelly isn't a *doll*. She isn't, er, an American Girl."

When I can't think of what to say while reenacting, I say "er" instead of "um." For some reason I believe that "er" sounds more authentically Colonial. I don't know why. This is probably not *true*.

"If you aren't Felicity," the girl said, yanking her bonnet back on her head, "and you aren't even an American Girl at *all*, then where *are* the real American Girls?"

I looked to the mother for help, but she just smiled and said, "We drove all the way down from New York to see the real-life American Girls. Jessica *loves* her American Girl dolls, don't you, sweetie?"

"I have all of them," Jessica confirmed. "Only not Kirsten's bed. I don't have Kirsten's bed." She glared at her mother.

"Er, you do know that the Colonial times actually happened, right?" I said, more to the grown woman than to her kid. "America was actually a bunch of Colonies that belonged to England. There was actually a Revolutionary War. A lot of people died. American Girl dolls are made-up."

They both stared at me blankly for a long moment.

"Let me get a photo of the two of you," the mother broke the silence. "Just go stand in front of that big grave so it looks real. Okay, say cheese!"

A click of the camera, and they were off, the girl tripping over her long gown.

It's funny how little time it takes for kids to stop being cute and start being annoying.

I wondered how many photographs I appear in that belong to people who I don't know, whom I will never see again. Thousands. It must be thousands. I imagined myself going to college and getting some boyfriend from really far away—like Oregon, or Ireland. And he'd take me home to meet his parents, and we would look through their old photo albums, and I'd come across a picture of myself, Miss Elizabeth Connelly, at the age of eleven, in full Colonial regalia.

Assuming, of course, that I would someday fall in love with a guy who wasn't Ezra Gorman. Which might or might not ever happen.

"You just killed that darling child's dream," Linda said, walking over. "While you were at it, why didn't you tell her that Santa Claus is fake too?"

I shrugged. "I was educating her. That's what they come here for."

Linda is a tall, sturdy, maternal-looking Colonial who always speaks in a dry monotone, so I can never tell when she's kidding, even though I've known her for years now. She couldn't *actually* think that brat was darling. But I wasn't positive.

A family approached us with a couple of young teenage boys in tow. "What a fabulous cemetery!" the mom enthused. Her sons rolled their eyes and looked like they wanted to die.

"In fact, it's called a burying ground or a graveyard," Linda said. "The word 'cemetery' doesn't come into use until the 1800s, during the Romantic period. In Colonial times, we don't use fancy words like that—we just call things what they are. Plus, cemeteries need not be connected to churches, but burying grounds almost always are."

"You hear that, boys?" the mom said. "Wow!" My heart went out to her poor children. They clearly wanted to be at home, playing video games. Couldn't she have just let them play video games?

"Do you have a question for the nice ladies?" the mom asked.

The boys shook their heads.

"Sure you do. Remember you were wondering why so many of the gravestones have skulls and crossbones carved into them?"

"Oh, yeah." One of the boys heaved a sigh. "Why do so many of the gravestones have skulls and crossbones carved into them? Like, are they pirates? Or what?"

"Nay," Linda said. "Colonial gravestones often have the skull and crossbones on them. It symbolizes mortality. We don't think it's scary."

"Oh." The boys seemed depressed to learn that they were not walking on the remains of pirates.

"While we may not have any pirates buried here, we *do* have two signers of the Declaration of Independence," Linda said.

This had no impact whatsoever on the boys, not even after their mother nudged them and said, "You know about the Declaration! Remember, you did that play about it in third grade?"

"Also," Linda said, "you see that small grassy mound over there? With the metal door built into the side of it?"

The boys shrugged their affirmation.

"That's where we bury the unbaptized babies. Every time an infant dies, we just open that door and stick it in. There are hundreds of dead babies in there."

The boys' eyes lit up. "Dead babies!" one exclaimed.

"Cool!" added the other.

They ran off to inspect the hillock more closely. Whoever said history was boring knew nothing about sudden infant death syndrome.

I went back to wandering atmospherically. I had never before spent much time in the burying ground, but I liked it here. It felt more peaceful than the silversmith's ever did, and not just because my dad wasn't stomping around, holding court. There was grass here, and big oak trees casting shade on the graves. I liked the slightly crumbling slate headstones and the engraved old-fashioned names. "Here lyes the body of Mary Jackson, wife to Jacob Jackson, aged 42 years." "Samuel Otis, born in Essex, January, 1734. Died May, 1818." "Here lyes the body of Elisabeth Connelly, daughter of Seamus Connelly, aged 15 years. Deceased February 12, 1706."

I stopped and reread it, in case I'd made a mistake. But no, that was the inscription, as clear as could be. *Here lyes the body of Elisabeth Connelly.* . . .

I wanted to show Fiona immediately, but she was working

down the road, so for now Linda would have to do. "Come here!" I called to her during a gap between moderners.

"Do you have a question?" Linda hurried over. Historical interpreters love to answer questions.

"Look at this headstone!" I pointed to Elisabeth Connelly's grave.

"I know," Linda agreed. "It seems unusual for Irish Catholics to be buried in the graveyard adjoining a Protestant church, but this is more of a town burying ground than a religious one—"

"Not that. She has my name! And she died when she was practically my age!"

Linda squinted at me, then at the grave, then back at me. She seemed maybe not as excited by this coincidence as I was. Of course, it would be out of character for Linda to act excited about anything, be it a coincidence, a bouquet of balloons, or a free pony.

"Don't you spell your name with a *Z*?" she asked. "'Elizabeth'?"

"Well, maybe. I mean, I never write it down. I could spell it with an *S* if I wanted. Anyway, don't you spell 'lies' with an *i*? Spelling is clearly not this gravestone's best subject."

"And aren't you sixteen?"

"I used to be fifteen, though. Not even that long ago."

Linda shrugged. "Okay."

"How do you think she died?" I asked, gazing at Elisabeth's

headstone. I didn't care what Linda thought; this was my doppelgänger. My *forebearer*. We had a soul connection.

"A fifteen-year-old girl in 1706? There are any number of ways she could have died. Childbirth, disease, an accident . . . There aren't very good records on these people, except for the famous ones. Tell whatever story you want, and it's bound to be true of someone in our graveyard."

Then Linda went off to yell at some kids who were climbing on the table tombs, and I went back to roaming around and reading headstones, even though I had already decided that Elisabeth Connelly was my favorite.

Eventually it was time for my lunch break. I walked along the dusty main road to Bristol House, where I found Tawny eating lunch under a tree. I crouched down next to her, and an overweight modern man snapped a photo of us, exclaiming to his overweight modern wife, "Lookit, a Patriot eating a sandwich!" Which is why there's a rule that we're not allowed to have lunch where moderners can see us. But Tawny doesn't care about rules.

"Thank God you're here," she said to me, immediately springing to attention. "I've had a brilliant idea."

"Great," I said. "Hey, how was your first day of work?"

Tawny furrowed her eyebrows at me, like I was completely insane for trying to discuss anything other than the War.

"Forget it," I said. "What's the plan?"

The spark flashed back into her eyes, and she leaned

forward conspiratorially. "We're going to take them down from the inside," she muttered, then quickly looked around her, as if for spies.

"Cool," I said. "How does it work?"

"We're going to make our own Civil War uniforms," she hissed. "And then we're going to waltz right in there like we belong, and they'll *think* we're Civil Warriors, and we'll use that inside access to tear the place down. You never suspect one of your own."

Now that I understood it, I saw that Tawny's plan actually *was* brilliant. More than a hundred people worked at Reenactmentland; they wouldn't all recognize one another, especially not this early in the season. Even if they thought we looked unfamiliar, they'd assume we were Civil War reenactors from a visiting regiment. If we were properly costumed, they would never suspect us of being Colonials.

"Except they'd recognize me and you," I pointed out to Tawny. "Since they just kidnapped us on Friday and all."

Tawny flipped her hand dismissively. She's a visionary, not a details person. This is why she needed a Lieutenant in the first place. "We'll send a few of the guys," she said. "No big deal. It doesn't have to be the two of us."

Too bad. I would have enjoyed taking Reenactmentland down from the inside, if only because it would have given me the chance to see Dan again. But all I said to Tawny was, "I like it."

"Good." She grinned. "'Cause I already enlisted the milliner girls to start sewing Confederate uniforms."

Ladies and gentlemen: Tawny Nelson.

Our strategizing complete, Tawny leaned back against the tree and returned to her anachronistic sandwich. I continued on to the silversmith's, to get my own lunch. The upstairs of the silversmith's workshop, like the upstairs of a lot of buildings at Essex, is modernized. There's a fan and a refrigerator, where my cheese sandwich was waiting for me.

A few moderners stopped me along the way, asking for directions to the cooper's or wanting to take a photo with me. I wanted to say, "No, I don't have to, I'm on my lunch hour." But I didn't. Because I am a professional.

"Hello, Mother. Good day, Father," I said when I entered the silversmith's studio. Even though I was on break, Mom and Dad were working. Bryan Denton was too, but I ignored him. The moderners watched us, waiting for something exciting and historical to occur.

"Good afternoon, Elizabeth!" Mom gave me a big hug. She was sticky with sweat, but I couldn't complain, because so was I.

"Would you like to see this silverware that I am engraving with our family's monogram?" Dad asked me.

"Nope!" I gave him a smile. No way was I going to spend my hour-long lunch getting dragged into historical playacting with my dad. *I'm on break here, people.*

I had almost made it to the stairs in the back of the

workshop when Bryan came out from behind his workbench and cornered me. "Miss Connelly," he said. "May I escort you?"

"Oh God, Bryan," I said, then noticed the moderners still watching us. "I mean, how kind of you to offer, but that shan't be necessary."

"I insist," he said, taking my elbow and leading me out on to the porch.

"Okay," I said once we were outside. "*What?* I have thirty-seven minutes left for lunch, if you were wondering."

"I've been thinking it over," Bryan said, "and I've decided that, because I am your dad's apprentice this summer, it would make a lot of sense for you to be my girlfriend."

"Really," I said.

"Yes. I've done a lot of research on this, and apprentices often court their masters' daughters. Then they get married and continue in the family business. So you and I would just take over being the silversmiths when your father gets too old."

"Gross, Bryan, I'm not marrying you."

"I'm not saying *us.* I just mean, that's what *they* would do. So we should too. It would be so historically accurate, for the silversmith's daughter to date the silversmith's apprentice!"

"Wow, how romantic of you." I heaved a sigh and leaned against the wooden porch railing. "This may be hard for you to believe, but I don't actually decide to date guys based on what would be the most *historically accurate.* And also?" Unbidden, a memory popped into my mind: Dan, lounging on a tree stump in Reenactmentland, half-grinning at me. "I don't want to be someone's girlfriend just because it would *make a lot of sense.* Making sense has nothing to do with it."

I curtsied at Bryan, then went back inside and stomped upstairs. The lamest guy I know wants to date me. My ex-boyfriend wants to be friends. The only guy who has any potential lives ninety years too late. I hate boys, and my life is a joke.

Chapter 7
THE TELEPHONE WARS

Tawny got right on everyone's case to come up with an awesome plan of attack that would prove to Reenactmentland that we were serious contenders. "They're just resting on their laurels!!!" she said in an e-mail to all of us on Monday night. "They think we don't have any game!! Let's prove to those farbs that they have underestimated us!!!!"

But so far they hadn't underestimated us, because so far we hadn't come up with any awesome counterattacks.

Of course we had Tawny's fantastic Undercover Operation battle plan, but according to the people constructing and sewing the uniforms, that was at least two weeks away from being ready to go. They needed materials and fabric to make the costumes, and they could work on them only when their supervisors weren't around. Tawny had sent another e-mail asking, "Can't this happen any faster???" to which Patience, the milliner girl and self-appointed costume designer, replied, "look tawny, we are not going to half ass this. just because theyre farbs doesnt make it ok for us to show up in some safety pinned old sacks. sewing is an ART & like any art it takes TIME & when you rush us like this i feel like you dont RESPECT OUR CRAFT."

So that's why we didn't have Civil War uniforms yet.

But Tawny was right that we had to do *something*. We couldn't afford to wait two weeks while Patience embroidered Confederate jackets.

As I was riding my bike home from Essex on Tuesday, I stopped by my favorite junk shop to see if anything cool had come in recently. You might think that because I spend all my time with antique goods they would no longer interest me, but I love junk shops; there's always the chance I might find a treasure buried in all the old crap.

As I coasted to a stop in front of the store, I saw an employee struggling out the door with a big trash bag filled with some sort of electronic gear. "What's in there?" I asked.

"Bunch of broken phones," the guy said, letting me peer inside the bag. "Rotary, touch-tone, whatever. They don't work anymore. The boss thought we could sell 'em as paperweights or something, but they were just takin' up space, so we're trashin' 'em."

I waited until he'd shuffled back into the junk shop, then I called Tawny. "Get down here," I said as soon as she answered her phone. "Bring your car. I have an idea."

Tawny and I sent emergency text messages telling everyone to meet outside Reenactmentland promptly at five thirty the next morning. Going there at night was too risky; the Civil Warriors might stay late, plotting strategy or just hanging out. Very, very early morning seemed safer.

I woke up at five a.m., feeling weirdly awake and pumped for the day. I put on my PUMAs and cute jeans and even ran a brush through my hair, all of which is a lot of effort in the middle of the night, but there was a small chance I might run into Dan at Reenactmentland, in which case I thought I should look like a person who wore real clothes instead of pajamas. I even found myself *wanting* to run into Dan while we were on our Telephone Mission, which was, as Fiona would have said, very Benedict Arnold of me, since if Dan were there, he would *stop* us because he was the *enemy*.

Also, he wasn't going to be there. He was going to be asleep. Get a grip, Glaser.

I ran downstairs and let myself out, locking the front door behind me as quietly as I could. Fiona was waiting in her convertible a little ways down the block, so my parents wouldn't hear her.

"Hi," I whispered, climbing into the passenger seat.

She grunted. "This plan sucks."

"It's going to be awesome."

"I hate it. And I hate you for coming up with it. And I hate myself for voting for you to be second-in-command."

Fiona hates a lot of things. Mostly mornings.

We drove in silence for a few minutes. I don't know how this is possible, but Fiona seemed to be driving with her eyes entirely closed. Finally she rubbed them and looked at me like she was actually seeing me.

"Why are you dressed like that?"

"Like what? Fi, I'm wearing jeans and sneakers."

"You're wearing your cute jeans and cute sneakers. God, Chelsea, is this because *Ezra* is going to be there? And at five thirty in the goddamn morning you want him to see you in your goddamn PUMAs and realize that he was a fool to let you go?"

"No," I said, even though this had, in fact, been my plan for the past two months, every day that Ezra and I had class together. "How crazy do you think I am? Anyway, Ezra won't be there. He's even worse at mornings than you are."

I said this and had a sudden flashback to the morning I woke up in Ezra's bed. We weren't *allowed* to spend the night together—"Not while you're living under my roof," my dad had said—so I had only this one memory, from March, when my parents were out of town at a historical interpreters convention in Philadelphia. (Yes, there are conventions for historical interpreters. There are conventions for everything.)

So I went over to Ezra's house, because his parents were almost always out of town, and we didn't *do* anything. That was the best part. We didn't eat a fancy dinner or go to a party or anything. We baked brownies and watched a couple hours of reality TV, and I remember leaning against his chest and feeling like we had all the time in the world. We had hours until the next morning, and we could spend every minute of those hours together, just us. We weren't doing anything except lying together on his couch, and it felt like the most exciting night of my life.

We fell asleep in his bed ridiculously late at night, his arms wrapped around my waist, his breath tickling the back of my neck. But we came apart in the night, and when I woke up a few hours later, the sun was shining through the windows and we were on opposite sides of the bed. I watched him sleep for a while, the hypnotic rise and fall of his bare chest.

Eventually I got bored, and I couldn't fall back asleep with him there. I whispered, "Ezra. Ezra," a few times. He didn't stir. I tried cuddling up to him, but he shrugged me off. "Leave me alone," he mumbled. "Stop it. Can't you just let me *sleep?*"

He probably wasn't awake enough to know what he was saying.

I lay on my side of the bed and stared at the ceiling for a while. I texted some friends. I finished the book in my purse. Ezra slept on like a dead man. Finally I just left.

When he called me later that day, we had a fight. He was mad at me because when he woke up I was gone, and I was mad at him for refusing to wake up, and I think both of us had pictured this perfect morning together, like the perfect night before it, and we were both mad at each other for ruining it. It was a stupid thing to fight about, and if I could go back in time, I would just let it go. I would lie right next to him for as long as it took him to wake up, even if it took all day. Because that way, whenever he woke up, at least we would be together.

I remembered all of this as Fiona pulled into Essex. I could still feel his arms around me, if I tried. "Yeah," I said to Fiona. "Ezra really hates mornings."

In the Essex parking lot we met Tawny, Nat, Bryan, two out of three milliner girls, and a half dozen other Colonials. The trunk to Tawny's car was open and filled with plastic bags of telephones. "Let's do this," she said in her commander's voice. "Time to show those farbs they've reached the wrong number."

We each grabbed a bag of telephones and marched across the street and into Civil War Reenactmentland. Although they keep the main gate locked overnight, nothing prevented us from just walking in through the woods. They really should pay more attention to their security.

Once inside, we split up. We had a lot of ground to cover and not much time in which to do it, since we had to get out before any Civil War reenactors showed—and I had to be home before my parents woke up.

Other than my kidnapping, I had never been to Reenactmentland before. I usually played more of a backstage role in the War. But I quickly found a big field of canvas tents. I peeked inside one and saw a few cots, kitchen supplies, and clothes. This must be where they lived. Perfect.

I placed a hot pink wall phone on one of the cots. I took a bludgeonlike rotary phone and stuck it in a big saucepan. I perched a cordless phone atop a pair of boots.

I loved this plan. I wished only that I could stick around to see the expressions on those farbs' faces when the first moderner asked, "So, like, do you guys make a lot of long-distance calls while you're out defending the Confederacy?"

I hid a few phone cords in a trunk, hoping some reenactor would be stunned to find them weeks from now, long after the rest of the plague of telephones had been forgotten. I opened another trunk and found in it a music magazine and a copy of *The Great Gatsby*. Far be it from authentic, indeed. Throwing in a telephone on top of that seemed unnecessary; these reenactors were screwing themselves.

I flipped over the magazine and read the subscriber's name: Dan Malkin.

It felt like the whole morning skidded to a stop, just for that moment. Like the birds took a breath between their chirps and the sun paused in its rising. This was where he lived.

I moved aside the reading material to see what else was in his trunk. For some reason, I wanted to know more about this guy. Anything more. I uncovered some clothes—though not, of course, his gray hoodie, which was still in my bedroom. *Whoops.* I found an iPod, which would be serious contraband at Essex. And I found a photograph, styled to look like a daguerreotype, of Dan leaning against a tree, his arm draped over the shoulders of a girl I didn't recognize.

"Chelsea?"

I dropped the photo as though I'd been caught shoplifting and whirled around.

"Oh, hey, Nat." It was just Nat, holding a telephone and tugging at the end of his ponytail.

"What's wrong?" he asked.

"Nothing." I threw a Mickey Mouse–shaped phone into Dan's trunk, on top of the photo, and closed the lid. "Let's head back, it's getting late."

Nothing's wrong, Nat, because what could be wrong? I just learned that some guy who was already off-limits might have a girlfriend and therefore be even more *off-limits?*

"That guy had an iPod in his trunk," I said as we walked out of Dan's tent.

Nat snorted. "Farb."

Of course, Dan was just a nineteenth-century farb who was probably some other girl's boyfriend. Of course he was; I'd known that all along. There are no surprises here. Suddenly my good jeans felt too tight, and my PUMAs looked ridiculous as I stared down at them.

We met up with the others in the parking lot.

"Done?" Tawny asked.

Everyone nodded solemnly. Fiona yawned.

"Good." Tawny smiled for the first time all morning. "I'm proud of you guys. These telephones are a super act of modern vandalism. And, Chelsea,"—she turned to me—"great idea."

Tawny's compliment was like a flower blooming in my heart, crowding out any thoughts of that stupid farb with his fake daguerreotype. I beamed the whole car ride home.

The rest of the day, in between telling moderners tales of the dead baby hill, I daydreamed about the Civil Warriors discovering telephone after telephone. I pictured the adults at Reenactmentland yelling at them. And the junior inter-preters would feign ignorance, blame the moderners, or even own up to it—whatever they had to do to keep the adults from finding out about the War. But as soon as their bosses were out of earshot, the Civil War kids would curse us and our brilliance, and they would plot their revenge. That's how war goes.

By the time work ended for the day, I had already been awake for twelve hours, and I had taken to sitting down and yawning directly in moderners' faces. Linda didn't say anything, just looked at me disapprovingly before she left. But she has a disapproving face, so I didn't take it personally.

The burying ground was empty, and I was about to go home and pass out for the night, when Ezra walked in through the gate. He was by himself, which made this the first time we'd been alone together since . . . Oh, right, since he broke up with me. I could hear Fiona's voice in my head, reminding me: *Is it August seventh already, Chelsea? Well, is it?*

"Glad you're still here." He tipped his hat.

I hated to think it, but Ezra looked good in Colonial costume. Really good. I guess he just looks good in everything.

I tried to will myself into looking alert and non-sweaty. "How may I assist you, sir?" I asked, hoping that, whatever Ezra wanted, it could be accomplished quickly and professionally. *Unemotionally.*

But he didn't get right to the point. He looked around a little, read a couple headstones. "So this is where you work, huh?"

"This is where the magic happens. Hope you're not scared of ghosts," I joked.

He laughed. "No worries. I don't believe in ghosts."

Of course, Ezra didn't believe in ghosts. I knew this.

It made me sad to hear him tell me, like I didn't already know. I remembered the exact brunch when we'd discussed this. I was eating French toast. He was eating an omelet. We'd seen an advertisement for some horror movie, and the next thing I knew we were discussing the afterlife, or lack thereof.

"When you die, you just die," Ezra had said that day in the diner. "No ghosts, no reincarnation, no heaven. People want to believe that their 'souls' live on or whatever, but that's only because they can't handle the idea of the world going on without them."

I didn't share Ezra's certainty. Not like I believed in a bunch of Caspers floating around and saying "boo." But I also couldn't believe that a person could live and then die, and suddenly it would be as if they'd never lived at all. An ending couldn't be that abrupt. When I pictured ghosts, I mostly pictured memories. Aftereffects. Ezra didn't get it, and told me I was being silly.

"I like this place," Ezra said now, glancing around the graveyard. "I can see why you wanted to work here."

My game plan for dealing with Ezra had been the same for the past two months: stony silence. Stoicism. Maybe the occasional death-glare, but mostly ignoring him to the point where he would wonder if he even existed at all.

That was the game plan. But when it was a beautiful summer day, and I was riding on the high of a successful military campaign against Reenactmentland, and Ezra was acting so *nice*, then I defaulted to plan B.

In plan B, I just try to make him happy. In plan B, I turn into a one-woman Entertaining Ezra Gorman show.

"You see this hill?" I asked him. "This is where the unbaptized babies are buried. Hundreds of them."

"Seriously? That's awesome. It looks too small for that, though."

"Well, babies are small," I pointed out. "That's, like, what they're known for. But this isn't even the best grave. Come look over here."

He followed me to Elisabeth Connelly's headstone. "See," I said, "she has my name!"

Ezra's expression was as blank as Linda's had been when I'd shared this with her. "I mean, my Colonial name," I clarified for him. "But it's the same thing. So random, right?"

"Sure," Ezra said, nodding.

Hearing him say *sure* was like swallowing a weight. I knew there had been a time when Ezra would have been excited about this, if only because I was excited about it. When he would have gotten it, gotten *me*. I could remember that time so clearly. But it wasn't now.

That just about pulled the curtain on the Entertaining Ezra show. It's a short show, and it doesn't get any applause, these days. I turned and walked out of the graveyard, him falling into step beside me.

"I came over to congratulate you on the telephone thing," he said. "The guys at the magazine can't stop talking about it. It sounds awesome."

"Oh," I said. "Thanks."

All I ever wanted was for Ezra to be like this, to choose to talk to me, to compliment me. But when he did, that made it even harder. Because I couldn't hear him say just, "Nice job with the battle plan." The ending I heard to that sentence was, ". . . and therefore I want to get back together."

I would take him back, if he asked me. I told Fiona I wouldn't, I told *myself* I wouldn't, but, walking side by side with him now, I knew that I would. Since we'd broken up, I'd constructed countless fantasies in which he asked me to give him one more chance, and in these fantasies I made him beg, or I lectured him on the despicable way he had treated me, or I gave him a long list of conditions and requirements—but in the end, I always said yes.

He adjusted the brim of his tricornered hat and said in a self-satisfied way, "See, I knew you'd be a good Lieutenant."

We reached the parking lot. My bike was locked to a sapling in the corner. "What do you mean, *see?*" I asked.

"Nothing. Just that I predicted you'd be a good Lieutenant, and, see, I was right."

"Are you taking credit for me coming up with this telephone plan?"

"No, I'm just taking credit for nominating you for this position."

"Okay, well, then congratulations to you." I unlocked my bike and strapped on my helmet. "You win again. Yay."

"Jesus, Chelsea, I just came to tell you that you did a good job. Why are you acting like such a bitch to me?"

My nose and throat felt pinched. "I guess I just keep acting like some girl who used to be your girlfriend. I don't know why I do that. That is pretty bitchy of me."

I hiked up my gown, pulled on my helmet over my mobcap, swung my leg over my bike, and pedaled away. The air rushing past felt good on my eyes.

The answer, Ezra, is that you broke my heart, and I want to hurt you even one-tenth of how much you hurt me.

But I wasn't going to tell him that. Because then I would have to tell him just how bad I felt about him, and I didn't want him to know he had the power.

Before I went to bed that night, I found myself sitting at my desk, wrapped in Dan's oversized gray hoodie and looking through my Ezra file. There's not much in my Ezra file. It's much skinnier than, say, my geometry file, which is depressing, because Ezra has had a far greater impact on my life than geometry ever will.

The Ezra file includes printouts of our first e-mails back and forth, from September; a Diamond Café napkin on which he'd written, "Meet me after work? xoxo Ezra P.S. Writing on a napkin is hard!"; a strip of photobooth photos showing us looking mad, sad, surprised, and, finally, happy; a twenty-year-old Coney Island postcard that he'd bought for me at a junk shop; ticket stubs from a midnight movie we once went to; a picture of us bundled up and sitting on a sled, his arms wrapped around me, both of us squinting our eyes and smiling up at the camera. That's the Ezra file.

"I shouldn't let you keep all this," Fiona said back in April, after she had already gone through and deleted every sweet text from him, every one of his e-mails. "You should really throw this whole thing away."

"I can't," I said.

"It would make you feel better."

I shook my head and held on to it. The few, flimsy items in this file were my only proof that Ezra had ever been mine, that we had ever happened. That he had ever once missed me, that we had ever gone sledding together, that he had ever thought about me for long enough to write my name. These were our historical artifacts.

"Fine, I'll let you keep it," Fiona relented, "but only if you never look through it."

I told her I wouldn't, and usually I kept to that promise, but it was harder in the nighttime, especially tonight, when I was too tired even to make myself go to bed. I opened the Ezra file more nights than I should have, though I can't say what I ever hoped to find in there. I guess I just wanted reassurance that it had been real; we had been happy together. That I hadn't made up the whole thing.

Two days later, I was showing Elisabeth Connelly's grave to a group of day-camp kids in matching neon green T-shirts when a cell phone started to ring.

"*I want to sex you up,*" the ringtone blared. "*All night, I want to sex you up.*"

The summer campers, startled out of their it's hot/I'm hungry/Jeremy stole my friendship bracelet stupor, started giggling. "Sex!" shrieked one of the boys.

Their counselor looked both embarrassed and downtrodden. "Whose phone is that?" she demanded as it kept ringing.

"We don't *have* phones," answered one of the girls, who looked to be maybe six years old.

"We aren't *allowed* to bring our phones," said another girl. "We're at *camp*."

"I want to sex you up!" sang someone else in time with the ringtone.

Linda marched over to me, her gown swishing around her ankles. "Miss Connelly," she said, "will you please *turn off* that sound?"

"I don't know where it's coming from! Some moderner must have dropped it." I hated that she assumed this was my fault. If there's one rule every Essex employee follows, even Tawny, it's that you don't carry your cell around with you, because you never want something like this to happen.

The ringing stopped for a minute, then started up again. The kids were in hysterics.

"Listen up," I said. "Treasure hunt! Whoever can find the cell phone wins!"

The kids scattered amongst the graves, screaming randomly.

"I found it, I found it!" One of the little boys ran up to me, holding a cheap-looking flip phone. "It was behind that grave!"

The phone was still ringing when I grabbed it out of his hand. "Hello?" I said.

"I heard you Colonials like phones," said a girl's voice on the other end. "So, here you go." Then the line went dead.

Okay, Civil War. You are asking for it.

"Miss Connelly, please *put away* that modern device," Linda snapped.

"It's not mine!" I said "I swear. Can I bring it down to Lost and Found? I'm sure someone's looking for it."

Lies, lies, lies.

Linda let me go, and I took off practically running down the road.

"Can you tell us where the bathroom—" An elderly couple tried to flag me down.

"Later!" I shouted, dropping them a curtsy without slowing

my pace at all. The phone in my hand started to ring again, so I turned it off.

I ran into the Bristol House, where Tawny was in the middle of re-creating a typical middle-class family experience for a handful of onlookers. "This is a sampler," she explained as I thundered into the room. "Young ladies practice their embroidery stitches . . . Oh, welcome, Miss Connelly."

"Miss Nelson," I replied, curtsying. "We have a bit of a problem."

The moderners crowded around. *Real slick, Chelsea.* They probably thought our problem was like "The King is taxing our tea!" and now they wanted to hear all about it.

I thought fast. "The fife and drum parade is about to start on Governor's Row," I announced. "It's an excellent performance. Very authentic!"

The moderners scrambled for the door.

"Nice," Tawny said once they'd gone. "You know the fife and drum show isn't until one."

I shrugged. "They should get there early to claim their spots. That parade route gets crazy-crowded."

"It's nine thirty."

"*Crazy*-crowded."

"Look, we won't have much time before more moderners come in," Tawny said. "What's going on?"

"There was a cell phone in the graveyard. Someone from

the Civil War hid it there. And then they called while I had, like, a full-on troop of Cub Scouts."

"Shit. Do we think it's just a one-off, or is this a far-reaching sabotage plan?"

As if to answer Tawny's question, tinny strains of a ringtone pierced the air. *"Let's talk about sex, baby! Let's talk about you and me!"*

"Classy." Tawny rolled her eyes and moved purposefully toward the sound.

"God, this is an old song," I commented.

"Unfortunately, it's not *two hundred fifty years old*, so it is still an *anachronism*." Tawny found the phone on the mantel-piece, tucked away in a silver sugar bowl, which had most likely been handcrafted by my dad. She flipped the phone open and barked into it, "Tony's Pizza! Pickup or delivery?" She paused. "I *said*, pickup or delivery?" Pause. "Listen, lady, I don't know what you mean by 'Colonials,' but next time you call this number, you better have your pizza order ready. Capiche?"

"You know, I've heard of prank phone calls," I said once she'd hung up, "but I've never before witnessed a prank phone answer."

Tawny was barely listening. "We're going to need a really good retaliation, but for now let's focus on damage control. Let's both spread the word, and hopefully everyone will be able to find the phones and turn them off before they ring."

"I'm on it." I headed out, nearly bumping into a kid on his way into Bristol House who was explaining to his dad, "See how the door is so short? That's because they were really short back then! Except for George Washington. George Washington was nine feet tall. And all the doors in his house were enormous."

I made a break for the silversmith's. I could hear a phone ringing as I walked inside, but fortunately both my parents were out of the room.

"Where is that coming from?" I snapped at Bryan.

"I don't know. It keeps ringing, though."

"So why haven't you found it and turned it off?"

Bryan looked thoughtful and toadlike. Technically, Bryan is much smarter than I am. But in any category that counts—like the category of "what to do when a phone is ringing 'Let's Get It On' in the middle of your living history village"—Bryan is not the brightest candle in the abra.

I found the phone in the box of silver shavings that my dad keeps. Every year or so, Essex sends them to Richmond and cashes them in for actual money. A year is about how long it takes to collect any significant amount of silver shavings.

I answered the phone, drawing inspiration from Tawny. "Thank God you called, Maurice," I said. "What did the test results say?"

There was a moment of silence. Bryan squinted his eyes

at me. "Uh, Chelsea?" said the voice on the other end of the line. "Is that you? Who's Maurice?"

"Yes," I said. "Wait, who's this?"

"It's Dan. You know, we met when I kidnapped you?"

"Right, of course."

"I've been calling you all morning, but no one answered."

"Oh, I don't work at the silversmith's anymore, so I wasn't here. I'm working the graveyard shift now."

"What's the graveyard shift?"

"In the graveyard."

"Elizabeth!" I looked up to see my dad standing over me, looking furious. "Mayhaps you could take this call *somewhere else*?" He gestured with his chin to the onlooking moderners.

I gathered up my skirts and edged out of the studio and upstairs to the break room.

"Sorry," Dan said as I climbed the stairs. "Did I get you in trouble?"

"Yeah. Just with my dad, though, so it's fine. Anyway, it's War. Getting your opponents in trouble is pretty much the point."

"Then I guess we're winning this War."

"You are not."

"Uh, pretty sure we are. Come on, ringing cell phones? Genius."

"Pshh. Clichéd. And 'Let's Get It On'? You've got a dirty mind, Dan."

He laughed. "That ringtone is purely coincidental. Maybe *you* have a dirty mind?"

I blushed.

"Listen," Dan went on. "Do you want to—Oh, shit. Tourists. Later." And the call ended.

I held on to the cheap, cracked phone for a minute, staring out the window in the break room. *Do you want to . . .* what? "Do you want to stop sneaking into my tent and going through my personal belongings?" "Do you want to take your lame Colonial friends and your poor excuses for pranks and get the hell out of town?" "Do you want to, in the immortal words of Marvin Gaye and this cell phone, get it on?"

I turned off that phone and threw it in the trash can. It didn't matter what Dan had been about to ask me; my answer was no. No, I don't want to. What I *want* to do is be the best Lieutenant Essex has ever seen. What I want to do is win. And that meant no chatty phone calls with Civil Warriors. So I smoothed my skirts, adjusted my mobcap, and headed back out to battle.

Chapter 8
THE FOURTH OF JULY

*E*ssex flirts with anarchy every day of the year, but on the Fourth of July, any illusion of control disappears, and the village disintegrates into a totally lawless land of petticoated women and uniformed men running wild.

First the British troops show up and set up camp on the Palace Green. I don't know who the British troops are. They're not employed by Essex. I don't know where they come from or where they go after the Fourth of July, and I *definitely* don't know why they choose to portray a losing team. I feel this way about Civil War Reenactmentland, too. Like—guys, guess what! The Confederate Army *lost the War!* That is why we're still part of the United States!

Anyway, these regiments of freelance historical interpreters descend upon Essex, and they march around in uniform and party in the taverns. There are skirmishes in the street, and we taunt them in a historically accurate fashion in the hopes of getting them to arrest us.

If you can swing it, getting arrested is the high point of the Fourth of July. Also, the reading of the Declaration of Independence is exciting. (Yes, the Declaration was written two years after Essex is officially set. No, this doesn't stop us.) Thomas Jefferson, aka my dad's friend Mike, stands in the Governor's Palace, overlooking mobs of tourists, and reads in a booming voice, *"We hold these truths to be self-evident, that all men are created equal, that they are endowed by their Creator with certain inalienable Rights, that among these Rights are Life, Liberty and the pursuit of Happiness. . . ."* It sends shivers down my spine every year. It makes me want to get out there and do something *American.* So the Declaration reading is pretty cool. But, all things considered, getting arrested is better.

"Remember when I got arrested last year?" Patience asked. I was standing with her, Anne, and Fiona, eating ice cream outside of Belmont's General Store and watching the British troops march down the main road. Independence Day is the only time when we can blatantly eat food in front of moderners without getting in trouble. Like I said: a lawless land.

"I got arrested too," Anne piped up.

Patience ignored her. "I was singing 'Yankee Doodle' as

loud as I could. I shouted at them, 'You'll never catch me, you lobsterbacks!' Then I ran away. They got me and tied my hands behind my back and marched me around as a prisoner of war. *Everyone* was taking pictures. It was very exciting."

"People also took pictures of me when I got arrested," Anne offered.

"The soldiers who arrested me were *hot.* I don't know if it was the fake British accents or what, but *roawr.* One of them even got my number before I escaped from their jail."

"But then he never called," Anne noted.

"Okay, well, did any of the Redcoats who arrested you even *ask* for your number?" Patience turned on Anne. Anne said nothing. "Exactly," Patience concluded.

Everything about Patience is pointy, from her stick-straight blond hair, to her angular nose and chin, to her jutting-out hip bones. I know her too well to find her pretty, but I guess she is, in a technical sense. Anne is rounder than Patience, and plain-looking. She highlights her dishwater-brown hair as if that might make her look more exciting, but the roots grow too fast for that to work. Maggie is the real beauty of the milliner girls, with thick, dark hair, pouty lips, and curves in the right places. But Maggie was back at the milliner's, presumably working, though it was hard to imagine anyone accomplishing anything on the Fourth of July.

"I want that one," Fiona said, gesturing at a British soldier with her spoon.

"How can you even tell?" I asked. "They're all wearing the same uniform, and marching in the same gait. They all seem equally hot. Which one are you pointing to?"

"The one with the long hair, see?"

"Fiona," I said, "you need to get over this hair thing. It's creeping me out."

"Down with King George!" Patience hollered.

Three adorable Redcoats descended upon her like flies to honey. Patience giggled and flounced a little until one of them grabbed her and proclaimed, "The King's name shall not be so blasphemed!" and frog-marched her off.

"Do any of the rest of you ladies have words to say against our king?" the long-haired soldier asked. He looked as menacing as a teenage guy can when he has a mane of luscious locks tumbling down his shoulders.

Fiona nodded solemnly and beckoned him closer with her finger. He leaned in, and she cupped a hand to her mouth and whispered into his ear. "Enough of that, miss!" he exclaimed, grinning at her. She twirled a strand of hair around her finger and grinned back. "I shall take you to explain yourself to the magistrate," he announced, presumably for the benefit of any nearby moderners.

Fiona poked me and nodded her head toward the unclaimed Redcoat. He blushed. I blushed. Neither of us spoke. Fiona rolled her eyes and thrust her cup of ice cream into my hand. "I give it a four," she said to me, though her eyes were on her soldier, not the ice cream. "I've had better, but it'll do in a pinch."

Then the soldier placed a hand on her lower back and guided her down the little brick path toward the garden behind the York House. She glanced over her shoulder and winked at me before they disappeared from view. I watched her go, the remains of her rum-raisin ice cream melting in front of me. The available Redcoat skittered away.

Patience and Fiona make it look so easy. To just run off with random cute boys. Unfortunately, the only thing I find easy is lusting after boys who are wholly unavailable.

I could tell Fiona wanted me to flirt with that Redcoat, as part of her "find Chelsea's true love this summer" scheme. She probably thought I was being prudish. I did know how to flirt, though. Sort of. Dan and I had been flirting when he called on the phone, or at least I thought maybe we had been. I wished that Fiona knew about that conversation. But of course she couldn't. She could proposition a British soldier in broad daylight, in front of everyone, but I wasn't even allowed to *think* about Dan.

I tasted Fiona's ice cream. It was only so-so, since I think raisins are gross and desiccated and should stay the hell out of desserts. But I finished it anyway, since mine was all gone, and even the worst ice cream is better than no ice cream. Though apparently the worst ice cream isn't better than making out with a long-haired Redcoat.

"I'm going to stop by the silversmith's to say hi to my parents," I said to Anne. "You can come along, if you want." So she did. Anne likes to follow people.

"Where's Bryan?" Dad asked me as soon as we stepped into his studio.

"And hello to you, too, Father."

Dad just raised his bushy eyebrows at me.

"Look, I have no idea where he is. I'm not his keeper, thank God. He's probably off discussing battleship repair with a British soldier."

"That boy has a good head on his shoulders." Dad nodded.

"Yeah, I mean, he definitely knows more about eighteenth-century sexual politics than anyone else I've ever met."

"Find him and bring him back here." When my dad's not asking unanswerable questions, he is issuing impossible commands. It's hard to say which is more annoying.

"I don't know where he is," I protested.

"*I* don't know where he is," Dad said.

"But I don't *care* where he is!"

"But *I* do."

"So why don't *you* go look for him?"

"*Because I am repairing this sugar bowl!*" Dad bellowed at me. Anne and I left.

"Bye, sweetie!" Mom called after me. "Come back any time!"

"Where are you going to look for Bryan?" Anne asked as

we headed down the road toward the milliner's.

"I'm not. He'll find his way back to the silversmith's on his own. He's a big boy. Excuse me!"

A band of British soldiers nearly crashed into us. They're great at marching in formation, but they seem not to handle obstacles so well. "Long live King George!" they hollered at me and Anne.

"Long live King George!" we shouted back, and scurried around them.

"Are you a Loyalist, then?" Anne asked me. "Wow, I didn't know that about you! Are your parents Loyalists, too?"

"No," I said. "I'm just a Loyalist when there are drunk Redcoats around. It's easier that way."

"Don't you want to get arrested, though?"

"Nah. I just got kidnapped like a week and a half ago," I reminded her. "I'm kind of sick of getting held captive these days."

"Hey!" A hand clamped down on my shoulder.

"Long live King George, okay?" I sighed as I turned around. But it was just Nat. "Oh, hi," I said. "Never mind."

He looked confused. "Where's Fiona?"

"God, why does everyone think I know where everyone is today?"

Nat shrugged and twirled his ponytail. "No idea. But you *do* know where she is, right?"

"Yes, of course." I didn't elaborate.

"So . . . ?"

Way to put me on the spot. "Um, I think she's, like, by York House or whatever."

"She's with a Redcoat!" Anne piped up. "He's cute. Actually"—she peered at Nat thoughtfully—"he kind of looks like you!"

"Oh, right." Nat's shoulders slumped. "Thanks. I guess I'll look for her later, or tomorrow, or something."

Independence Day must be rough for the Essex guys. All these hot strangers show up and make off with the Essex women, but they don't bring along any British *girls*. That is gender inequality in action.

Nat walked away. "Nat!" I yelled after him. "Do you know where Bryan is?"

"No," Nat called back, that one syllable somehow wavering with heartbreak and loneliness.

Goddamn theater kids.

Anne and I kept walking. We passed by the courthouse. Outside of it was the pillory, and lo and behold, who had his hands and head trapped in there but Bryan Denton. You're welcome, Dad.

Moderners surrounded Bryan, snapping photos. "Can it decapitate you?" worried one woman.

"No," Bryan answered, sounding unusually depressed about sharing his historical knowledge. "It's for public shaming. You get put in the pillory when you commit a petty crime, and then you're trapped in here for a few hours, usually."

"What petty crime did *you* commit?" a man asked, smiling broadly.

"Disrespecting the King," Bryan answered, sounding like he was going to cry. "No taxation without representation!" But his voice was thin.

"Good day, sir," I said. Anne and I both curtsied.

"Miss Connelly! Miss Whitcomb!" Bryan struggled to raise his head.

"Mr. Denton, sir, your presence is required by the silversmith," I said.

Bryan's eyes bulged, and he twisted his neck from side to side like a beached eel. "Miss Connelly . . ." he said.

"*What*, Bryan?"

"The Redcoats put me in the pillory, and now I'm stuck," he hissed. "Help me."

"Oh my God, oh my God!" Anne flew to his side and tried, uselessly, to lift the wood panel off of him. "How did this happen? Are you okay?"

"I am suffering," Bryan moaned, his head and hands hanging limp.

"Elizabeth, help us!" Anne cried, scraping at the wood with her fingernails.

I cracked up. I laughed and laughed. I had to sit down on a rock, I was laughing so hard.

"It's not funny," Bryan sniffed.

It's true, I'm usually not a Loyalist. But today? Those British troops were on *fire*. I just wished we could use them to our advantage.

And that gave me an idea.

Leaving Bryan writhing in the pillory and Anne fawning over him, I continued down the road. I bumped into the same British unit from half an hour ago. Apparently they were just pacing up and down the main street on a loop.

"Long live King George!" they yelled, like we hadn't *just* had this conversation.

"Ditto!" I cried. "Hey, guys, come here. Huddle up."

The troops broke formation and clustered around me. "Look," I said. "I know you're strangers to Essex. But as fellow members of the eighteenth century, we need your help with something. So I'm just going to ask you one question: How do you feel about the Civil War?"

Essex stayed open late that night, for the holiday. Our patriotism cannot be constrained by an eight-hour workday. After the sun set, I sat out on the Palace Green with Fiona and her Redcoat fling and watched the fireworks explode overhead.

Tawny found me there. "Did you hear the news?" she asked, squatting next to me. "Today a unit of Redcoats marched out of Essex, across the street, and straight into Civil War Reenactmentland."

"Well, *that* sounds historically inaccurate." I shook my head in mock horror.

"Extremely. Apparently they told the moderners there that the Civil War began at a cricket match between England and South Carolina in 1861. It took the Civil Warriors close to an hour to run all the Redcoats out of there."

I snorted. "What enterprising young chaps they are," I said. "Tally-ho, and all that. I wonder *how* they got such a good idea?"

Tawny gave me a high five so powerful that it nearly knocked me over. "Whoever's idea this was, she's the greatest Lieutenant I could ever hope for." A firework boomed, as if in agreement.

"Hey, you're the Essex Lieutenant?" asked Fiona's Redcoat, leaning over to address me.

"Depends who's asking," I replied.

"Well, if you are, I have something for you." Using his hand that wasn't wrapped around Fiona's waist, the Redcoat pulled a folded piece of paper out of his breeches pocket and handed it to me. FOR ESSEX'S LIEUTENANT (CHELSEA), it read.

"What is this?" I asked him.

He shrugged. "I didn't open it. Some Civil War guy gave it to us when we were across the street."

I unfolded the paper and read the words inside. YOU STOLE MY HOODIE. WHAT DO I HAVE TO DO TO GET IT BACK?

"What's it say?" asked Tawny.

I quickly folded it back up. "Nothing."

"Who's it from?" Fiona was studying my face.

"It's not signed." That much was true. "It's just some trash talk from the Civil War. 'The Fourth of July sucks.' Typical stuff."

"If that's the best they can do, they might as well surrender today." Tawny spat on the ground.

"Why are you smiling?" Fiona asked me.

"Am I?"

"Yup," Fiona said. "You're definitely smiling."

You stole my hoodie. What do I have to do to get it back?

"I'm just really excited now. About . . . fireworks."

"Fireworks," repeated Fiona.

"Yes, fireworks. I love the Fourth of July." And I shouted, "Long live the King!" as a shower of red, white, and blue rained down above us.

Chapter 9
THE ENCOUNTER

"So what happened to your Redcoat boy?" I asked Fiona over ice cream the following evening. She had driven us two towns over, to Plainville, so we could go to Abbott's. Abbott's is an old-fashioned soda shop that puts Essex's ice cream options to shame. Abbott's handcrafts its own ice creams and then serves them in massive sundaes with names like "Dentist's Nightmare" and "Diabetics, Beware."

"What do you mean, 'what happened to my Redcoat boy'?" Fiona asked, swirling her spoon around her dish.

"I mean, where did he go?"

"He went . . ." Fiona gazed off into the distance and shook her head slightly. "He went the way of all things."

"You mean he *died*?"

Her focus snapped back to me. *"No."*

"Well, you made it sound like he died."

"I just meant that he went wherever it is that boys go when they go." She waved a hand. "Into the ether. Into the great beyond."

"It's still sounding like he died. Did you at least get his number?"

Fiona paused with a spoon full of nuts, caramel, and salted-caramel ice cream halfway between the bowl and her mouth. "Why would I want his *number*?"

"Hmm, let me think . . . Oh, I've got it: so you could call him."

"And talk about what?"

"Whatever it is that you two talk about," I said. "For example, what did you talk about yesterday?"

"Me, mostly."

"Fine. So if you'd exchanged numbers, you could have phone conversations where you talk more about you. Doesn't that sound fun?"

"Or," Fiona suggested, "you and I could go out to ice cream, and *we* could talk about me, and that would spare me the trouble of having to interact with that guy ever again."

"That dumb, huh?"

She tossed her hair. "The beautiful ones always are."

"He wasn't *that* beautiful," I pointed out.

She sucked on her spoon, considering. "In that case, he was disproportionately dumb," she determined. "Let me tell you what he said when I told him about the Essex Cheerleaders. . . ."

I leaned back in the booth, half listening to Fiona, half trying to digest the quart of cake batter ice cream I had just devoured. I noticed a guy and a girl ordering at the counter. I have never understood people who go to Abbott's for takeout. The walls are overflowing with colorful knickknacks; every table and plate is unique; and all the waiters wear 1950s-style soda jerk uniforms. Abbott's is not a take-out place; it's an *experience.*

I overheard the girl at the counter say, as if she were reading my mind, "But why can't we stay and eat here?"

"Because I told Mom we'd be home by nine."

And I recognized that voice, that gentle Southern drawl. I stared at the guy to make sure, but there was no real question. It was Dan. It was Dan, ordering ice cream with the girl from the daguerreotype.

"Mom wouldn't notice if we were a few minutes late," the girl wheedled.

"Are you kidding? Are we talking about the same mother? If we were a few minutes late, she'd become convinced that we'd abandoned her too. No question. Do you have her Rocky Road?"

The girl halfheartedly lifted a container of ice cream.

"Great. Let's roll."

They started to walk toward the door, which meant that they started to walk toward *me*. Toward the table where I sat with Fiona, who was still talking, maybe about cheerleaders, maybe about genocide now, I didn't know, I wasn't listening. I was panicking.

Time felt like it slowed down and sped up all at once. Dan was coming closer and closer to where I sat, while I kept staring at him, my eyes searching for his eyes.

When he was only a few feet away, Dan noticed me. He smiled directly at me and opened his mouth as if to say hi. So I responded as any reasonable girl would: *I ignored him.*

I dropped my gaze to my bowl, scooped up an overflowing spoonful of ice cream, and shoved it so far back into my mouth that I gagged on its watery sweetness. Some of it dribbled out of the corners of my mouth, so I had to snatch up a big wad of napkins and swipe at my chin. When I was done with all of that, I looked up again, and Dan was gone.

Fiona was laughing at me.

"What?" I demanded.

"*What*, you just attacked that ice cream like a slobby snake who's been starving itself for weeks. Do you know that guy?"

"Which guy?"

"The one who almost made it necessary for me to give you the Heimlich maneuver."

"You don't know the Heimlich maneuver," I pointed out.

"Chelsea! Do you *know* him?"

"No."

Fiona narrowed her eyes at me. She required a better lie.

"I just thought he was cute, that's all." He *was* looking cute, too, all disheveled hair and pale skin. He was as cute here as he had been in my mind.

Not that it mattered, since I had just blanked him in the middle of Abbott's.

"I guess he was cute," Fiona granted, "but he was with that girl. You need someone who's actually available."

"She's his sister."

"I thought you didn't know him?"

"I *don't*. I just heard them talking at the counter. They're brother and sister."

"You were listening to some strangers when you could have been listening to me talk about myself? Chelsea, how could you?"

I rolled my eyes at her.

"I give this sundae a nine and a half," Fiona continued peacefully. "It's perfect, but I just want to hold on to that ten in case something more perfect ever shows up, you know?"

And that was it for Fiona. I had seen a hot guy, I had almost killed myself on a spoon of ice cream, that was all. Only I knew the truth: I had *completely* blown it.

Chapter 10
THE MILLINER GIRLS

*W*ednesday was hot. Even by Virginia-in-July standards it was hot. By lunchtime, the "How can you stand to wear that dress in this weather?" tally had reached double digits, and I had lost the will to lie.

I knew I had to blame somebody, so I decided on Fiona. I marched over to the milliner's, where I found Fiona and Maggie putting away scrap fabric, while Patience and Anne crowded around a moderner trying on a dress, telling her how awesome she looked in it.

"Good day, Elizabeth," Fiona said.

"We could be at The Limited right now!" I leaned across the counter to whisper-scream at her. "At this *very moment,* we could be in an air-conditioned mall. We could be taking a break from our air-conditioned jobs to eat ice cream in the air-conditioned food court. In some parallel universe, luckier, smarter versions of Chelsea and Fiona are doing exactly that, while *we are stuck here.*"

"It's really hot," Fiona agreed.

"Damn straight it's really hot!"

The moderner paid Maggie for the gown. "I look just like you all now!" she exclaimed, which I guessed was true, if the five of us looked like middle-aged preschool teachers.

After she had pranced out the door in her new Colonial outfit, I asked, "Since I'm here, can I see the Civil War costumes?"

Patience narrowed her eyes, as if trying to figure out whether she could trust me.

"I'm the *Lieutenant*," I reminded her.

She shrugged, still suspicious, then dug around in the back of the armoire before producing two snazzy Confederate soldiers' uniforms.

"Perfect!" I reached for one, but Patience whipped it away from me.

"They're not done yet."

"Really?"

"Of *course* not. See, they need another row of buttons here. And you might think it wouldn't *matter* if the shirt isn't hemmed, since it's going to be tucked in, but honestly . . ."

The other milliner girls all nodded seriously, even Fiona. I had no clue what they were seeing that I wasn't. The uniforms looked good enough to me. If we truly lived in the past, I would make some historical man a totally useless wife.

"So when do you think all this will be done?" I asked.

Patience widened her eyes and took a step toward me. "Oh, I'm sorry," she said. "Are we not working *fast* enough for you? Does this seem *easy*? Could you just whip up an authentic Confederate uniform in an *hour or two*?"

"Nope." I shook my head quickly. "Definitely no."

"Then have. Some. Patience," snapped Patience.

I made a mental note to tell Tawny that some of our soldiers seemed overworked and possibly on the verge of an insane meltdown.

"Can we *please* go to the brickyard now?" Fiona asked as Patience stuffed the costumes back into their hiding spot. "We're wasting our break."

This was the first good idea that I'd heard all day.

We hustled out the door and down the small dusty lane to the brickyard. Once there, we stripped off our boots and stockings, hitched up our petticoats, and waded into the treading pit. The clay and water felt cool on my calves. This was almost as good as air-conditioning. I completely understood how pigs felt.

"So, about the Lenny and Elissa thing . . ." Anne started, but the rest of the girls all groaned.

"He's not worth it," Fiona said, stomping through the clay. "Honestly, you can do so much better."

"He has that weird thing going on with his chin," added Patience.

"And not to minimize your suffering or anything," Maggie said, "because I totally get that you are suffering, but you guys hooked up, what, once? A year ago? It's not like you have any claim over him. If he wants to bang that skank, that's his prerogative."

"I'm not saying I have a *claim* over him," Anne protested. "I just want to know what she has that I don't."

Maggie answered by holding her hands about six inches in front of her chest, miming Elissa's D-cup. The rest of the girls cracked up.

"She is such a slitch," Patience said, thus saving herself the effort of having to use two full syllables to call Elissa both a slut and a bitch. She was also wrong. As far as I knew, Elissa was just a normal history nerd who worked as a waitress at the White Horse Tavern.

Anne said, "I'd almost feel better if Lenny was dating a Civil Warrior."

"Ewww," we all cried in unison—even though a picture of Dan flashed through my mind as I squealed.

"Elissa's bad, but she's not *that*," Fiona said. "Those Civil War girls are such whores. Chelsea told me they left old bras and panties draped all around the shoemaker's yesterday."

"True," I confirmed. "I didn't even want to pick them up for fear of contracting an STD."

"We need to fight back harder." Maggie looked at me pointedly.

I put up my hands. "Hey, if anyone's got ideas, by all means, bring them on."

"The thing about Lenny—" Anne tried to return to her favorite topic, but Patience interrupted.

"How's it going with Nat?" Patience asked Fiona.

Fiona squished the mud between her toes. "It's *not* going with Nat."

"Maybe he's scared," I offered.

"Oh, please," Fiona scoffed. "I'm not scary."

"Sure," I said. "You're just gorgeous—"

"Only if you're into brunettes," she argued.

"And rich—"

"Not anymore."

"And charismatic—"

"Eh, it comes and goes."

"Oh, and you've made out with practically every worthwhile guy at school."

"At least twenty percent of them were drunk at the time." She fluttered her long lashes.

"Right, so I can't imagine why Nat would be scared of you. Plus, Fi, you *just* hooked up with a British soldier. Like two days ago. So maybe Nat has some reason to believe you're not that into him."

"He didn't need to know that I was making out with a

British soldier," Fiona said. "What he doesn't know can't hurt him. But no, someone here just *had* to tell him."

"Sorry!" Anne bleated.

"It's truly a wonder that anyone ever manages to date anyone," Fiona observed. "When you think about how complicated it is."

"How about you and Bryan, huh?" Patience nudged me so hard that it hurt. "He's obviously still carrying that torch for you."

I rolled my eyes. This is how the milliner girls are. Constant boys and dating and hookups and crushes, like there's nothing else going on in their lives. Maybe there's really not. I don't know how Fiona stands working with them.

Of course, I'd spent an unhealthy amount of time over the past few days thinking about Dan Malkin. But at least I *knew* it was unhealthy.

"What's wrong with Bryan?" Maggie asked me. "Okay, he's a little weird, but I think you guys would make a cute couple."

I blanched. This was probably the worst insult I had ever received.

"Speaking of cute couples," Anne said to Maggie, "do you know where you and Ezra are going tomorrow night?"

Maggie glowed. Maybe it was just the sweat or something, but she positively *glowed*. "He won't tell me," she said. "Just that it's a surprise and that I should look cute, like I always do."

A collective sigh from all the girls, except for Fiona. And

me. Fiona stared down at the mud. I stared at her. *Come on, Fi, just look up and tell me that it's nothing. Tell me that nothing's going on.*

Maggie was on a roll. "He bought me candy from Belmont's yesterday. Seriously. A little box of truffles, all wrapped up with a bow and a note about how he couldn't wait to see me. He's so sweet, guys, it's unbelievable. And did I tell you what he said when we were watching the Fourth of July fireworks together?"

"*Yes,*" Patience and Anne chorused.

"Like eight times," Patience added.

Fiona was still refusing to look at me. And I could have let that be my answer, but I had to know for sure. "Ezra who?" I asked, in my best attempt at a normal voice.

"Ezra Gorman," Maggie answered. "You know, the new guy who works in the magazine? The hot one?" She gave a loud, braying laugh.

"Of course Chelsea *knows*, idiot," Patience said. "She used to date him. During the school year." Patience goes to school with me and Ezra. Maggie does not.

Maggie stopped laughing. "Is that true?"

"Yeah," I said.

"You just have a thing for people's ex-boyfriends, don't you?" Patience asked her.

"Well." Maggie shrugged. "Everyone is *someone's* ex-boyfriend."

"It's okay," I said, even though no one had asked me whether it was okay or not. "It was a long time ago."

"He's a great guy," Maggie offered, like my consolation prize was that I had great taste in guys.

So I said, "Thanks." And then I tried to get out of the treading pit, but in the process I dropped the hem of my petticoat into the mud.

"Ugh," Anne said, with great sympathy. "It's *so* hard to get mud off these clothes." All the girls nodded in solidarity.

"You're right," I said, pulling on my stockings without even bothering to wipe the mud off my feet. "It is really, really hard."

A family of moderners showed up then, exclaiming, "Look at the Colonial girls in the mud!" The milliner girls posed and pouted and splashed around while the moderners took photos, and I made my escape.

Fiona caught up to me on the small road behind the brickyard. She was barefoot, holding her boots in her hand. "Are you okay?" she asked.

"Yeah, it'll be fine." I stopped walking and gestured toward my muddy dress. "I was going to have to do laundry one of these months, anyway."

"I meant about the Ezra and Maggie thing."

"Oh." I played with the drawstrings on my petticoat. "You knew already."

"Yes. I work with her. I can't help but know."

"Why didn't you tell me, Fi?"

"I didn't think you could handle it." She gazed at me steadily.

"Then you were wrong. I can handle it. Look at me handling it."

"Chelsea—" Fiona began.

"Seriously, what does it have to do with me? If he wants to date Maggie, or anyone else, how is that my concern? If he wants to buy her *candy*, and include a *note*, does that mean anything to me? We broke up months ago. It's not like he's cheating on me. It's not like he needs to ask my permission. His love life is none of my business, and *I don't care.*"

"Well," Fiona said, "that was very convincing. Color me convinced."

I kicked a pebble and said nothing. Ezra gave me a box of chocolates once too. It was for our two-month anniversary. Who the hell remembers a two-month anniversary? Ezra Gorman, that's who. And there was a note with my truffles too. That's not original. It said, "The past two months have been the happiest of my life. Let's have so many more. Love, Ezra." That was in the Ezra file too, if I ever needed to look at it, if I ever managed to forget what it said.

What, had I thought I was the first girl, or the last girl, or the most important girl? I am everygirl. I am this easily replaceable.

"I thought I was happy on the Fourth of July," I said quietly.

"I didn't see Ezra once, and I barely thought about him at all. And now that I know that the reason why I didn't see him is that he was off with Maggie, well . . . It's like now it turns out it wasn't such a great day, after all."

Fiona shook her head. "That's revisionist history. While it was happening, it *was* a good day. You *were* happy. You shouldn't let whatever Ezra was doing ruin that for you."

"I know that I shouldn't," I said. "But I do. I can't help it." I leaned against the low fence bordering the road.

Fiona said, "Yes, he's moving on. Yes, it's sad. But he's not the only one who can do that, Chelsea. You can move on too."

"I'd be glad to," I said. "How?"

"Just . . . stop thinking about how it used to be all the time. Live in the present."

I laughed bitterly. "What does that even mean? It's hard to live in the present when the 'present' is two hundred fifty years ago. It's hard to live in the present when my job is literally called 'living history.' And I'm really good at it. I've spent most of my life perfecting the craft of living history. I have no practice at living in the present."

"Not that you asked me," Fiona said, "but I think a good start at living in the present would be going on a date with someone else." She leaned against the fence beside me and started to put her boots back on.

"No one else wants to date me." Briefly, I pictured Dan. But that wasn't real. That was only wishful thinking. I had sabotaged that before it could be anything more than a note saying, basically, "Give me back my belongings so that we'll never have to deal with each other again."

"Bryan Denton wants to date you," countered Fiona.

"*Gross.* Bryan is, for all intents and purposes, an amphibian. Given the choice, I would rather go on a date with an *actual* toad."

Fiona nodded—this was a hard point to argue. "Jared Fitch asked you out after Ezra."

"But, as we discussed at the time, Jared and I have literally nothing in common. He asked me to go out *bowling* with him. And what is the one sport I hate most in the world?"

"Boccie." Fiona volunteered, lacing up her boot.

I furrowed my brow. "I've never played boccie."

"It's like bowling, only worse."

"See, I rest my case. On my first date with Ezra, we went to see a concert of one of my favorite bands, who also happens to be one of *his* favorite bands. *That* is a first date. I can't believe you're presenting Jared like he was ever a viable option."

"Okay, Ari Hester."

"Has no interest in me."

"False. Ari would have asked you out this spring if you had given him half a chance. Why else do you think he was always hanging around outside of your locker, asking you what the math homework was?"

"Because otherwise he would have failed math?" I suggested. "Anyway, Ari, good guy, *unbelievably* boring. Have you ever tried to have a conversation with him?"

"Have you?" Fiona countered. She straightened up from her shoes.

"You know how there are some people who can light up a room just by walking into it? You, for example. Ezra, for another example. Well, Ari sucks the light out of a room by walking into it. He starts to speak, and you become aware of how drab and pointless all of life is." I mopped the sweat off my forehead. "It's very depressing."

"Fine, forget dating. You could have at least made out with that Redcoat on the Fourth. No strings attached."

"I didn't feel like it."

"What I hope you're noticing here," Fiona said, "is that some boys *do* want you. You just don't want *them*, because they are not Ezra Gorman."

"Look, Ezra was amazing."

Fiona snorted.

"I'm serious. You heard Maggie going on about how he's taking her on a surprise date and telling her she's adorable and whatever. Why should I go from a guy like that to a guy who wants to spend his life rolling a ball down an alley?"

"Because you need *somebody* new so you can get over Ezra and move on."

"Do I *need* somebody new?" I asked. "Can't I just be a

liberated woman and not have my day-to-day happiness be dependent on boys?"

"Absolutely," Fiona said. "By all means, be a liberated woman. But you actually have to *do* it. You have to start making yourself happy *now*. Because I'm getting sick of watching you be unhappy. This summer is supposed to be about *us*, remember? Us having fun. Us being friends. Not you moping."

"Enough." I felt stung. "I'm not moping. I am transcendently happy. We're winning the War, and nothing could be more fulfilling. And I get to spend my summer in the company of my wonderful best friend, in thirty pounds of clothing, in three-hundred-degree heat. It's all fantastic. And now I am going to return to my graveyard. The land where dreams and Colonials go to die. This has been an intense amount of advice for one lunch hour. How exactly did you become such a relationship expert?"

Fiona made as if to swish her hair, then remembered it was all pinned up under her mobcap. "I watch a lot of movies," she answered.

"That's true."

"Really, Chelsea, if you spent as much time as I do thinking about movies, then you'd know everything there is to know about love. And if I spent as much time as you do thinking about the past, then I'd probably be a lot better at my job."

"But, instead, I'm supposed to think about the present."

"Right. I think the present should be our main summertime focus."

"Also, ice cream," I reminded her.

"Yes," Fiona said as we continued our walk down the road. "Also ice cream."

Chapter 11
THE TRAITOR

A few days after my conversation with Fiona, I made a decision: I was going into Civil War Reenactment-land. Not as a hostage. Not as a saboteur. Not as a spy.

I was going into Civil War Reenactmentland to return a sweatshirt.

In front of my bedroom mirror, I rehearsed what I would say if anyone from Essex saw me across the street. "It's my day off and I got bored. Thought I'd go just for a laugh."

Right, because that sounded like the kind of thing I'd do.

"I'm returning this sweatshirt to one of the Civil Warriors who kidnapped me."

True, but unacceptable. If anyone knew I had a sweatshirt from the Civil War, we'd have to find some way to use it against them.

"I'm going to scope out their territory and report back on any weaknesses."

That would have to be my answer. That was the only answer my friends would accept.

I sighed and made a face at my reflection. *Please, just don't let anyone see me.*

This was the first full day I'd worn modern clothes in what felt like forever, and I was overwhelmed by choices. I dumped pile after pile of clothes onto my bed. Practically the only items left in my closet were the recently completed Civil War uniforms that had been put in my care until the day of the mission.

I pawed through my options. I could wear open-toed shoes! As if it were *summertime*! I could wear earrings! I put on a pair of dangling, interlocking silver hoops, just because *I could.* I could even paint my nails but decided, regretfully, that it wasn't worth it, since I'd just have to remove the polish before I went back to work tomorrow. Mr. Zelinsky always carried around a bottle of nail polish remover to help out the girls who conveniently "forgot."

I had stupid tan lines from my costume. There was a square cut-out across my chest that had turned a lovely bronze, while the rest of my skin was as pale as winter. I put on a pair of short-shorts and hoped one day of full-on sun exposure would help my legs perk up.

It's not even that I think I look better tanned. I don't. It's just that being tan makes me feel like I have accomplished something quantifiable with my time outside.

I spent a while on my makeup, then washed off nearly all of it, because I didn't want Dan to think I'd gone to any lengths to impress him. I was just returning his sweatshirt. That's all. Common courtesy.

Finally, I put on a floppy sunhat and big sunglasses. This was my disguise, so that when Civil Warriors glanced at me, they wouldn't immediately recognize me as Elizabeth Connelly, the silversmith's daughter and the Colonials' Lieutenant.

One final look in the mirror. I looked like a pasty-skinned, hat-and-shades-wearing sun-phobic. Fine. At least my earrings looked good.

I biked in the direction of Essex, but then turned left instead of right, past a garish sign proclaiming, "Welcome to Civil War Reenactmentland, winner of the Barnes Prize for Historical Interpretation!" I made a mental note that we needed to find a way to target that sign in an upcoming attack. Maybe graffiti.

I pulled the brim of my hat down low over my eyes while buying an entry ticket, and no one shouted anything like, "That girl is a Colonial! Don't let her in!"

Also, by the way—the Reenactmentland entry fee? *Not*

cheap. I was probably spending more money on returning this sweatshirt than it had cost Dan in the first place.

Reenactmentland barely resembled the barren place where I'd hidden telephones less than a week earlier. Under the midafternoon sun, it was swarming with families of squabbling moderners, summer-camp groups in matching T-shirts, couples holding hands, and people in period dress cutting purposefully through the crowd. For all intents and purposes, it looked like Essex.

I stood still for a moment, trying to orient myself toward the big field where Dan's tent had been set up. A little boy, focusing on his Popsicle, crashed into my legs.

"Michael, say sorry!" his father scolded him.

"It's fine," I said, and they pressed on.

It was more than fine, actually. It was remarkable. No one wanted to take a photo with me, no one asked me for directions. I just blended in.

The crowd swept me along until I came to the big field of tents. I walked into a few different ones before I found Dan, crouched down to explain a bayonet to a wide-eyed little girl.

In his suspenders, loose-fitting vest, and felt hat, he looked even better than when I'd seen him in a T-shirt and cut-offs. What can I say, I have a thing for guys in period dress, okay? That's just who I am.

He glanced up from the moderner, then did a double take when he noticed me. "Chelsea?"

"Hey." I waved.

He stood, towering over the little girl. "What are you doing here?"

"Um . . ." I suddenly got a fluttery feeling in my stomach. This was a bad idea. Why was I the last one to understand that this was a bad idea? "I wanted to return your sweatshirt." As proof, I held it out to him.

He looked pointedly at me, then at the moderners. I slowly dropped my arm to my side.

"Mama, I'm hungry," the girl whined.

"Okay, sweetie. We can get lunch." To Dan, the modern woman said, "Thanks for your time," and she pressed a five-dollar bill into his hand.

"You guys get tips?" I asked once they were out of range. "No wonder you could afford to buy credit for a bunch of cell phones that you're never going to see again."

"Unlike some historical interpreters, we *earn* tips." Unsmiling, he reached out his hand. "I'll take my sweatshirt now."

I am an idiot. I'm simply an idiot. Dan hadn't called me to say, "Do you want to go out on a date with me." He had called to say, "Do you want to give me back my stuff." He hadn't sent a note asking about his sweatshirt because he secretly wanted to kiss me. He had sent a note asking about his sweatshirt because *he wanted his sweatshirt.* As Fiona sometimes tells me, boys are not that complicated.

And if Dan had ever wanted anything more, then I had

127

killed that by ignoring him at Abbott's. That had been my one chance to confront him not as warring reenactors, but as two people, a girl and a boy, and I had *killed* it. I am the Charles Manson of relationships.

I was all set to give him the hoodie, walk out of Reenactmentland, and chalk up Dan Malkin as just another failure in my so-called love life—but then I stuck the sweatshirt behind my back and said, "What'll you give me for it?"

Dan blinked. "You're not seriously holding that thing hostage, are you?"

"Why not?"

"We captured your General and Lieutenant, and you captured my *sweatshirt*. Have you ever even been in a War before?"

"Well, if you don't want it . . ." I pulled on the hoodie over my tank top, shoved up the sleeves to stop them from dangling over my fingertips, and walked out of the tent.

I made it about three yards away before Dan caught up to me. "What exactly do you want for it?" he asked.

"I haven't decided yet. I'm willing to bargain."

Dan groaned. "Let's go for a walk. Let's talk this out."

"Sure," I said. "Unless you're worried about people seeing us together."

"I am." He took my elbow. "That's why we're going to walk down by the creek."

"*That* hurts my feelings," I protested as he led me past tents bustling with clothing, pottery, and dry goods vendors.

"And you're wearing an enormous hat, and sunglasses the size of basketballs, because you *want* to be seen with me?"

Fair point. "Are you taking me down by the creek so you can drown me in a place where no one will hear me scream?"

"Maybe." He half-grinned. "Do you trust me?"

"I don't trust Civil Warriors."

I followed him out of the big field, over a grassy hill, and down through some trees to the creek. We were the only people there. We walked along quietly for a moment.

"You know, if you just keep following the water, eventually you wind up in Essex," I said.

"I do know that. Two living history villages set along the same creek. The only difference is which side they're on."

"And which century."

"And that," he agreed.

"So why *do* you guys hate us so much?"

"Why do you hate *us* so much?" he shot back.

"I asked you first."

Dan was quiet for a moment, thinking, as we walked through the bluebells and Queen Anne's lace alongside the stream. Then he asked in reply, as if this cleared up everything, "Well, why did Biggie hate Tupac?"

I shrugged. "I don't know, why?"

"I don't know why, either," Dan said, "but I would guess it's because they were both doing pretty much the same thing at pretty much the same time."

"And they got jealous?" I suggested.

"Sure, or they felt threatened, like, 'This world is big enough for only one of us!'"

"'This town is big enough for only one American living history settlement,'" I said. "Sure. I buy that."

"Or, why did the Patriots hate the British?"

"Oh," I said. "Well, that's a really complicated question. Part of it was their concern about taxation without representation, as I'm sure you learned in school. It also had to do with philosophical developments of the time. After studying so many Enlightenment thinkers, the Patriots had big ideas about natural rights and the social contract, and under British rule—"

"Never mind," Dan said. "Bad analogy. I was thinking that maybe we hate you guys for the same reason that the Patriots hated the British, but I'm going to say that's unlikely, since the Enlightenment has nothing to do with it. As far as I know."

"Then how about, why did the Montagues hate the Capulets?"

He shook his head, flopping his hair a bit over his eyes. I wanted, suddenly, to reach out and brush it away, but then he fixed it himself. "I read that freshman year," he said. "I don't remember."

"They don't remember, either. They just do. They just always have. 'Two households, both alike in dignity, in fair

Verona, where we lay our scene, from ancient grudge break to new mutiny, where civil blood makes civil hands unclean.'" I quoted.

Dan laughed, and I blushed and looked down at my sandals as we kept walking. "Now, that's what I've always imagined it's like in Essex," he said. "A bunch of genteel Virginians, sitting in parlors and quoting Shakespeare."

"For your information, I can't thank Essex for that one. My best friend, Fiona, played Juliet last year. After you sit through enough performances, you start to memorize lines whether you want to or not."

"That's an impressive commitment to a friend," Dan noted.

"I guess. Or it's just that Fiona would have killed me if I'd missed a single show."

"Is Fiona the other girl we kidnapped?"

"No, that was Tawny." I didn't want to reveal too much information about Tawny, in case I accidentally told Dan something the Civil Warriors could use against us. But I couldn't help saying, "She's great. She could win this War single-handedly. The rest of us are probably just holding her back."

"It's cool that there are black kids working at Essex."

"Uh, I don't think it's particularly *cool* or *uncool*, except insofar as 'being racist' is not super-fashionable these days. I don't know if the Civil War got that memo yet. About how racial discrimination is passé."

"Oh, we got the memo. But everyone's still concerned

about, you know"—Dan made air quotes with his fingers—
"authenticity."

"Believe me, Tawny is as authentic as they come."

"I believe you. Does she know you're here, consorting with
the enemy, right now?" Dan asked.

I didn't reply, just sat down on the grassy slope leading
down to the creek. I felt guilty, all of a sudden.

Dan sat down next to me. "I'll take that as a no."

"Is that what I'm doing?" I asked. "Consorting with the
enemy? It sounds really bad when you put it like that."

"Sure," he said. "We're consorting. We're cavorting.
We're . . ."

"Carousing?" I suggested.

"Okay, if you want, we can carouse."

I sighed and started picking petals off a flower. "Tawny
would not be happy to hear that I'm carousing with the
enemy."

"So is that why you ignored me at Abbott's?"

I'd been hoping we could pretend like that hadn't happened. "Um, yes," I said. "I'm sorry. That was rude. I just . . .
panicked."

"It *was* rude," Dan agreed, but he bumped me with his
shoulder, so I could tell it was okay. "Well, if it makes it
any better, *no one I know* would be happy to hear that we're
carousing."

"I'm not too happy about it myself."

"Oh." Dan's voice was surprised, and a little hurt. He looked away.

"I didn't mean it like that," I said. "You're . . ." Clever. Interesting. Hot. "Nice."

He snorted. "I don't know that I've ever been described that way before."

"Look, I just meant that Essex is important to me. It's where my family and friends are. I've grown up there. I don't love feeling like I'm betraying them by being here."

"Yet here you are."

I hugged my knees to my chest and echoed, "Yet here I am." Just to return a sweatshirt, obviously. To return a sweatshirt and gather information that we can use for the War. Purely innocent.

"Who was that guy who rescued you?" Dan changed the subject.

I purposefully misunderstood him. "There were a few of them. Lenny, Ezra, the girl was Caitlin . . ."

Dan was shaking his head. "Which is the one who picked you up and threw you over his shoulder like you were some wounded maiden and he was Fabio?"

I giggled. "Ezra."

"What's his deal?"

"Oh . . ." I stared across the river and shrugged. "He's, you know, my ex-boyfriend."

"Figured."

"What, it's that obvious?"

"No, it just seemed like you two had some kind of history. I mean, to someone who's paying attention, it's fairly clear that something is or was going on there. The way you reached out your arms to him after they untied you."

"Did I do that? I don't remember. Anyway, whatever. We were together a long time ago." I didn't want to discuss Ezra with Dan. They existed in separate worlds, and I wanted to keep them that way.

"Why did you guys break up? If you don't mind my asking."

I didn't mind Dan's asking, exactly, but I also didn't know how to answer him. I had never known why Ezra and I broke up, though I had thought about it, of course, thought about it until I drove myself—not to mention Fiona—crazy.

To just come out and ask Ezra *why* seemed like it would give him too much satisfaction. So it ended and I don't know why. So what? So many things come to an end—dinosaurs, my mother's garden, British Colonial rule. Who knows why? Who would care enough to ask?

"I'm not sure," I said to Dan now. "He decided one day that he didn't want to be my boyfriend anymore, and that was that. I think he just . . . got tired of me." There was a hollow feeling in my chest, which had been there since our breakup, which never fully went away.

"Did you get tired of him?"

I was so surprised that I let out a quick burst of laughter. "Of course not."

"What a dick. Do you want me to punch him for you? I could say it's part of our War effort."

I smiled. "Thanks, but don't bother. I don't care about it."

"If you say so." Dan leaned in close and asked, "Was he your first?"

"What?" I whipped off my sunglasses. "Oh my God, did you actually just ask me if I lost my *virginity* to Ezra? Dude, I, like, *barely* know you."

Dan busted out laughing. "All I meant was, was he the first guy you ever fell in love with."

"Oh." I felt myself turning red. "Well, then you should have *said* that."

"I know, I could have said that . . . but the expression on your face was priceless."

I smacked his chest with the back of my hand, and he collapsed backward into the grass, pretending I had really hurt him. We both laughed, and then he said, "I have a theory that the first person you fall for creates a model for how you approach relationships going forward. Like, it frames how you'll look at every person who you date after that. So that's why I asked. Does that make sense?"

"I guess so . . ."

I thought about Dan's question. I was no Fiona Warren, but I'd dated a few guys before Ezra. A brief summer romance with a pensive, historically minded blacksmith's assistant. My freshman-year boyfriend, who was adorable and earnest and devoted and who had probably never read an entire book cover to cover, including *Goodnight Moon*. The first boy I ever kissed, when I was twelve, who I supposedly "went out with" for three weeks, even though we never actually went anywhere, or even spoke to each other. The guy I dated in eighth grade, who was the region's best speller, but who never had time to do anything with me other than study spelling words. All good people, who went on to make other girls very happy.

My dumb, adorable freshman-year boy started dating a dumb, adorable cheerleader right after he and I broke up, and they're still in dumb, adorable heaven. My first kiss now spends his time writing and filming artistic movies with his girlfriend. In ninth grade, the region's best speller found the region's sixth-best speller, and they would sit together and quiz each other on words for hours.

These are all good people. I know they are. And I, unable to hold on to anything good, threw each one away, or let each one slip through my fingers like water.

Ezra was the only one I really tried with, really *wanted* to keep. But even trying, and wanting, didn't save anything. That was the only loss that actually counted for me.

"Yes," I said to Dan, "Ezra was my first. First love. First heartbreak. First everything."

"Well, you can't have heartbreak without love," Dan pointed out. "If your heart was really broken, then at least you know you really loved him."

"I suppose that's true. But you *can* have love without heartbreak. Why didn't I get to have that kind?"

Dan rolled his eyes and leaned back on his elbows. "I think love without heartbreak is a myth. A pretty myth, but the kind of myth that ultimately makes us all feel worse about ourselves because we're somehow not able to make it come true."

"You sound like you're speaking from personal experience." I pushed up the sleeves on the hoodie. It was too hot for sweatshirts.

"I've never been in love like that. I guess I'm speaking from my personal experience with my parents."

"Not a great relationship there?" I guessed.

"Really not. My dad took off a few months ago. Technically, this is a good thing, since he was breaking my mom's heart in very small ways each day that he stuck around. But then he broke her heart in one final, big way when he left. Like I said, technically, it's for the best. But no one looks at their lives *technically*. I don't."

"I'm sorry."

"I am too. If he were still here and everything between them was still fine—technically fine, that is, since it hasn't been *actually* fine since I was really little—but if he were still here, then I wouldn't have to be. I would be touring with my band this summer. I'd be, right this moment, probably asleep with two other guys in the backseat of the van, or eating eggs at a diner in rural Pennsylvania, or practicing for a gig . . ."

"But instead you're stuck sitting out by the creek with me," I finished for him.

"Aw, this part is okay." He playfully shoved my shoulder, and I had to resist the urge to grab hold of his arm. "It's the rest of it that I can't handle. Feeling like I *have* to be here. The only things that really matter to my mom are family and Reenactmentland. I'm not going to take either of those away from her. She's batshit, though. She keeps telling people that her husband isn't here because he's fighting the Yankees in North Carolina . . . and of course she knows that it isn't *actually* the Civil War, and that Dad's not *actually* fighting anywhere . . . but sometimes she acts like she believes it. Because she wants to. Everyone else plays along with her, even though they all know that he got fired at the end of last summer."

"That's rough," I said. I couldn't imagine what my father would do if Essex fired him. Essex was his life. "What did he do to get fired?"

Dan shrugged and looked away. "Some stupid political issue. It doesn't matter." He quickly changed the subject. "Why are *you* in the reenacting business? If not to keep your mother from having a meltdown?"

"Oh, I don't know. I'm not a huge history buff or a natural

performer, but I don't mind it, as a job. I like the people—with a few notable exceptions. My best friend is there, and she wants me there. My parents want me there." All of these reasons were completely true, but they weren't quite enough. After Dan had opened up to me about his father, I felt like I owed him some honesty. So I said, "Fiona says that I have trouble moving on. That I cling to the past."

"'The past,' meaning 1774?" Dan asked.

"Sure, 1774, or six months ago, or four summers ago . . . I wasn't going to come back this summer, but I did, and it's not entirely because Fiona or my parents asked me to, or because I didn't know if I could find a better job. It was also because I knew that I would miss it. I'd miss the way my life used to be, when I worked there. I always miss the way my life used to be, and the best way to prevent that is to not change my life very much. I don't know." I leaned back onto my elbows, too, so that our arms were nearly touching. "I guess I don't handle change very well."

"I think most people don't handle change very well." He looked at me. "Of course, *this* is a change. You're hanging out in the Civil War—and not even to hide telephones in our trunks!"

"Ha. Yeah, this is a change."

"And how would you say you're handling it?"

"So far, better than expected."

We sat there for a long moment, just staring into each

other's eyes. All I could think about was the nearness of him.

"We shouldn't be doing this." Dan broke the silence, his voice low. "We would both get in trouble." He stood up. "Let's go back."

"We shouldn't be doing what?" I scrambled to my feet. "What exactly are we doing?"

"This."

"You mean consorting?"

"Sure, consorting. Cavorting. Carousing." He paused to take a deep breath. "Kissing." Then he leaned in and pressed his mouth to mine. His lips were warm and soft, moving against my own. And then I was kissing him back, and I closed my eyes to block out everything else except this, this here and now.

A noise that sounded like zippering made me pull away. "What—" I began, before I realized that I *had* heard a zipper. Dan had tugged down the zipper on his hoodie, and now, with an expression of wide-eyed innocence, pulled it off my arms and quickly put it on over his uniform.

I was still breathing hard from our kiss, but I managed to get out, "Do you undress all the girls that fast?"

"No," he answered. "Honestly, I've never been in quite this situation before."

I wet my lips. "Did you kiss me just to distract me? Just so you could get your sweatshirt back?"

Dan shook his head slightly, his eyes fixed on mine. "No," he said quietly.

I wanted him to come back. My mouth, my whole body, wanted him back. I wanted him to hold me, wanted his arms wrapped around me here, in the tall grass, with the water rushing by and the sunlight shining down upon us.

But that's not what happened. In my life, that's never what happens. What happened was that he turned to go, like there was nothing between us.

"Dan!" I said, and he turned back around. But then I didn't know what to say.

"Chelsea." He ran a hand through his hair so it stuck up in tufts. "I want to. God, obviously, I *want* to. But think what all our friends would say. Think what your Tawny and Fiona and all of them would do if they knew their Lieutenant and a Civil Warrior were together. I've been thinking about it ever since I met you. Is it worth it?"

I remembered how one of my friends at school had started going out with one of the popular guys last fall. It was a *huge* scandal. Fiona and I gossiped about it constantly. Our group of friends cut her out almost entirely. We didn't like the popular kids, because they were casually mean to us, and shallow, and manipulative. And if this friend of ours was going to *date* one of them, then obviously she just wasn't the person we had thought she was, and we didn't want anything to do with her.

And we weren't even at *war* with the popular clique. We just didn't especially like them.

"No one would have to know," I suggested to Dan.

"But *we* would know."

Which was true, of course. Already, I felt ashamed of what we had done—and we had barely done *anything*.

"Is it worth it?" he asked again, but I didn't know the answer.

"I wonder if this ever happened during the historical wars," I said as we started walking together back up the hill from the creek. "Did a Patriot ever make out with a Loyalist? Did a Confederate soldier ever have a thing for a Northern woman?"

"I'm sure they did," Dan answered. "If there's one common thread throughout all of history, it's that people have always fallen for the wrong people."

I gave a little laugh. "Somehow they didn't mention that in Essex's historical training."

"When am I going to see you again?" Dan asked.

"Do you think we should see each other again?"

"No," he said. "Of course we shouldn't."

"Right." I felt so sad all of a sudden, so *trapped*. "Let's exchange numbers, anyway. Just in case we later find out that we should see each other again." So we did. And those ten numbers that I knew I could never dial helped a little, but not enough.

"Look, Chelsea, I meant what I said." Dan grabbed my

hand, interlocking my fingers with his. "I guess it doesn't make any difference. But I really do *want* to."

We held hands all the way back up the hill, until we came into view of the big field, busy with reenactors. Then we immediately dropped our hands apart and walked away in opposite directions.

Chapter 12
THE UNDERCOVER OPERATION

"So I said to Mike, 'Look, the King had porphyria. All the studies point to that explanation. It explains why he had his worst attacks of madness when he was older. It explains why his medical treatment just made him act crazier and crazier. To my mind, there is no doubt.' And do you want to know what Mike said?"

This was my father talking, obviously. We were out to dinner at the Italian place in the mall—me, Fiona, and my parents. My father had talked for roughly eighty percent of the meal, Fiona was sneaking in at around fifteen percent, and my mother and I were tied for dead last.

"Do you want to know what Mike said?" my father repeated.

He was already laughing. I could tell that, whatever Mike had said, it was a doozy.

"What did Mike say?" Fiona rose to the bait, claiming her dwindling corner of the conversation.

"He said—listen to this! 'Then you must be out of your mind'! Get it? Because King George was out of his mind? Ha!" To the approaching waitress, "No, I'm still working."

"Wow," I contributed.

"Mike still thinks the King had a 'simple case of mental illness.' As though mental illness is ever simple! He says—honey, listen to this." Dad laid his hand on Mom's arm. "He says claiming that the King drove the Colonies out of his empire because he had porphyria is the same as claiming that El Greco painted elongated figures just because he had astigmatism!"

"Well, El Greco *might* have had astigmatism," Mom pointed out. Yes, that would be seven times the number of words that I said. Assuming you count "El Greco" as two words.

"That's exactly what I told Mike!" Dad crowed.

I gave Fiona a *why is this my life?* look. Fiona smiled back beatifically.

"What do you think, Elizabeth?" Dad turned to me.

"Um, my name's still Chelsea. Remember, you named me that yourself? When I was born?"

But pesky details cannot deter my father from his quest for

historical truth. "Why do you think King George went mad?" he asked again. This was a test.

"What are my options?" I asked.

"Because he had a metabolic condition. Because he had bipolar disorder. Because he had lead poisoning." Dad ticked them off on his fingers. "No, I'm still eating"—to the waitress.

I knew what answer Dad was looking for, but still I couldn't give it to him. "Does it matter?" was what I said instead. "I mean, if he was crazy, does it matter *why* he was crazy? If the outcome's the same?"

Does it matter *why* we're at War with Reenactmentland? We just *are*, and that means Dan can't kiss me, and that's all there is to it. Does it matter *why* Ezra broke up with me? No, because we are not together, and I could know every little thing, and still we wouldn't be together. Does it matter *why* King George was crazy? He just was, and he's dead now, and we will never put together the pieces.

This was the wrong answer for my father, obviously, who shook his head with disgust and muttered about how I "disrespected the past" and excused himself to the bathroom. The waitress saw her chance and swooped in to clear his plate.

"Can we see the dessert menu?" I requested.

"Are you really hungry for dessert?" Mom asked, clutching her stomach.

"Yes!" Fiona and I said at the same time. "Mom," I went on, "we are becoming ice cream connoisseurs this summer. I already explained this to you."

"Ah, yes." Mom sighed. "Now that you mention it, it seems that I do remember something about ice cream connoisseurs."

"And we can't be connoisseurs if we don't *eat ice cream*," Fiona continued.

"Then we will just be like *normal people*," I agreed.

"And no one will respect our expertise," Fiona concluded.

So we ordered a scoop of every flavor on the menu. The vanilla was the best, which was surprising. Usually vanilla provides a good base for hot fudge or nuts, but unadorned vanilla rarely impresses me. I once read that vanilla is the most popular flavor of ice cream, but I don't believe that—if vanilla is the most frequently ordered, that must be because it's the most readily available, not because it's truly the most *loved*.

"Is this vanilla bean ice cream?" I asked the waitress.

"I'm not—" she began.

"Well, *obviously* it's made from vanilla beans; it's vanilla flavored," Fiona said, rolling her eyes.

"I know that, but vanilla and vanilla *bean* are two different flavors, and vanilla *bean* is a much more intense experience. Is this vanilla bean?"

The waitress looked uncomfortable. "I can ask the chef—"

"Is it gelato?" Fiona demanded. "It feels much softer and meltier than normal ice cream. Like gelato."

Fiona's family went to Italy two years ago, and ever since then she hasn't shut up about Italian gelato and how it is this amazing taste sensation and how no American gelato knockoffs can even pretend to compare.

"Fiona, if this were *gelato*, don't you think they would have mentioned that on the menu? Don't you think that would be a selling point?"

The waitress said, "I'm not sure I know the difference between vanilla ice cream and vanilla gelato . . ."

Fiona's and my jaws dropped. "Oh my God," I said.

"They are two totally different things," Fiona said.

"See, when you talk about freezing points . . ." I said.

My parents dragged us away.

"That waitress was flirting with me," Dad announced once we were out of the restaurant. He said it in his "whispering voice," which meant it was still loud enough for the waitress, all of her coworkers, and the shoppers at every other store in the mall to overhear.

"Ew," I said. "She was not."

Dad chuckled with delight over how hot and eligible he imagined himself to be. "She kept coming over to 'try to collect my plate' . . ."

"Because that is her job," I reminded him.

"And the way she looked at your mother? Pure jealousy!"

Dad slipped his arm around Mom's waist. "Poor thing. I left her a big tip."

"Mom, are you going to let him get away with imagining this nauseating *affair de coeur* with the nineteen-year-old waitress at Basta Pasta?"

But for no good reason, my mother doesn't mind that Dad is delusional. "He's a handsome man." She kissed his cheek. "I wouldn't blame any woman for flirting with him."

Fiona giggled. This must all be so hilarious when you don't live with it every day.

Once in the parking lot, we let my parents get ahead of us so we could talk without them overhearing. "You're in a good mood tonight," Fiona said to me.

"What makes you say that? The part where I didn't scream at my father in the middle of a crowded restaurant?"

"Sure, that part. I don't know, you just seem unusually smiley. Kind of soft around the edges."

"Hmm," I said.

"Anything going on you want to talk about?" She nudged me with her hip. "Any *boys*?"

I looked at her. I wanted to tell her, *Yes, I went to Reenactmentland, and I had a really great time with a really great guy.* I had never in my life *not told* Fiona about a kiss.

Except I knew what Fiona would say. She would accuse me of being Benedict Arnold again. She would worry about the War, and if I had told Dan anything that they could use against us.

And as much as I was excited about kissing Dan and wanted the world to know, I also didn't want anyone to know. I didn't want to admit this to anyone, because it was wrong.

So I just laughed at Fiona and said, "*What* boys? I still don't know any. You're spending too much time with the milliner girls. I'm in a good mood because we're winning the War, that's all."

"Sending those British troops over there on the Fourth was a genius move," Fiona agreed.

"You know what they say: The enemy of my enemy is my friend."

"Except in this instance, I think it's like, my enemy is actually my friend if I have another enemy who is also the enemy of my first enemy."

"Totally," I said. "That's totally what it's like."

We got in the car and my father began to drive toward Fiona's house. "Chelsea," Dad said, all of a sudden putting on his somberest, most silversmith-ish voice. "Your mother and I need to talk to you about something."

"Am I in trouble?" I asked. It definitely sounded like I was, only I hadn't done anything wrong recently. Other than . . . Oh, right. Going to Reenactmentland. To visit a boy who could never, *should* never be mine. My guilty conscience kicked into high gear. I would make a terrible criminal. My father hadn't even accused me of anything yet, and already I felt like throwing up and confessing to everything. Or maybe confessing first just to get it out there, and saving the throwing up for afterward.

"Chuck, I thought we were going to wait until we had dropped off Fiona," my mother murmured.

"Don't worry about that," Fiona said. "Whatever it is, Chelsea will tell me all about it later. So you might as well talk about it while I'm here, to spare her some time." She smiled at me reassuringly.

This is my parents' favorite tactic, by the way. To go through all of dinner acting like everything is fine, and then to bring up a serious, horrible issue once I'm trapped in the car with them. That's their guarantee that I can't run away. They broke the news to me about how "Someday, you will be a woman, and you will get your period" on a three-hour road trip to Washington, D.C.

"Chelsea, we found something in your room," Dad said.

From his tone, the only follow-up I could imagine was "drugs" or "pornographic magazines." Except that I didn't own any drugs or porn.

"What were you doing in my room?" I demanded, because if there's one thing I've learned from the War, it's that the best defense is a good offense.

"I was looking for my gray belt," Mom replied.

"Well, that's not even *in* my room."

"I noticed that. Where is it, by the way?"

I pondered that for a moment. "I don't know. Fi, is it at your place?"

"Maybe?" Fiona said.

"Can we focus on the issue at hand?" Dad snapped.

"Right. Okay, so you snuck into my room, into my *private space*, to look for something that *wasn't even there*, and you found . . . something."

"But not my belt," Mom contributed.

"We found two historical costumes that look remarkably like . . . Well, there's no way to couch this in polite terms. They're Civil War uniforms, Chelsea." Dad cleared his throat. "You have two Civil War uniforms in your closet."

"Oh," I said. "Those." I had a sudden vision of my closet door hanging wide open, the Undercover Operation uniforms center stage, with all my clothes spread out on my bed as I tried to decide what to wear to see Dan.

"Chelsea, do you want to stop reenacting the Colonial times and start reenacting the Civil War?" Mom asked, and I could hear in her voice that no question could pain her more. "I know you were thinking about not coming back to Essex this year, but I just never imagined . . . Were you trying to tell us that you didn't want to work at Essex because you wanted to work across the street?" She paused. "Over *there*?"

"No!" I protested.

"Denial," Dad noted, gung ho about staging this intervention. "You're sixteen years old, and that's mature enough to make your own decisions, *some* of the time, but in this instance your mother and I both feel that you're making a serious mistake. Which war fought for equality and democracy, the foundation of our society? Meanwhile, which war had casualties exceeding the United States' losses in all our other wars combined? Which document do you hear quoted more often: America's Declaration of Independence or the Southern States' Declarations of the Causes of Secession?"

Okay, *whoa*, attack of the rhetorical questions!

"Who's pictured on the penny?" Dad went on. "Abraham Lincoln! Who's pictured on the quarter? George Washington! A quarter is worth twenty-five times as much as a penny, just as the American Revolution is worth twenty-five times as much as the American Civil War!"

"Oh my God," I said. "Dad, do you have porphyria or something?"

Next to me, Fiona was shaking with silent laughter.

Mom's turn: "Honey, we love you, and we'll love you no matter what. But I feel so disappointed that you would choose the Civil War over the community that you were raised in, that has always supported you."

I wanted to bang my head against a hard surface. This thing with Dan was making me careless. That was the problem. I saw one cute boy, and then all of a sudden I couldn't even remember how to keep a secret from my parents.

"Wow," Fiona spoke up. "Chelsea and I *had* been thinking

about joining the Civil War. We weren't sure, but we were considering it. But you've brought up so many persuasive points that we hadn't thought of. I'm really feeling now like I *don't* want to quit Essex."

And this is a credit to Fiona's talents as an actress: She sounded one hundred percent genuine. That is how good she is.

So I took the cue and said in *my* best acting voice, "Gosh, I feel silly now for even thinking about leaving Essex."

We dropped off Fiona, who gave me a *good luck/I'm so sorry* pat on the shoulder, and my parents continued their pro-Colonial propaganda the rest of our drive home. I bit my tongue and agreed with everything they told me. This is probably what it's like when you're a heroin addict, and your parents try to convince you to quit smoking cigarettes.

At the end of the drive, I said to them, "I'm really not going to join Reenactmentland. I promise. It was just a dumb phase. You know how teenagers are."

We went into our house. I paused on the stairwell up to my bedroom. "Um," I said, all casual, "where *are* those Civil War costumes now?"

"We gave them to Reenactmentland," Mom said.

Dad snorted and muttered, "As if they deserve them."

"Oh, Mom," I said, horrified. "No, you did not. Please tell me you're joking."

"We'd want them to do the same for us. These are

wonderful costumes and they belong with people who will wear them well," Mom said firmly. "That's just not you."

I stared down at her for a moment, but I didn't speak. There was nothing I could say. Then I retreated to my room to call Tawny and report that our army had lost some ground.

Chapter 13
THE TOP FIVE

*S*aturday evening, after Essex had closed for the day, we were having a War strategy meeting.

Okay, no. Not quite true. It was indeed Saturday evening, and we were *going* to have a War strategy meeting. But Tawny was running late. Until she showed up, we were all waiting for her out by the creek, playing Top Fives.

"Lenny, Nathaniel, Ezra, Robert, and, um . . ." Anne twirled a strand of hair around her finger and gazed up at the night sky, trying to think of her fifth name. "Bryan," she said at last.

I made an involuntary gagging noise. Both Anne and Bryan glared at me.

"Well, you *have* to have five," Anne defended herself.

"Bryan's turn," Patience declared. Patience is usually the person in charge of Top Fives.

Bryan squinted his eyes and rested his chin on his fists, deep in contemplation. "Hmmm," he drawled. Hardly anyone ever asked for updates on Bryan's Top Five because no one cared. Now that his moment had come, it was obvious he was going to drag it out for as long as possible.

"Fiona," he began at last, "Rosaline, Caitlin, Patience, and Anne."

"Whoa," Fiona said. "Stop the presses. When did Chelsea get knocked out of your Top Five, Bryan?"

I wasn't going to complain, but I had been wondering the same thing. When the boy who has had an untreatable crush on you since you were eleven years old suddenly ousts you from his Top Five, you know you've hit rock bottom.

Bryan puffed out his chest in a way that was maybe intended to look self-important, but actually just resembled a toad preparing to *ribbit*. "After Chelsea undermined the Undercover Operation, I stopped seeing her appeal."

"Hey, my *parents* are the ones who trashed our Civil War uniforms!" I protested. "Do you think I *wanted* that to happen?"

"Well, you let them." Bryan shrugged, like *there you have it.* Everyone else nodded along.

"I should never have trusted Chelsea with the uniforms," Patience said for the millionth time since Wednesday. The look on her face implied that not only had I lost the costumes, but also I had probably handed the Civil Warriors a kitten with a sign tied around its neck reading, "Please torture me." Patience went on, miserably, "We worked so hard on them. I should have given them to someone who would have been more careful."

I wondered if Lieutenants during the Revolutionary War had to put up with this sort of bullshit too.

"I'm sorry," I said, also for the millionth time. "It was my parents' fault, but I'm sorry." And I did feel sorry because, even though it was ninety-eight percent my parents' fault, it was two percent my fault. My fault for thinking about Dan so much that I forgot to think about the War.

Fiona said, "Even if she *weren't* sorry, Bryan, that's no reason for you to take her out of your Top Five!"

Because obviously my standing in Bryan's list of hottest girls was the *real* issue here.

Fiona was correct, though: Top Fives are supposed to be purely appearance based. The rules are that you're not allowed to account for things like personality or intelligence or whether someone's parents destroyed a top-secret military operation. It's not a list of "people you want to date." Top Fives are exclusively superficial. But Bryan's too dense for superficiality.

"Ezra's turn," Patience decided.

"Where *is* Tawny?" I muttered, since if there was one thing I really didn't need today, it was to hear my ex-boyfriend's

Top Five list. I could just stand up and walk away. Except that there were a dozen of us sitting in a circle, having this conversation together, and everyone would notice if I left, and everyone would know why. Chelsea Glaser, the bitter loser. Chelsea Glaser, the girl who can't get over anything.

"This girl here, for starters," Ezra said, draping his arm around Maggie. "Obviously."

She giggled and leaned into him, resting her head on his shoulder.

So they were officially together now. They had cuddled during fireworks, and they had gone out on a date, and now they were a couple. Boom.

I had assumed as much, of course. I wasn't shocked. But it was harder, seeing it in action. It was harder to know it for a fact.

"Four more," Patience prompted him. When it comes to Top Fives, Patience does not kid around.

Ezra rubbed Maggie's arm with his hand as he listed, "Elissa, Rosaline, Chelsea, and Dahlia."

Chelsea.

He said my name. He said it. I was still in Ezra's Top Five.

And I knew that Top Fives are about physical appearance only, that you can hate someone, want nothing to do with them, and still include them in your Top Five. . . .

But still.

And I knew that being in Ezra's Top Five was meaningless,

because he was dating Maggie now, so everyone else on his list was just space-filler. . . .

But still.

And I knew that he could have been lying even, could have been including me in his Top Five just as a pathetic little consolation prize for pathetic little me. . . .

But still.

Ezra didn't find me abhorrent. And that was worth something, right? That was worth something to me.

Fiona was watching me for a reaction, so I showed none. I'm not an idiot. I knew it didn't mean anything real. It felt like it meant something, but I knew it didn't.

"Chelsea's turn!" Patience ordered.

"Why is it never *your* turn?" I shot back.

Luckily, it was nobody's turn. Tawny showed up then, so it was back to War business.

"Let's get this meeting started!" she said. "We're running late enough as it is."

This is what makes Tawny such a stellar General: We were running late *because she was late*, but she wasn't going to apologize. The General never says sorry because the General's never wrong. Meanwhile I could apologize over and over for inadvertently ruining the Undercover Operation, but no one was going to forgive me.

I stood a little bit behind Tawny. Because I was her Lieutenant, I was supposed to be up front, helping to run this meeting, but I wasn't the greatest public face of our army at this moment in time.

"First order of business," Tawny began. "I know a lot of you have been feeling discouraged over the past few days."

A few nods and glares, mostly directed at me.

"So it's time to boost our morale," Tawny concluded. "Bring on the Essex Cheerleaders!"

Everyone applauded as the three cheerleaders raced to the front, pom-poms ablaze. Wait, actually—four cheerleaders. I had been right. Fiona had totally joined the squad.

Breaking into synchronized dance, the cheerleaders chanted,

We don't need no muskets.
We don't need no swords.
We'll hit you where it hurts you.
We've got class you can't afford.
We don't need your cotton.
We don't need your slaves.
We don't need your ugly chicks
'cause we've got all the babes.
Keep your Emancipation Proclamation
'cause we proclaim:
You're farbs!

From my vantage point, I had a clear view of not only the cheerleaders, but also the audience. I watched the way Nat watched Fiona, how he didn't take his eyes off her as she shimmied and strutted. Fiona's captivating when she's performing, it's true. She stands in front of a crowd and she's immediately taller, her skin clearer, her eyes brighter. No one could help noticing that. But the way Nat watched her was special. It was as if no one else was there at all.

But of course other people *were* there. Like the other cheerleaders, and me, and Rosaline, who, everyone knew, had made out with Nat in the stables over the weekend.

Fiona and Nat were clearly meant for each other, and I wished they could both stop hooking up with randomers for long enough to notice that.

After the motivational cheering portion of the strategy meeting, Tawny said, "Next order of business—"

Patience raised her hand and said, without waiting to be called on, "Tawny, what are you going to do about Chelsea?"

"*Do* about her?" Tawny narrowed her eyes.

"Well, she totally screwed up the Undercover Operation," Patience whined. "And a lot of us are really upset about that. It was going to be our best attack!"

"Look," Tawny snapped. "All of you. We are going to accept the casualty and move on. Chelsea Glaser is your Lieutenant, and you will treat her with the respect due a Lieutenant."

I let out a breath that I hadn't known I'd been holding. Tawny is not usually so forgiving.

"How long will it take to make new uniforms?" Tawny asked.

Patience's jaw dropped. "We can't! They're incredibly hard."

"It's okay if it takes more time," Tawny said. "If we could have them within two weeks . . ."

"Two *weeks*?" Patience shrieked.

Maggie spoke up, "But this time can they be girls' costumes?"

"Hey!" Bryan objected. "Boys didn't even get the *opportunity* to go!"

Because of course Bryan would have been the first man picked for the job.

"We could dress as ladies of the night," Maggie proposed. "That would give us a lot of, ahem, *inside access*. The Civil Warriors would take us into their confidence."

"That means whore, right?" Ezra asked. "You're proposing dressing up as whores?" He threaded his fingers through her hair and yanked it lightly.

"'Whores' sounds so tasteless," Maggie objected. *"Courtesans."*

"Harlots," Anne said.

"Strumpets," Maggie said.

"Slatterns."

"Women of ill repute."

"We could have really shiny, colorful dresses," Anne pointed out.

"With fantastic hats," Maggie added.

This is who Ezra is dating now. He is now into girls who are into dressing up as nineteenth-century prostitutes. For the *hats*.

Suddenly, I thought of Maggie in her lady-of-the-night costume prancing into Reenactmentland. I thought of her in a shiny dress and a fantastic hat running into Dan and taking him, just as she had already taken Ezra.

It was stupid, I know. She hadn't taken Ezra from me, and she couldn't take Dan from me, because neither of them were mine at all.

Nonetheless . . . "We're sticking with the original plan," I decided. "Men's military uniforms. Have them ready in two weeks."

"In the meantime," Tawny spoke above Patience's groans, "let's get something simple in motion. Here's the plan: Late tonight, we go over there and dump horse crap in their tents."

"Ewww," the milliner girls squealed.

"That's how I hope they'll feel about it too," Tawny said. "Now! All together! Who is going to help me collect shit from the stables?"

If I asked that, I know exactly how many people would raise their hands: zero. But when Tawny said it, it sounded like a really vital duty, perhaps even an honor. A full three Colonials volunteered.

"Chelsea?" Tawny said.

"Hmm?"

"You're in, right?"

Make that four volunteers.

I would gladly gather horse turds with my bare hands if it

would prove to Patience and Bryan and everyone else that I *was* dedicated to the War effort, and that my parents finding our Civil War uniforms had been a mistake, nothing more.

"Absolutely, I'm in!" I said, with a wide, shit-eating grin on my face.

Not literally, of course.

"That's what I like to hear," Tawny said. "Team, meet by the stables at twenty-two hundred hours. If you have any old backpacks that you don't mind getting a little dirty, bring them along. As for the rest of you . . ." Tawny continued, but I stopped paying attention when I felt my phone vibrate in my pocket. I pulled it out to see what my parents needed. They were the only people who might want to talk to me who weren't at the creek with me right now.

Only it wasn't my parents. Instead, my phone screen said, 1 NEW TXT FROM DAN CIVIL WAR.

Chapter 14
THE RENDEZVOUS

I didn't open Dan's text while I was at the strategy meeting. I didn't open it while I was in Fiona's car, heading home. I didn't open it until I was alone, sitting on my front porch. This took monumental self-restraint, but I didn't know what his text was going to say, and I wasn't sure I could handle it calmly.

I opened it. "U around?" is what it said.

So, that was an anticlimax.

"Yup," I texted back.

My phone buzzed again. "Want 2 hang out 2nite?"

"I thought we shouldn't see each other again," I typed back.

"We shouldnt. So is that a Y or a N?"

I paused for a while, staring blankly down my driveway. Yes, I do want to. No, we shouldn't. Yes, I honestly think this could be something real, something new. No, I'm supposed to be busy scattering horse manure in the tents where you and your friends work. Yes, no, *Y, N*, this is my life.

I didn't reply until after my parents and I had eaten dinner, after they had gone up to their room for the night. I didn't reply because I didn't know what to say, and I think I was subconsciously hoping that, if I gave it a couple hours, the right answer would present itself to me.

It did not.

And maybe I should have taken the loss of our undercover costumes as a sign, a warning of what could happen to our War efforts while I was focusing on Dan. Maybe I ought to have seen a sign there, but I didn't. Around nine o'clock I texted, "Y."

Dan wrote back almost immediately: "Where r u? Ill meet u there."

I sent him my address, then another text that said, "I'll wait for u outside so we don't wake up my parents." My dad had never specifically set any rules about Civil War boys coming over after dark. But I could imagine what the rule might be.

Then I texted Tawny to say, "Sry cant make it tonite after all. Family stuff came up. Good luck w operation horseshit! ☺"

She could handle this without me for one night. She was *Tawny Nelson*, for Lord's sake.

I sat out on my porch and pretended to read a book, but

my head jerked up every time a car drove by. After a dozen cars had passed, it occurred to me that maybe Dan wasn't coming at all. Maybe this was just a War prank, like he had said, "Guys, the Essex Lieutenant totally digs me! Let's mess with her! I wonder how long she'll sit outside alone, getting eaten by mosquitoes, before she figures out that I'm not coming." And then all of his friends were like, "Haha, what a dumb Colonial bitch!"

By the time Dan's car finally pulled into my driveway, I had fully convinced myself that the only reason he was here was because he had a pack of his friends trailing behind him, all ready to vandalize my house or kidnap me again or who knew what. There was no question in my mind. And I had only myself to blame, because I had invited him. I had *invited* this.

"Hey." I stood up, and he made a move as if to hug me, but I kept my arms wrapped tightly across my chest, so he didn't.

"Hey. Uh, is everything okay?"

"Sure. Are you alone?" I scanned the road behind him.

"Of course. Was I supposed to bring someone?" Dan's forehead wrinkled, and I started to think that maybe he was a really talented drama kid, or maybe I was just being kind of . . . paranoid.

"No, no, never mind." I put a smile on my face and walked down the front stairs, but he got it anyway. He got it, and he got mad.

"Oh, you mean, like, did I bring the entire rest of the Civil War with me? Is that what you meant?"

"No, of course not—"

"God, Chelsea. What kind of person do you think I am?" he spat out.

"Look, I don't *know*. It's War, okay? Sometimes people do things like that. They want to win. You do what you have to."

"Well, that's not what I'm doing. Jesus. Is it so hard for you to believe that I just like you? That I just wanted to see you?"

I paused. "Yes," I said at last. "It is so hard."

Dan sighed. "Do you want me to go?"

"No," I said. "Sorry. I want you to stay."

"Okay, then." He exhaled again, some of the anger leaving his face.

"Since you're not planning on smashing the windows of my mom's car or booby-trapping my trampoline or whatever, then I want you to stay."

"Dude, you have a trampoline?" Dan's eyes lit up. "Can we jump on it or something?"

"Yes," I answered, relieved to have something neutral between us. "In fact, that is exactly what we can do with it."

We ran around to the backyard, kicked off our shoes, and climbed on to the trampoline. It was a warm, clear-skied night, with an almost-full moon overhead. The air felt cool rushing into my lungs as I started jumping.

"I'm sorry I snapped at you," Dan said. He jumped up,

landed on his butt, rebounded to his feet, then did it again.

"No, I'm sorry." I started doing seat drops too, facing him. "I was being ridiculous."

"It's War. We're enemies. I'd react the same way, I think." He did a few more seat drops. "This is good," he said, as if to himself.

"The trampoline? It should be. It's a top-of-the-line back-yard trampoline."

He laughed. "Yeah, I don't know, the trampoline, the weather, everything. I've had a crappy day. It's nice to know things don't have to suck all the time."

"What happened?" I asked, still jumping back and forth between sitting and standing.

"Nothing, really. Nothing important."

"It doesn't have to be important," I told him.

"I don't know, it was just . . . I called Nevin—he's the lead guitarist in my band—and they're having this amazing tour, apparently. They played Philly last night, and the crowd loved them, and one of the other bands on the bill invited them to go to New York and open for them."

"That's great," I said.

"Sure, it's great for them." Dan sounded dubious.

"But not for you," I supplied.

"Right. Because I'm not there. I wrote some of those songs that they're playing, but I'm not *there*." Dan stopped jumping and lay down, staring up at the sky. I kept going, so his body bounced above the trampoline every time I landed. "Nevin says they're all crazy about the bass player who they brought in to replace me on tour. He's really funny and a really great musician and whatever. I'm getting the sense that they want to keep him in the band permanently, instead of me, and they just haven't figured out how to break the news."

"Bastards. Traitors. I hope that's not true."

"Me too."

"I guess this is just an off week for everybody," I said.

"For you too?"

I nodded.

"Want to talk about it?" he asked.

I paused in my jumping for a moment, thought about it, then shook my head. "No. It's War stuff."

"Forget it, then."

I returned to my seat drops.

"Anyway, look, I didn't come over just to complain to you," Dan said. "I don't have anyone in my life to talk to about this, which is why you, lucky girl, are the beneficiary of all my whining."

"I'm not in your life?" Sitting. Standing. Sitting. Standing.

"Not officially, no. Why, am I officially in *your* life?"

"Nope," I answered. "No way."

"Great. Glad we're on the same page. Anyway, I'm not going to say anything to the band, because what kind of asshole would that make me? 'Psyched you guys are having so much success on the road, but I wish you were having a worse time because I'm not there'?"

"Yeah, say that. I mean, they should be dedicating every performance to you," I suggested. "They should light a candle onstage in your honor every night."

"They should have a giant cardboard cutout of me sitting in the van with them."

"They should change all the lyrics of their songs so they're just singing 'Dan Malkin, Dan Malkin' over and over."

"Good plan, that doesn't make me sound petty at all."

"I can't help you there. Non-pettiness isn't really something that I strive for," I said.

"My friends at the Civil War don't . . . get it." Dan clasped his hands behind his head. "They have reenacting, they have the War, and that's *enough* for them. They don't want anything more. And I like reenacting fine, but I've *done* reenacting, and now I want to do the music thing. I want to see if I can make it. I'm so close to making something happen in my life, but then I never do."

"Yes," I said. "I'm with you on that. I have no idea how to make a change in your life."

"Well, I think sometimes you just text a girl, and you see if she'll let you come over."

We locked eyes for a second as I landed across from him— then I bounced back to my feet, and he looked away.

"Sometimes I feel like I understand my dad."

"Whoa," I said. "I never feel like I understand my dad. What's that like?"

"Creepy!" We both laughed. "Okay, to be honest, I don't understand why someone would marry the wrong girl a couple months after graduating from high school, knock her up three times in rapid succession, and then have some messed-up early-onset midlife crisis and take off in a trailer at the age of thirty-seven. He has shitty priorities and he's a cheater— he cheated on my mom, and he cheated on the application for the Barnes Prize, and he'll cheat on whatever he does next. I'm not saying any of that makes sense to me. But I understand how he could look at his life and want to make it into something more, something that mattered. Because that's what I do every day."

"It makes me sad that you can't share that with your friends," I said. "Though I'm not surprised, since the Civil War sucks in every regard."

"The Civil War is the best," Dan replied, as if automatically. "It's just that everyone there has known me for years, and they've known me in this particular context, so that's the context they expect me to stay in. But I knew *you* would get it. I knew that from the first time I saw you."

"Tied up like a trussed pig and screaming my head off? Yeah, I'm sure that did make me seem like the empathetic type."

"Less empathetic, more just plain pathetic."

"It's truly amazing how your wordplay never grows old for me," I said.

"I *meant* last summer, at the silversmith's," he said.

"I honestly don't remember you there at all."

"Right, because I was *spying*. I kept a low profile."

"You're tall, though. You'd think that would stand out in my mind. Maybe you were *so* tall that I couldn't even see your face, and that's why I didn't know you were there."

"Chelsea, I'm, like, *maybe* six feet."

"A giant," I said. "A freak of nature. A redwood tree."

"I'm trying not to be offended that you didn't notice me. But I noticed you. I saw you reenacting, and it just . . . you *wowed* me."

No one had ever said anything like that to me before. Not even Ezra during our glory days, when he passed me notes and sent me flowers and asked me every day if I wanted to hang out every night. Not even when we were perfect together did he ever say that I *wowed* him.

"Thank you." I hoped the darkness hid my blush.

"Seriously, you're an incredibly natural historical interpreter. And what can I say: Talent is a turn-on."

The phrase *turn-on* made me feel shivery inside, so I acted like he hadn't said it. "I *should* be natural at it. I've been doing it for long enough."

"And *I've* done it for long enough to know that you're better at it than other people."

I flopped down onto my stomach, next to him. "I guess I just don't look at it as *history*. So it's easier for me."

"What do you mean?"

I'd never explained this to anyone before. I pressed my face to the trampoline, staring at the grass underneath, as I tried to figure out how to put this into words. "Okay," I said at last. "I don't know if you do this at Reenactmentland, but at Essex, we always talk about history in present tense. 'This is the hill where we bury the dead babies,' or, 'That's where the cabinetmaker lives.'"

"Of course."

"But we do this with *every* moment in history, not just 1774. 'That's where two signers of the Declaration of Independence are buried'—even though there was no Declaration of Independence until 1776, and even though they weren't buried until 1807 and 1815, respectively."

"We do that too, I guess. I hadn't noticed, but we do."

This was the hard part to explain. "So it seems like all of history is concurrent. It's not a linear series of events. It's all happening simultaneously. There is one moment, and that moment is now, and we are always present in it. So I'm not reenacting history so much as just living every time at once." I looked up at him. "Does that make *any* sense?"

"Yeah, I get it." Dan nodded his head a few times. "That's brilliant. I don't know if it's true. But it *sounds* true."

"I don't know if it's true, either. But I believe it."

"So that's why your friend says you have problems moving on?" he asked.

"Well, she doesn't know about my whole theory, but yeah. How am I supposed to move beyond the past when it is still happening, when it is always, endlessly happening?"

"You ask tricky questions, Chelsea Glaser. I think the answer is that you have to make something *else* happen."

Dan got to his feet, so I started to stand too, but he said, "Just lie down while I jump. That's what I was doing while you were jumping earlier. It feels good."

So I did. I lay on my back and watched the stars in between the crisscrossing tree branches overhead. I let my body go limp, and every time Dan jumped, I sank into the trampoline, and every time he landed, my body lifted into the air.

He screwed up the rhythm of the jumping so that he double-bounced us, both of our bodies flying into the air at the same time, twice as high. I shrieked, then clapped a hand over my mouth so my parents wouldn't hear. We landed simultaneously, him half on me.

"Ow," I grumbled. "You're not really a natural gymnast, are you?"

He didn't reply. He shifted his weight so he was lying completely on top of me, pressing me into the trampoline. I could feel his heartbeat stuttering against my own.

"Oh," I whispered.

"Oh," he replied, staring into my eyes, his head only

inches from my head, his mouth so close to my mouth.

"Dan . . ." I wrapped my arms around him, pulling him closer to me. "Look. I know we're not actually kissing."

"Right."

"Because that would be a really bad idea."

"Really bad," he echoed.

"But we're still . . . This is still . . . I mean, it's not technically kissing, but we'd still get in trouble for it. If anyone found out."

"I see what you mean," Dan agreed, touching his forehead to mine, his lips even closer. I could almost feel them brushing against my own as he murmured, "You mean, since we'll get in trouble either way, then we might as well do something really wrong."

That was the opposite of what I meant, but as I opened my mouth to explain, he closed the space between us and kissed me. It was a long, purposeful kiss, one of his hands tangled in my hair, the other holding on to my hip, our legs entwined, as we breathed in and out of each other. The trampoline swayed underneath us, and my hands slid up and down his back as if on their own accord. It might have lasted a minute, or it might have lasted forever. I couldn't tell and wasn't curious. I felt like all of time was happening in one moment, and that moment was now.

Ever since Ezra had broken up with me, I'd worried that maybe I had forgotten how to kiss entirely. Or maybe I didn't know how to kiss any boy who wasn't Ezra. But when I stopped thinking about it, it turned out that my body remembered. Apparently kissing is like riding a bike.

Dan pulled away just a little bit. "Wow," he said, and inhaled a quick, ragged breath. "I've spent a lot of time imagining doing that."

"And how was it compared to what you'd imagined?"

"It was almost as good."

"*Almost?*" I gave his shoulder a small shove.

He grinned. "I have a really well-developed imagination."

He started nibbling at my neck, and if I weren't already flat on my back, I would have had to lie down, that's how dizzy it made me. I closed my eyes and kept my chin up, so he could have maximum neck access. Then, because I am very successful at romantic situations, I said this:

"What did you mean when you said your dad cheated at the Barnes Prize?"

My words came out sounding dreamy and spaced-out. Dan bit down on the skin above my collarbone, and the question swam out of my mind.

"I don't know," Dan said a minute later, his lips tickling my neck as he spoke. "I just think he did. I think that's why he got fired." His voice, too, had the unfocused quality of someone who's thinking mostly about making out, and not so much about living history.

Dan propped himself up on his elbows to look me in the

eye. His expression reminded me of Nat watching Fiona in the Essex Cheerleaders. Like nothing could distract him from me. I held on to the back of his head with both my hands. Now that we were here, now that we were touching, I didn't want to stop touching him. I didn't want any part of my body not touching his.

"I'm glad you came over tonight," I said.

He touched his nose to mine. "Me too."

"Though you did pass up a golden opportunity to set fire to our car or assault my parents or something."

"You're right, that would have been smarter of me. But"—he tightened his arms around me—"then I wouldn't have gotten to kiss you." Which he started to do again, his hands on my back, then on my stomach, under my shirt, on my ribs. I could hear him breathing faster—and then I felt a vibration against my thigh.

"Your phone," I whispered.

"It can wait." He kissed me harder.

This impressed me enormously. Ezra had never made his phone wait for *anything*, least of all me. No matter what we were doing, it was never as interesting to him as what *might* have been happening on his cell phone.

I kissed Dan back . . . but then his phone vibrated again. Then my phone chimed in from my back pocket.

"Let's put them on silent," I said. "So we can focus." We both managed to work our phones out of our pockets without letting go of each other for a second. I glanced at my screen.

1 NEW TXT FROM LENNY.

Lenny had been with Tawny on Operation Horseshit tonight. I frowned and opened his message.

"Hi everyone the civil warriors caught us tonight there was a fight tawnys in the ER we're having a war council with reenactmentland after work on monday be there Lenny"

"Shit," I said. Dan said it too, at the same moment. I looked up at him.

"My sister was in a fight," he explained, his face drawn.

"With Tawny," I guessed.

"I don't know. Is that what your text says?"

"Yes. Tawny's at the emergency room now."

"My sister's home. They had to carry her there. Her friend says she's really banged up, and she can't even use her hand to text. I hope Mom's not awake. This is the last thing she needs."

"Oh, God." I let my arms drop to my sides, away from him. "I should have been there."

"Why, so *you* could have been the one fighting?" he snapped.

"No, so I could have stopped them!"

He shook his head, looking angry. "You don't get it. Nothing could have stopped them." He rolled off of me. "I need to go home," he said.

"Right."

"That's war," he said, making a face like the word tasted sour.

"What, had you forgotten?" I asked.

"For a few minutes," he said wistfully.

He climbed down from the trampoline and tied his sneakers on.

"Hey, Chelsea," he whispered. I scooted to the edge of the trampoline, and he grabbed my face between his hands and kissed me so thoroughly that I felt it from head to toe. Then he turned and walked away.

I lay back and listened to his car start, then drive off. I wanted to call Fiona and tell her: "I kissed a boy! And it wasn't even Ezra!" But I couldn't. I couldn't tell anyone that I had been making out with a Civil Warrior on my trampoline while his sister was beating up the Colonial General. Because I should have been there.

I found myself, as happened so often, thinking about Ezra. I had loved Ezra for real, for many reasons—for his confidence and charm and cleverness. It had been so *easy* to love Ezra.

But this? This was really hard.

Chapter 15
THE WAR COUNCIL

"W hat's on your neck?" Bryan asked me as we sat in the ice cream shop on Monday, waiting for the War Council to begin.

"Nothing," I said. This was a lie. It was something. Specifically, it was a hickey from Dan.

I am truly a class act.

"Did someone hit you?" Bryan looked creepily concerned for my welfare.

"No, it's just a trick of the light," I answered. Bryan wouldn't recognize a hickey if one was staring him in the face, which, in fact, this one was.

Maggie, on the other hand, is a veritable hickey expert.

"Why do *you* have a hickey, Chelsea?" she laughed, her hand resting on Ezra's knee.

"Or if you're going to have a hickey, why didn't you put concealer on it?" Patience added.

I *had* put concealer on it. In the morning, before I left for work, before I sweated for eight hours. I even had my compact in my purse, but I hadn't gotten the chance to touchup between work and the War Council. For some reason, I had imagined the other Colonials wouldn't be constantly and vocally assessing every aspect of my appearance. I, of course, turned out to be wrong.

"A *hickey*?" Bryan wailed. "That's not *fair*!"

"Chelsea is so obviously still in your Top Five," Fiona said to him.

"Yeah," Nat said, in a quick-thinking agreeing-with-Fiona moment.

"She is *not*!" Outrage from Bryan's corner.

"She is," Fiona assured him. "Otherwise you wouldn't care so much that she's making out with other guys."

"I'm not—" I began.

"Oh, now, I'm not sure those things are connected," Ezra said to Fiona. "For example, Chelsea's in my Top Five, and *I* don't care that she's making out with other guys."

Okay, and *screw you too, Ezra Gorman.*

I glanced at the door, hoping for Tawny to show up and put an end to this soul-crushing conversation, but, typically, she was running late. Of course, she had a sprained wrist, which was a better excuse than she usually had.

I'd run into Tawny at Essex earlier. Just for long enough to see her bandaged arm, and for her to tell me that the Civil Warriors were going to pay for this. Just for long enough to say that I was sorry for not being there when she got hurt, and long enough for her to reply, "It's okay, Chelsea. Family stuff comes up sometimes, and there's nothing you can do about it. It's not your fault."

I stood up and said to the other Colonials, "I'm getting ice cream." Ice cream is the best method that I have ever discovered for dealing with guilt.

"That's a good idea," Maggie said. "Because if it comes with a cold spoon, you can press it to your neck. That's great for getting rid of hickeys. Trust me." She pretended to bite Ezra just under his chin, and he laughed and pulled away.

"Thank you," I said. "Thank you, Maggie, for that thoughtful advice."

Fiona followed me as I went to the counter to order as much chocolate as I could stuff down my throat. "So . . . ?" she said, gesturing toward my neck. I ignored her to focus on my ice cream options.

"I'd like a large Mudslide," I said to the cashier. When he turned around to prepare it, I said to Fiona, "You see this? This guy wearing a T-shirt and surrounded by ice cream? This could have been us. He has no special talents. There is no reason why *he* gets to wear T-shirts and scoop ice cream while *we* are trapped in this horrific panopticon of the eighteenth century."

"That'll be six fifty," the cashier said, shooting me a dirty look, like maybe he didn't appreciate my saying that he had no special talents.

"Chelsea, come on. Who were you making out with?" Fiona asked in a low voice.

"No one!" And I felt bad about this, lying not through omission, but lying straight to my best friend's face. But I rationalized it as . . . well, Dan was a Civil Warrior. So he was practically, effectively, no one.

"Are you really not going to tell me?" she snapped. "What, was it Ezra?"

"Right, like that would even be a possibility. After all, it's not August seventh yet. And did you miss the bit where he said he *doesn't care* if I'm kissing other boys?"

Fiona heaved a long-suffering sigh. "Don't believe that for a second," she said. "He didn't say that he 'doesn't care' because he means it. He said it to make you feel bad about having anything else going on in your life that isn't him."

"Really?"

"I wish you wouldn't look like you find that a *good* thing."

"It doesn't matter," I said as we carried our ice cream to join the rest of the Colonials. "Because I'm really *not* hooking up with anyone. I'm not."

Fiona just shook her head, looking massively pissed off. And yes, I felt bad, but I would have felt worse if she knew the truth.

"You know what's so great about your hickey?" Maggie said to me. "You would be a shoo-in for the role of lady of the night, if we ever made those costumes. You'd look so authentic."

"You're still on that, huh?" I said.

"Can't those Civil Warriors be on time to anything?" Patience complained. "It's already six forty-five!"

"They must run on Confederate time," Bryan joked.

Ezra groaned. "What's Confederate time, Bryan?"

Bryan looked confused, as usual, to find that he knew a fact that the rest of the world did not. "You know," he said. "The Confederacy ran about half an hour behind the Union. Because they relied on apparent solar time, while the North used mean solar time. This was before there were standardized time zones. So that would explain why the Civil Warriors are *late* today, get it?"

"Yet more proof that time is just a social construct," I commented. And I wanted to ask *why* Bryan knew this esoteric piece of nineteenth-century trivia, but most likely it was because he had already run out of esoteric pieces of eighteenth-century trivia.

Tawny stomped in the door to the ice cream parlor. Other than the stark white bandage on her arm, it would have been impossible to tell that she had just been in the hospital. There should be a video game made about Tawny. She's that indestructible. "Where's the enemy?" she snapped.

"Running on Confederate time, apparently," I replied.

"How are you feeling?" Patience flew to Tawny's side. "Do you need anything?"

"I just need those farbs to show up," Tawny growled, shaking off Patience. "If this weren't a War Council, I'd kick their asses right here."

"And if your arm was working," Bryan added.

Tawny glared at him. "I'd kick their asses with both arms tied behind my back."

"We're getting ice cream," Patience said, clearly bummed that Tawny the Victim was no more vulnerable or needy than Tawny the General.

"Try the Mudslide," I suggested to her. "It's a total eight."

"My strawberry is an eight point five," Fiona countered.

"No. That is, in fact, impossible," I said. "Excellent strawberry cannot compare to excellent chocolate, and this is notably excellent chocolate. Strawberry spans the scale from maybe two through seven. But even the worst chocolate can't be less than a four, and the best chocolate, well, that's a ten. That is straight-up a ten, Fiona."

"This sounds more confusing than Confederate time," Maggie muttered. She, Patience, and Anne headed to the counter, but along the way, they encountered a group of girls with slender tanned legs, either tiny sundresses or booty shorts, eye shadow, flat-ironed hair. It was immediately apparent to me that these girls had never sweated a moment in their lives. They had never dealt with an unsupervised five-year-old trying to yank off their petticoats. And I guarantee that none of them had ever been unable to date a boy because he *came from the wrong time.* I could not figure out what they were doing in an ice cream shop, since they couldn't possibly eat actual calories. I imagined they just fed off the misery of less cool people.

"Oh, God," sneered the one with the most fashionable sunglasses. "It's some of those history losers."

She looked Patience up and down, and immediately the three milliner girls caved in on themselves. "Hi," Patience, Maggie, and Anne murmured in unison, eyes cast downward.

The girl sighed loudly and tossed her hair. "Let's get out of here," she said to her friends. "This place is just *overrun* with them tonight. Freaks."

The group of girls sashayed away, leaving Patience, Maggie, and Anne staring longingly after them. They were so entranced, they didn't even remember to get their ice cream.

The whole scene was mind-blowingly phenomenal. There is nothing like *real* popular kids to put Essex's popular kids in perspective. I gave Fiona a nudge, but she seemed not to feel it.

I caught Ezra's eye for a brief moment, and, before we

both looked away from each other, I noticed the small smirk on his face.

He and I had had our own encounter with our school's popular clique, a few months ago. One of the girls—the one who always wore tube tops, even in the depths of winter—accused Ezra of having a crush on her. And I do mean *accuse*. It was a very Salem Witch Trials moment.

We had been in chem lab, centrifuging some stuff, when she extended her arm, dramatically pointed a finger at Ezra, and said, "*This guy* is obsessed with me. He's like *constantly* staring at me. Give it a rest, psycho, I am *way* out of your league."

I remember watching this with my mouth hanging open. How are you supposed to respond when a girl says that to your boyfriend? And I remember Ezra laughing in her face and saying, "Actually, I'm good," and then dipping me over our work station and kissing me for the whole lab to watch.

Maybe Ezra was remembering that moment too as we watched those girls stalk away.

Or, maybe he wasn't.

The door hadn't even closed behind the real-world popular kids when the Civil Warriors marched in. They were all wearing matching Confederate flag armbands, which I had to admit looked good, if a bit National Socialist for my tastes.

Dan stood in the thick of the Civil Warriors. He was wearing jean cutoffs, a scruffy T-shirt, and the hoodie that I'd returned to him. It was a soft, comforting hoodie. I kind of regretted giving it back. His mouth was set in a hard line, a soldier off to battle.

The Mudslide churned in my stomach. There's something nerve-wracking about seeing someone in public after you kiss them. How were we supposed to act now? The same as we had before? Was that even possible? Something changes after you kiss someone. You can't ever again really act the same as before.

I gave Dan a small smile, but his eyes swooped past me. Like he didn't even see me. Like I was the same as every other Colonial.

"Let's get this War Council started," said the short girl who had orchestrated my kidnapping that first night, weeks ago. I assumed she was the Civil War's General. With her leathery skin, upturned nose, and hicktown accent, she reminded me of a pit bull. A Southern pit bull. "Unlike y'all, we got War plans to take care of, so we don't have all night to hang around and chat."

"*We're* not the ones who are twenty-six minutes late," I heard Patience whisper.

"Okay," Tawny said, staring the Civil War General straight in the eye. "For starters, what happened on Saturday can't happen again. We can't tell our bosses and our parents that there *isn't a War going on* when I suddenly show up with a sprained wrist."

"Maybe y'all should have thought of that before you

decided to attack us with crap," the Civil War General replied.

"Oh, please," Maggie interjected. "There's a difference between throwing around some manure and physically assaulting someone. In one, the worst that happens is your shoes get dirty. Boo-hoo. In the other, someone can get seriously hurt!"

"It was self-defense," spoke up one of the Civil War boys. "You infiltrated our land; we protected it."

"That's not self-defense!" Nat argued.

"In case none of you had noticed," said a Civil Warrior, "this is *War*. We work at a Civil War living history museum. We spend all day demonstrating weapons and talking about battle formations. If you're surprised that we know how to fight, then you're a pack of idiots."

"We are *not* idiots!" Anne squawked.

"We didn't do anything outside the rules of the War," Ezra said. "We spread around horse shit. Big deal. You're so anachronistic, we could have been spreading around video game consoles and no one would have noticed."

"And you're so anachronistic, you let *her* be your General," one of the Civil Warriors sneered, jabbing a finger at Tawny.

"What the hell is wrong with you?" Patience screamed. "This isn't the 1860s. You can't just *say* stuff like that!"

Then everyone started yelling at once. Except for me. I was horrified into silence. Dan's voice won out. "You're saying you didn't do anything outside the rules of the War?" he said. "That's bullshit. My kid sister has barely been able to get out of bed for the past two days. One of her eyes is swollen shut, her lip won't stop bleeding, our mom is freaking out, and *you* didn't do anything against the rules?"

"She started it!" Patience protested.

"I don't give a shit who started it," Dan spat out. He looked around the room at everyone, his gaze again slipping right over me. "You're all hooligans. Get it together. It's *just War*."

He headed for the door.

"Where are you going?" demanded his General.

"To take care of my sister." And he left without a backward glance.

The room erupted into more shouting, but I tuned it out. I kept staring at the door, like he might turn around and come back in. I wanted to run after him. But everyone would notice. And I didn't even know if he would want me to chase him down, anyway.

Two nights ago, Dan had been kissing me so desperately that I hadn't been able to focus on anything else since then. And tonight he wouldn't look at me once.

This was good, of course; this was for the best. No one could know there was anything between us. No one suspected a thing. And that was the goal. Wasn't it?

Chapter 16
THE VANDALS

"*E*xcuse me, miss. When in the course of human events does it become necessary for one people to dissolve the political bands which have connected them with another?"

This was a moderner in my graveyard, talking to me. He had a Southern drawl way thicker than Dan's, a plaid shirt, a self-satisfied smirk, and three friends with him.

It had been three days since the War Council, and we were in a temporary détente. Tawny's vowed revenge on Reenactmentland was on hold until she got back more of her energy, and until we thought of an awesome act of warfare that would be sufficiently vengeful. Tawny wanted to make them pay, and a simple act of sabotage wasn't going to accomplish that. She was thinking more along the lines of launching a nuclear warhead across the creek.

I hadn't heard from Dan since the War Council, either. I texted him afterward just to wish his sister a speedy recovery and to ask if there was anything I could do. He didn't reply. I didn't know what that meant, and if he were any other boy, I would have brought the issue to Fiona and analyzed every possible explanation for Dan's silence. But he wasn't any other boy.

So for now, it was just me in the burying ground, turning the issue over and over in my mind. Me and some modern men with attitude.

"That's an interesting question, sir," I lied, while gazing longingly to the other side of the burying ground, where Linda was entertaining a batch of delighted-looking youngsters. I wanted to delight youngsters. I wondered if she would swap places with me.

"And?" the moderner prompted me.

I quickly ran through the rest of the Declaration's opening sentence, but it turns out that our Founding Fathers didn't exactly tell us *when* it becomes necessary to dissolve political bands. Just that it does, sometimes.

Thanks a lot, Founding Fathers.

Fortunately, Plaid Shirt Man wasn't looking for my answer. He had an answer at the ready. I am accustomed to that style of questioning. "Would you say," he boomed, "that whenever any Form of Government becomes destructive of the ends of Life, Liberty, and the Pursuit of Happiness, it is the Right of the People to alter or to abolish it?"

"Yeah!" his friends cheered. Presumably as in, "Yeah, our friend has memorized the Declaration! What a cool guy!"

"I might say that," I replied. "I can't think of a particular instance where I *have* said it, but . . ."

"And would you say that time is now?" the man went on. "Would you say that this left-wing, hippie, socialist Congress is ruling without the consent of the governed? Would you say that it is tyrannical? Would you say that it is our *duty*, as *Americans*, to resort to arms to fight for *our* liberty?"

Another day, another moderner who ought to be committed to an insane asylum.

"With all due respect, sir," I said, "I am a lady. We ladies do not participate in the menfolk's talk of politics and war. Furthermore, I know not of this 'hippie,' 'socialist,' or 'Congress' of which you speak."

The moderners were silent, looking disappointed.

"Also, I am a Loyalist," I added. Which, again, I'm not, but it's a handy claim to whip out sometimes.

Plaid Shirt Man shrugged and walked off with two of his buddies, presumably in search of a more militant Patriot. The third friend lingered for a moment. "What's your name?" he asked.

"Elizabeth Connelly, sir." I curtsied.

He smirked. "Elizabeth Connelly, huh? Yeah, I see that. I like me an Irish girl. They're feisty."

I didn't say anything.

"Nice dress," he went on. "That Colonial look is hot. Makes you wonder what's under all them petticoats. What about your boyfriend? Does he like your dress?"

Enough was enough. This wasn't the worst thing I'd ever heard from a moderner. They'll say anything to you if you're in costume. But on this particular afternoon, I didn't need sexist libertarians asking after my nonexistent boyfriend.

"Sir," I said. "I'm not really Irish. Essex is a tourist destination; I don't know if you've noticed. Everyone here is an actor. Also, I am still in high school. I'm sixteen. My parents work down the road. And they're strong. My father was a wrestler in college. Now get the hell out of my graveyard."

He did.

Of course Linda had come over just in time to hear the end of my spiel. "Elizabeth," she said in an exasperated tone.

"I know, I know, but he was hitting on me!" I protested. "It was gross!"

"Nonetheless, we must never break character," Linda said. "Our job is to give every tourist an authentic experience of the past, no matter who that tourist is."

"If we want to give him an authentic historical experience, then I'll tell my father to challenge that guy to a duel," I said. But Linda was, predictably, unmoved.

In my next life, I want a job that never requires me to interact with the public. Like maybe I'll pursue a career as a hermit.

I called Fiona after work to tell her stories about the day's sexual harassment, but she didn't answer her phone. I called her again after dinner, but she *still* didn't answer, and so then I called her once more, intending to leave a detailed message, but this time she picked up.

"You realize you've called me three times over the past three hours, right?" she said. "That's an average of one phone call per hour, *every single hour.*"

"Wow," I said. "Division, Fiona? Really? What's next, exponents?"

She didn't laugh.

I opened my bedroom window so I could better hear the rain. "This is the value of friendship," I explained to her. "I can call you whenever I feel like it without coming off as crazy and obsessive. This is why friends are better than boys. Can you imagine if I had a crush on someone and I called him three times in a row? He'd think I was a psychopath. But you already know me, which is why it's okay."

"You mean I already *know* you're a psychopath."

"Sure. But you love me for it, I promise."

"You used to try to call Ezra three times in a row," Fiona pointed out. "I had to physically restrain you."

I chose not to respond to that. Instead I said, "So what

have you been doing all evening that was more important than taking my calls?"

"Hanging out with Nat."

"By 'hanging out,' do you mean 'making out'?"

"*No.* If Nat and I had spent the past three hours making out, you can rest assured that I would just *tell* you about it."

As with her comment about Ezra, this struck me as a pointed jab straight at me. I made a face at my reflection in the mirror on the back of my door. "So explain to me why you and Nat were 'hanging out' but not 'making out.'"

Fiona was momentarily silent. "I don't know," she replied at last. "I think he and Rosaline are still hooking up. I think he doesn't like me that way."

"Really?"

"Plus, maybe I don't like him that way either."

I rolled my eyes so hard that it hurt. *"Really?"*

"We had a great conversation, though. I was telling him about this theater group I'm trying to start. It's going to be loosely based off the British pantomime style, but also drawing inspiration from big sketch comedy shows like *Saturday Night Live.* The other Essex Cheerleaders are all about it, and Nat had a lot of ideas for me tonight."

"Oh." I frowned.

"'Oh'?" she repeated.

I tried again. "That's awesome, Fi. I mean it, it sounds really amazing, and you know I'll cheer you on in every single performance. It's just . . . I didn't even know you were work-ing on this at all."

"Well, it's still in early stages. There's not much you could have known about it at this point. And . . . ." I heard her take a deep breath. "You've just seemed so caught up in your head this whole summer, Chelsea. We spend eight hours a day down the road from each other, but there are always other people around, and I feel like you're always working on the War or thinking about *something* that has nothing to do with me. So this theater project I'm working on, well, it never really had the chance to come up."

"I'm sorry," I said. I couldn't tell Fiona the reason why I'd been so distant, but I *was* sorry.

"Okay," said Fiona, her voice still sounding small.

"Want to come over on Saturday night? My mom will make dinner and we can just hang out. We can have all the Fiona-Chelsea quality time we want."

"By 'hang out,' do you mean 'make out'?" Fiona asked.

"Only if you're very lucky," I said.

"In that case, yes. I accept your dinner invitation."

Fiona sounded happier, and I felt better. This wasn't a serious problem. This wasn't like Dan, or Ezra, or the War. I could fix this one.

The next morning, my parents drove me to work, like nor-mal. My dad talked the entire car ride there, like normal.

The one time I interjected something, about how Fiona was coming over tomorrow night, he thought I had said the word "kite" instead of "night," which started him off on a long, self-absorbed anecdote about a boy who he once saw flying a kite. So that was incredibly normal, too, and then I put my lunch in the fridge in the break room above the silversmith studio. When I came downstairs Bryan tried to talk to me about bundling, a Colonial practice where unmarried couples would share a bed but keep their clothes on and supposedly not actually Do It (though probably some of them did). And while it was nauseating to hear Bryan talk about bedroom cuddling, it was still completely normal early-morning conversation for us. Then I walked down the road and let myself into the burying ground. And that's when things stopped being normal.

Linda wasn't alone. She was standing with Mr. Zelinsky, a couple other administrators, and a security guard. I paused at the entrance. Maybe I was in serious trouble because I had mouthed off to those moderners yesterday. Or maybe those modern men had since started an anarchist uprising and overthrown their local government, and now the police were trying to figure out exactly who at Essex told them this would be okay.

Then I decided that I was being ridiculous and started forward to ask Mr. Zelinsky what was going on. But I saw the problem before I reached him.

Three of the headstones were knocked over.

One was by the stone wall in the back. One was near the dead baby hill. And one was the Elisabeth Connelly stone.

I ran to it and crouched beside it, hoping I had made some mistake, but there was no mistake. There was Samuel Otis on one side, and there was Benjamin Hall on the other. And there was Elisabeth Connelly in the middle, laid out flat on the ground. Part of the stone had broken off and lay a couple feet away.

Unsure what to do, I stood up and approached the huddle of Essex employees. They would know what was going on. Maybe there was a good explanation for this. Routine maintenance or something.

"Good morning, Miss Connelly," Mr. Zelinsky said, unsmiling. No one was smiling. The routine maintenance explanation wasn't seeming too likely.

"What happened?" I asked.

"We are still trying to ascertain that," Mr. Zelinsky said.

"It could have been the thunderstorm last night," one of the other office workers suggested. "There were pretty strong gales. I could hear it outside my window."

I felt hopeful for a moment. Then I thought about it. "Is it likely that a gravestone could stand for more than three hundred years and then get knocked over by some 'pretty strong gales'?"

Mr. Zelinsky coughed into his handkerchief. "Not *likely*, no."

"So what is likely?" I asked, already knowing the answer.

"Vandals," the security guard answered.

"It's those Civil War punks across the street," Linda said. "It's got to be. They have no respect for the past."

"We don't know that," Mr. Zelinksy cautioned. "We would do best to check our facts before we go pointing fingers."

"Who else would have a reason?" asked Linda.

"Why would the Civil War have a reason?" Mr. Zelinsky replied.

But of course they did have a reason. War. That was their reason.

I didn't realize I was about to cry until I already was. All the adults turned to me, alarmed. "Miss Connelly!" Mr. Zelinsky exclaimed. "Chelsea! Are you all right?"

I had no idea he even knew my modern name. "I'm fine," I sobbed. "It's just . . . I just really loved that headstone." Saying it made me cry harder.

In most other places in the world, crying over a felled gravestone doesn't garner much sympathy. But in Essex, everyone gets it.

"It's a beautiful one," Mr. Zelinsky agreed, which was kind of him, since it really looked no more or less beautiful than any of the others.

"I remember your showing me that stone on your first day working here," Linda said with more compassion than I had ever before heard in her voice. I felt like we were at a funeral for a grave, only a grave is dead from the beginning.

"We'll get them back up, young lady," the security guard promised. "They'll be standing again and as good as new before you know it."

Mr. Zelinsky lent me his handkerchief so I could dry my tears, and then they set to work hauling the gravestones off the paths so no moderners would trip over them. Once that was done, everyone left the graveyard except for me and Linda, and it was back to a mostly normal day of work.

Only it felt nothing like normal. Once I stopped being heartbroken over the Elisabeth Connelly gravestone, I started getting mad. I was mad at all the Civil Warriors. But at one of them in particular, I was absolutely furious. Because he could have stopped it. If he really cared about me, he could have stopped it.

The minute that work ended for the day, I ran out to the main road separating Essex from Reenactmentland. I didn't even take the time to change out of my gown. I stood by the exit across the street, waiting, arms crossed. Moderners stared as they passed me on their way out of Reenactmentland, and some snapped pictures, but I didn't care. Let them gawk. Let the Civil Warriors see me on their way out of work, and let them do their worst to me. Just let them try. I was untouchable. And until I saw Dan, I wasn't leaving.

Finally, after the crowds had dwindled, I saw him, still in uniform, walking down the driveway. He was listening to his headphones, so I had to shout "Dan!" to get his attention.

"Chelsea!" he exclaimed. "What are you doing here?"

"We need to talk," I said.

Dan's forehead creased with concern. "Okay," he said. He took my arm and led me down into a little ravine, so we weren't quite so visible from the road. "You look amazing," he said in a low voice. "I'd forgotten how pretty you are in costume."

I glared at him. "I look *amazing*? You ignore me for days, you knock over my gravestones, and now when I show up you tell me that I look *amazing*?"

"What makes you think that I knocked over the gravestones?" Dan asked, still holding my arm.

"Are you telling me you didn't?"

He paused for an instant, then said, "No. I did."

I shook off his hand. "Why?"

"Are you kidding me?" He laughed, then stopped when he saw that I wasn't laughing. "*Why?* Okay, because we're at War, where property destruction is perfectly accepted and encouraged for both sides. Because I hadn't done much for the War since kidnapping you, and it was my turn. Because my sister's injured, and I wanted to get some nonviolent revenge." He gave me a look like *this is totally logical*, and of course it *was* totally logical, but . . .

"You know I work in the burying ground," I said.

"Sure." He frowned. "Does that make it off-limits or something?"

"They're real headstones, Dan. They commemorate real people, who actually lived, and actually died. They're not American Girl dolls."

"I didn't think—" he began.

"Did you know that one of the headstones you knocked over was for a fifteen-year-old girl named Elisabeth Connelly?" I asked.

Dan shook his head slowly. "No. I didn't know that."

"Really?" My voice rose. "You mean you came into my graveyard and you just knocked over three completely random headstones?"

"Yes."

"Without thinking about whose *names* were on them? You really expect me to believe that?"

"Yes!" Dan grabbed my shoulders, forcing me to look at him. "It was the middle of the night, it was pitch black, we were trying to move fast, we went for headstones that seemed like they'd be easiest to knock over. Chelsea, that was it. I promise. I wasn't trying to hurt you. I would never try to hurt you."

"Of course you would," I snapped back.

"I swear I wasn't trying to—"

"At the War Council," I said. "You just . . . ignored me."

"Oh." Dan tilted his head. "And that hurt you."

"Yes." I swallowed hard.

"Then I guess this will sound stupid, but I thought that

was what you wanted. I thought you didn't want anyone to know about us, and I knew that if I even *smiled* at you, people might suspect. I spent the entire time trying not to look at you, when all I wanted to do was look at you."

"Oh." I leaned into him.

"And frankly, Chelsea, *you* could have talked to *me*. But you didn't. You seemed to want to act like we were enemies, starting from that first time I saw you at Abbott's. So I acted like we were enemies."

"Huh." I frowned. "I guess we didn't really set any rules for this. Like, how to do it without hurting each other's feelings."

"No," Dan said. "We definitely did not set any rules."

"The thing is . . . my ex-boyfriend—"

"The one who sucks?" Dan supplied.

"He doesn't suck. He's great. But . . . well, he used to do that a lot. Act like I didn't exist. Like he didn't notice me. Like I didn't matter to him. So when you looked past me at the War Council, I felt like . . . God, I just never really matter to *anyone*."

"Chelsea." Dan cupped my face in his hands. "I promise you really matter to me." He touched his lips to mine. "I *promise*."

"And you didn't know it was my headstone?"

"I promise," he said.

I pulled him toward me and kissed him again. His hands moved to cradle the back of my head.

I moved my lips away from his for a moment. "You know, if you really didn't want anyone to know about us, here is something you could have done: not given me a hickey."

His eyes flew to my neck. "Oh, crap, did I really?"

"Well, it's gone *now*," I said.

"I'll do it again," he promised in a tone that made me feel breathless.

We kissed again, and I wondered, *why hadn't we done this for nearly a week? We're* awesome *at it. We should be kissing* all the time! I found myself lost in this world of him: the taste of his salty-sweet mouth, the smell of his skin, the feel of his hands pressing into my lower back—and then I heard a sound, a cross between a giggle and a gasp, that was definitely not part of the world of Dan. That was a sound that belonged to the real world. I couldn't tell if Dan noticed it or not. Instinctively, I pushed him away, and I turned around.

And saw Patience, Maggie, and Anne, staring straight at us.

Chapter 17
THE SECRET

*T*he milliner girls told everyone. I couldn't blame them. Girls like that are basically invented to spread gossip. To hold that against them would be to deny them their lifeblood.

The next morning started with me dropping off my lunch at the silversmith's. Bryan didn't talk to me about bundling, or menopause throughout history, or how the Colonials referred to French kissing. All he did was pretend to ignore me until I was almost out the door, and then run up to me and say, "Hey!" He glanced around to make sure my father wasn't listening, then continued, "You suck."

"I know," I said.

"How *could* you?" Bryan asked, his chin quivering. I couldn't tell whether he was asking how I could betray our troops, or how I could fall for a Civil Warrior, or how I could fall for any guy who wasn't him, Bryan Denton. But no matter what he meant, I could tell that he was truly hurt. He looked like his slimy, toadlike heart was breaking.

"I'm sorry," I said.

Bryan just sniffed and walked away. "This time you are *really and forever* not in my Top Five," I heard him yell after me.

I went and hid in my graveyard. Linda didn't know what I had done, Linda didn't care, and everyone else in a graveyard is dead. But the fallen stones, still prostrate on the ground, kept reminding me that even this place wasn't safe from the horrors of War. And Tawny showing up midway through the morning confirmed that.

With her unbandaged arm, she pulled me behind the Hawthorn family tombstone and said, "I will give you two options."

I felt sweat trickling down my chest. Ever since joining the War at the age of thirteen, I had been glad to have Tawny on my side. I always said that I would never want her as an enemy.

And now I was her enemy.

"Option one, you can resign as Lieutenant," Tawny said. "Walk away with whatever scraps of dignity you have left. But don't you *ever* show your face at another one of our strategy meetings, because I don't trust you.

"Option two, you can come to the meeting tonight, and

we'll have a democratic impeachment vote. Maybe someone will vote to keep you on. But I wouldn't bet on it."

"Tawny," I squeaked out. "He's a really good guy . . ."

Tawny spit on the ground in front of me. "You are such a *girl*."

A flushed, overweight woman approached us, dragging a Goth-looking preteen behind her. "Can my daughter take a picture with you?" she asked. "She is so excited to be here!"

The Goth daughter looked like she'd rather be dead. I knew exactly how she felt.

"Of course, good lady," I said to the moderner. To Tawny, I said, "Option one. I quit."

I smiled for the camera while the Goth girl held up devil horns behind my head.

"Then we're done here," Tawny said. "Have fun with the Civil War. But stay out of our way."

"Huh?" asked the Goth girl.

Tawny hitched up her petticoats and strode away.

I let out a deep breath and tried to focus on the positives. For example, now I'd have a lot fewer reasons to break character. Now that I didn't have all those pesky distractions of "friends" and "fun." Maybe my dad would become so proud of me.

And wouldn't that be just a super-great trade-off.

It was going to be okay, though. So I had lost Bryan and the milliner girls—I hadn't wanted them, anyway. So I had lost Tawny and the War—I would deal. So I had lost Ezra—

I lost Ezra long ago, nothing had changed now. As long as I had Fiona and as long as I had Dan, I would be fine.

When it was time for my lunch break, I decided to brave the milliner's. Fiona was there. And I didn't care what Patience, Maggie, and Anne thought about me, but I needed to talk to Fiona. She hadn't replied to any of my calls or texts last night, and I needed to hear her say that everything was going to be okay.

When I arrived, all four milliner girls—Fiona included— stood lined up behind the counter, glaring at me from under ribbon-adorned, wide-brimmed straw hats.

"Oh, look, it's the traitor," Patience muttered under her breath.

"I can *hear* you," I told her.

She gave a *who cares?* shrug.

"Seriously, Chelsea, if you wanted to make out *that* badly, I'm sure you could have found someone here," Maggie sneered. "I know you feel all wah-wah-wah about Ezra breaking up with you, but he's not the *only* guy at Essex. It's not like your only choice was to run across the street."

"You don't," I said, my voice catching in my throat, "know *anything* about how I feel about Ezra breaking up with me."

"At least now we know what *really* happened to our Civil War uniforms," Patience said, stabbing a needle into a nearby pincushion. "I should have figured it out then. But I guess we all made the mistake of trusting you."

"That's ridiculous," I insisted. "Everyone is being ridiculous. I kissed him a few times; it's no big deal. I never did anything to hurt Essex."

Four blank stares.

"Fiona," I tried. "Can I talk to you? Alone, please?"

She flicked her hat ribbon behind one shoulder and came out from behind the counter. Already I was getting this sense like maybe my best friend wasn't on my side.

I led her into the back room and pulled her behind the dressing screen.

"Are you really mad at me about this?" I whispered, in case the other three milliner girls were eavesdropping, which they almost certainly were.

"What do you think?" Fiona's voice was hard, and she didn't bother to whisper.

"We've been friends for eight years, and now it's all over just because everyone thinks I sabotaged the War? A War that you weren't even *fighting* until a few weeks ago?"

"It's a little more complicated than that," Fiona answered. "In case you hadn't noticed."

"Fiona, I wouldn't *be* here this summer if it weren't for you. I would be working at The Limited, and the worst that could happen would be if we were at war with the Abercrombie across the hall. But *you* wanted us to spend the summer together. So I just want to know—" I swallowed hard. "I want to know when a made-up War became more important than our friendship."

"Good question," she snapped. "Maybe you should ask yourself that." And she shoved past me to get out of the dressing room and rejoin the other milliner girls.

There was nothing left for me there, so I walked out.

I wallowed away the afternoon in my graveyard of self-pity. The only thing that took my mind off my predicament for even a few minutes was when a mind-bendingly hot moderner showed up with his parents and little sister. He looked to be a little older than me, wearing board shorts, and all sandy-haired and tanned and muscular.

I saw him, and I was like, This is *it*! This is the solution to all my problems! I will forget about Dan and date this random dude here, and no one at Essex will care, because he is not "the enemy." He's just a super-hot normal person. I will have a happy relationship without having to trade in everything and everyone who I care about. Fiona won't be mad at me anymore, and neither will Tawny, and possibly Ezra will be jealous, which would be a bonus. Also I won't care about anything so petty as War, because I will spend all my time catching waves with my new boyfriend. Or hanging ten. Or whatever it is that we surfers do all the time. We will lie on beaches and apply sunscreen to each other's backs.

So for a few minutes I followed him and his family around, their personal Colonial stalker. I noticed Linda approaching them, but I shot her this very intense look of, *Back off, I've got this*. She turned and walked down another row.

When I heard the little sister exclaim, "Look, it's George Washington's grave," I saw my opening.

I swooped in and announced, "Actually, President Washington is buried at his home of Mount Vernon. But a few of his relatives are from Essex and are buried here, so that's why there's this big Washington monument. It's mostly to attract attention!"

The family stared at me blankly for a moment, and it occurred to me that I had been so nervous about talking to my boyfriend-to-be that I had swallowed half of my words.

Then he said to his sister, "See, Mel, I *told* you Washington wasn't really buried here."

Ah, I thought. *And he is also good with children.*

The family started to walk away, so I launched into another story. "In the 1830s, they discussed moving President Washington's remains from Mount Vernon to a crypt in the Capitol. But already there were rumblings of secession. Virginians worried that if the South seceded from the Union then Washington would be stuck buried in a foreign country. So they kept him at Mount Vernon. And they threw the key to his vault into the Potomac River, so that his body could never be moved."

"That's cool," the guy said. "I didn't know that." He smiled, his teeth pearly white.

"Would you mind taking a photo with our kids?" the father asked me.

"I would be delighted," I replied with great sincerity.

The little sister put her arm around me, and the presumable love of my life put his arm around my other side. This was probably the most fulfilling physical contact I was ever going to have with a person so gorgeous. Unless Fiona started being my friend again, and then became a movie star, and then invited me to hang out with her and her movie-star buddies, and then one of them somehow accidentally kissed me.

But for that to happen, I'd have to start with Fiona being my friend again.

The father snapped the photo, and his kids took their arms off me.

"Be sure to send me a copy of that one!" I said.

The whole family chuckled and moved on.

"I wasn't kidding," I mumbled.

This is one of the saddest things about my job. If he could see more of my body than the space between my forehead and my shoulders, then maybe he would be interested in me. Probably not, but at least he would know that I was a genre of person whom he *could* be interested in. I was a girl, and I was sixteen. But in costume, I was like a walking, talking Disney character. I could recite as many charming stories about George Washington as I could find in the library or invent myself, but still he would never see me as an eligible human being.

So was it any wonder that I had a fallen for Dan, a fellow

interpreter? I mean, was it really that big a surprise?

"So," Linda sidled up beside me, and asked in her usual deadpan voice, "did you get his number?"

Sometimes I feel like I am the comic relief in everyone's life but my own.

At dinner that night, even my parents noticed that something was wrong.

Slight overstatement. One parent noticed that something was wrong. The other parent was busy sharing the story of the time when he won an argument with the Thomas Jefferson interpreter about what sort of ink the Founding Fathers used to sign the Declaration of Independence.

"I will never let Mike live this one down." My father chuckled. "The look on his face was priceless. Priceless!"

"Wasn't Fiona supposed to be joining us for dinner tonight?" my mother asked me. "I didn't put peppers in the salad, just for her."

"Yeah." I shrugged. Even shrugging felt like too much effort. Speaking felt like too much effort. Thinking about Fiona felt impossible. "I guess something came up."

"What's wrong?" Mom asked.

If I really wanted to tell them everything that was wrong, I wouldn't even know where to start. With all my friends turning on me? With meeting Dan? With Ezra's breaking up with me? With joining the War? With Colonial America?

How far back do I have to trace something before I can start to understand it?

"The headstones," I answered. "My favorite headstone in the graveyard got knocked over. I feel really sad about it."

Saying that I had a favorite headstone might have sounded weird to anyone who's not my parents, but surprisingly, they knew exactly which one I meant.

"The Elisabeth Connelly stone." Dad nodded. "Nice piece of slate."

"You know the Elisabeth Connelly stone?" Even granting that my father knows everything, this was remarkable. It was one grave in a yard with hundreds of marked graves, and there was nothing special about it. Even its decoration, a skull with wings, was the same as so many others. And my father never spent much time in the graveyard. He was a silversmith. He hung out at the silversmith's workshop.

"That's always been your favorite grave," he said.

"It's because of that grave that your name is Elizabeth Connelly in the first place," Mom said. "You don't remember?"

"*I* remember," Dad said, because obviously every question is actually directed at him. "When we first started working at Essex, what was it, ten years ago? You were so shy, you just wanted to be alone. You spent most of your time climbing the trees in the graveyard and eavesdropping on people's conversations, as I recall. For some reason you were drawn to that particular grave. I don't know what it was, but you insisted that we call you Elizabeth Connelly."

"You wouldn't even answer to 'Chelsea' for a while," Mom added.

"We compromised that you would be called Elizabeth at Essex, but Chelsea at home."

"That's how we all wound up with the last name Connelly." Mom drained her glass of water. "I'd been advocating for Gutenberg, but you were wedded to Connelly. You could be so stubborn when you were younger."

"Gutenberg." Dad rolled his eyes to show how he'd felt about *that* idea.

"Is this true?" I asked, setting down my fork.

"Of course it is," Dad said. "How did you think you wound up with that name?"

"Well . . . I knew I picked it myself, but I didn't remember that it was *because* of that gravestone. I don't remember hanging out much in the graveyard when I was little."

"Well, that's no surprise. It was years ago." Mom started clearing dishes.

"You don't remember everything," Dad said, then followed her into the kitchen to wash dishes.

I sat alone at the table for a few minutes longer, trying to picture myself as a little girl, falling for a long-dead name and the stories it suggested. Before I knew Fiona or Tawny or anything about boys or wars or broken hearts.

That night, I stayed up hours too late, just leafing through my Ezra file. It was more like an addiction than because I really wanted to. It reminded me of happier times, but it didn't actually make me feel any happier.

The next week passed in silence. My only conversations were with moderners, who mostly wanted to talk about where the nearest bathroom was. And with my dad, but that's a one-sided conversation, and it's not my side. I was starved for conversation, but all the Essex kids had cut me out entirely. Other than Bryan, they didn't even bother to tell me that I was a traitor or a farb-lover. They simply acted like I wasn't there.

The War seemed to continue as usual. I noticed miniature Confederate flags stuck under windshield wipers in the cars in Essex's parking lot, which seemed like a classic, if unremarkable, attack. I didn't know if Tawny had yet exacted revenge for her injury. I assumed not, because I hadn't heard anything about it. But since everyone was refusing to speak to me, how would I have heard?

Here is who actually wanted to talk to me: Dan.

He called me in the middle of the week, after work, while I was miserably watching TV in my living room. "How's it going?" he asked.

"Rotten," I replied, not taking my eyes off the flickering of the TV screen.

"I'm so sorry," he said. "I feel like this is my fault."

"It's probably my fault. I think I started kissing you first."

"Really? I thought I started kissing you first. Either way, is there anything I can do?"

I snorted. "Like what? What exactly could you do?"

He was silent for a moment. "I guess telling the other Colonials that you didn't do anything wrong wouldn't help you."

"Yeah, I don't think they would listen to you."

"Want me to come over to your place tonight? Would that make you feel better?" His voice was low and suggestive.

I changed the television channel and answered, "I'm pretty busy tonight. Maybe this weekend or something. I'll call you." And we hung up.

It should have been easier for me to be with Dan, now that everyone knew. The worst had already happened, so now I might as well live it up and tongue-kiss him all over town.

Except that wasn't what I wanted to do. What I wanted to do was avoid him completely and pretend like none of this had ever happened. Like maybe if I pretended hard enough, then things would go back to the way they used to be. I could get back Fiona and Essex and everything that really mattered. Dan was attentive and smart and good-hearted and good-looking—okay, not like my surfer soul connection, but still hot in his own right. He was all of that, but that didn't make up for losing my entire world. He couldn't even come close.

* * *

After many days, I got sick of moping alone at home. I felt that it would be more poignant to mope out in the open, where I could peer through restaurant windows and see groups of friends, couples, connections that didn't include me.

I was moping my way past the bank when I saw a guy turn around from the ATM. Ezra. He stood a couple feet away, so it would have been hard for me to pretend that I didn't notice him. Nonetheless, that's exactly what I was prepared to pretend, until he said, "Chelsea! Hi!" like I wasn't Public Enemy Number One.

I stopped walking. "Hi, yourself." I wished I had worn something a little more appropriate for a Friday night ex-boyfriend run-in. Instead, the look I had going was for ease of moping, which meant old gym sneakers (so I could walk away my blues without getting blisters) and no makeup (so I could burst into tears without mascara dripping down my cheeks). Ezra always catches me off guard.

"What are you up to?" he asked. He, of course, was looking great in worn-in jeans and an Essex High soccer T-shirt which tastefully proclaimed, "We'll kick your balls."

I shrugged. I didn't know why Ezra was talking to me like I was a human being. No one else was.

"Can I take you out for a scoop of ice cream?" he asked.

The thought of ice cream without Fiona turned my stomach. "No, thanks. I've kind of lost my taste for that," I said.

"Wow. That doesn't sound like the Chelsea Glaser I knew. I guess you really *have* changed."

I stared at him and tried to figure out whether he meant that I had changed over the past week, or that I had changed since we were together. I *felt* like I was still the same girl who he broke up with, three and a half months ago now.

Well, no. I didn't always feel that way. But when I thought about him a lot, or when I saw him like this, I was exactly that girl again. The girl who was his other half, waiting to be made whole again.

But all I said in response to his comment was, "It changes you a little, when all your friends stop being your friends overnight. You know you're not supposed to be talking to me, right?"

"Yes, I know that."

I started walking and Ezra fell into step beside me. It wasn't August 7th yet, but Fiona wasn't my friend anymore, so I didn't even have to try to follow her rules.

It had been an oppressively humid day, but when darkness fell, it had cooled into the perfect summer night. Fairy lights twinkled on the trees and streetlamps lining High Street. Ezra and I walked past wood benches and potted flowers and a parked car that was blasting an old doo-wop song.

Ezra had been my boyfriend from November to April. I didn't know what it was like to date him in summertime because I had never done it. But I missed it anyway; I missed these moments that we had never had. Maybe it would have been something like this.

"Where's Maggie tonight?" I asked.

"Hanging out with Patience and Anne," he replied. "Seeing a movie about shopping or something. I figured I didn't need to be there for that one. We can each do our separate things sometimes, you know? She can be a bit much."

I wasn't responding to that. There was nothing I could say without coming off as a bitch or a liar.

"Why did you do it, Chelsea?" Ezra asked suddenly.

"Why did I do what, exactly?"

"That Civil Warrior."

"Well, I didn't *do* him," I answered.

Ezra laughed. "Nice," he said. "Well played. And I'm glad to hear it. But, come on, you know what I'm asking."

I did know. And it occurred to me that Ezra was the first person to ask *why*. All the other Colonials just instantly turned against me, because no reason I could give would be reason enough.

"Because . . ." I began. "I thought I really liked him."

"Oh." This made Ezra look tense for some reason, his face briefly transformed into a scowl. "You said *thought*, not think. So now you don't really like him?"

"I think I don't really like him enough to be worth all this."

This seemed to relax Ezra a little, and his next words came out sounding less severe. "Personally, I don't know how you could like him at all, after what he did to you."

223

"After he did what to me?" I asked.

"Knocked over that gravestone you like!" Ezra said.

"You remember which gravestone I like?" *You pay attention when I talk?*

"Yeah, Fiona said it was your favorite. Seriously, how could you want anything to do with a guy who would show such total disregard for your feelings?"

Ezra made a good point. How could I? "I *was* mad about it," I said. "But he didn't know that grave was special to me."

"Of course he did."

I stopped walking and looked at Ezra. "No, it was too dark for him to read any of the names. . . ."

"*That* time, maybe. But he'd been to Essex before. Last summer, for example. Remember when he spied on you? However he did it, he knew that one was yours. I heard them all laughing about it when I went undercover."

I sank down on to one of the benches lining the sidewalk. "So the Undercover Operation finally happened," I said stupidly, like that was what mattered here.

"Yeah." Ezra sat down beside me, leaving space between us. "It went really well. I'd tell you what we did to them, but—well, I'm not allowed to talk about it with you. You know."

"Dan told me he didn't know about my grave," I said. And he'd meant it. Hadn't he?

"Chelsea, he *lied* to you," Ezra said gently.

I realized right then that I had traded in everything I

had, in exchange for nothing. Really nothing worth having, nothing at all.

I needed to find my way back. And here was Ezra, sitting beside me, listening to whatever I had to say.

So without stopping to think about the consequences, I started talking.

Chapter 18
THE BEST FRIEND

The Essex summer interpreters welcomed me back with open arms. After a week of the silent treatment, it was a hero's homecoming when Tawny invited me to the next War meeting. She pulled me up onto the big rock with her, and it was like the first day of the summer all over again, before I got kidnapped and everything changed.

"Chelsea Glaser," Tawny announced, "is a daring double agent! She went behind enemy lines without the enemy knowing—without *us* even knowing—and she uncovered a secret that will win us this War. She single-handedly learned that certain Civil Warriors forged historical documents to make their lame-ass battlefield seem like it actually mattered.

They cheated on their application for the Barnes Prize, and their superiors *knew* that they cheated, and fired them for it—but kept the prize as though they had rightly earned it."

"Farbs!" everyone shouted.

"I am not ashamed to admit that, though I've been fighting this War for seven years now, Chelsea's courage and instincts surpass any of my own. Soldiers—Chelsea Glaser!"

The Colonials applauded madly. There was even a performance of a cheer that had been written specially about me:

> *Keep your Stonewall Jackson.*
> *Keep your General Lee.*
> *Both of them are cowards*
> *compared to our Chelsea!*
> *Chelsea is the best!*
> *Chelsea is the one!*
> *If you don't have Chelsea*
> *you'll lose the Battle of Bull Run!*

The three original Essex cheerleaders followed up this cheer with a confusing pantomime portraying how I supposedly wrested secret information from Dan. The girl who was playing me batted her eyelashes at the boy who I guess was representing Dan, even though he was close to a foot shorter than Dan and wearing eyeliner. After she had looked coquettish for a while, he ran over and pretended to whisper a secret in her ear, after which they did a lot of fake kissing, him holding his thumbs between their two mouths.

The thing about historical reenactors is, they'll reenact *anything*. Even if it just happened a couple weeks ago.

Although Fiona was at the meeting, she was surprisingly absent from both the cheer and the pantomime. Either she was bored of cheerleading, or she was still mad at me.

But how could she still be mad at me? I was on the right side again. I had told what Dan's father had done, so now we had the ammo we needed to reveal those farbs for the fakes they were. I couldn't have planned it better if I had planned it.

Bryan ran up to me once the meeting was adjourned. "I just wanted you to know," he said, "that when I said you were really and forever not in my Top Five . . . well, I didn't mean *forever*."

"Good to know," I said.

"So if you ever want to pretend to be betrothed to me, well, I would be okay with that."

"Thank you, Bryan," I replied. "Thanks."

As my friends and I left, we spotted some Civil Warriors trying to steal one of the street signs pointing to Colonial Essex. They bolted as soon as they noticed us.

"Should we go get them?" Lenny asked, already lunging after them.

But Tawny just waved her hand dismissively. "Let them

go," she said, so over their petty thievery. "We have bigger fish to fry."

And fry them, we did. Tawny proceeded to call the director of the National Register of Historic Places; the local ABC, CNN, CBS, and Fox affiliates; and the editors of *The Washington Post* and *The Essex Courier-Journal*. She went on to every travel website and left comments panning Reenactmentland. "If they lied to win the Barnes Prize, who knows what else they're lying about????" read her review on historicalholidays.com. "How can you trust anything these so-called historians say now???"

My parents were scandalized by this news. Scandalized and I think a little thrilled, or at least my father was. On Tuesday we sat glued to the TV as the eight o'clock news reported, after its usual rapes and murders, that the director of Reenactmentland had resigned under allegations of corrupt business practices.

"The Barnes Prize for Historical Interpretation moves tourism dollars," explained the bobbed blond anchorwoman, for the benefit of those viewers who don't spend nine-tenths of their waking lives on reenactment. "When Civil War Reenactmentland falsified documents to prove the existence of a ship that could have altered the outcome of the Civil War's most important naval battle, they secured this award for themselves. The director, Lindy Steussel, claims she did not know that her living history museum had applied for—and been awarded—this prize under false pretenses. However, she did let go employee Robert Malkin last August, after he spearheaded the Barnes Prize application committee. This act indicates to many that Steussel was, in fact, aware of what was going on."

The TV screen flashed a color photo captioned "Former Reenactmentland employee Robert Malkin." The photo must have been taken a few years ago. It depicted a gangly young man in full Civil War regalia, toting a rifle. His wife stood next to him in a plain muslin dress, her hair hidden under a starched white bonnet. Two girls in similar outfits flanked their parents. And off to the side stood a dark-haired boy, maybe twelve years old, his shoes untied, staring straight at the camera.

I recognized that look.

The camera cut back to the anchorwoman. "The truth will always out," she said solemnly, before moving on to a story about a holdup at the Plainville Toys "R" Us.

I sat on the couch between my parents and thought that I don't know if that's true, that the truth will always out. I think a lot of truths are lost to time. In this case, the truth was outed because Dan told me, because he liked me. And I told Ezra, because I missed him. And Ezra told Tawny, because he wanted to, And Tawny launched a media blitz that told everyone, because she is a warrior, and that's what warriors do to win.

"They had it coming to them," Dad announced, turning off the TV and putting his feet up on his ottoman. "I said this last year—how could an organization that is so filled with anachronisms win the Barnes? Even *we* haven't won the Barnes. It didn't make sense. Didn't I say that it didn't make sense?"

"I feel bad for them." Mom took a sip of tea. "Most of the people at Reenactmentland are innocent bystanders in all of this, just trying to do their jobs. And now they're the laughingstock of the historical interpretation community. And their director is gone? Can you imagine what we'd do without Myron Zelinsky?"

"I think they deserve it," I said, even though I didn't think they deserved it. I kept seeing Dan's family in my mind, that photo of him staring directly at me. "If you cheat, you shouldn't be allowed to just get away with it. Right?"

"Right," my father agreed. To my mother, "Your daughter is right."

But instead of feeling right, I felt nauseous. "I'm going to go lie down," I said, but on my way out of the living room, the doorbell rang.

"Go see who that is," my father called.

It was Dan. From my TV screen to my front porch, from five years ago to right now. I stared at him through the keyhole for a moment, taking in his clenched fists, his hollow eyes, his gray hoodie that had once, briefly, been mine.

What was sad was that, despite everything standing between

us—the hills that had grown into Kilimanjaro-size mountains—I saw him and my heart still jumped, and I still wanted this to work. I wanted to fling open my door and have him sweep me into his arms and kiss me. I would kiss him back.

Instead, I opened my door, and he took a deep breath and said, "You are a bitch, Chelsea. You're a bad person with an ugly heart."

I didn't say anything.

"This is my *father*, Chelsea. And maybe you can't get that, because you have your perfect little family all together in your perfect little house, and you carpool in your perfect little car over to your perfect little Colonial tea party.

"But here's what I have: a sister with a busted face. A mother who can't deal with the real world at all. A lying, cheating father who doesn't give a shit what happens to us. A dream that is never going to get off the ground. A girl who *I really liked*, who turned out to be just another goddamn actress. That's *it*.

"And you? You could have anything. So you used me. You just used me, because you could have me so easily."

I could hardly breathe. I hadn't thought it was going to be like this. I hadn't thought at all. I hadn't told anyone Dan's secret, really. I just told Ezra. I had been mad. It had spiraled out of my control.

"I don't know if you noticed," Dan went on, "but I have a lot of people in my life who I can't trust. And for some stupid

reason, I thought you could be . . . Whatever, I *wanted* you to be someone I could trust."

"I'm sorry," I whispered.

"Why did you do this?" He was shaking. "Just tell me *why*."

I tried to muster up some of the righteous indignation that I'd felt on Friday night as I said, "You knocked over my gravestone!" But even to my ears, the words sounded tinny and pathetic.

Dan's face was pale. "It was a gravestone, Chelsea. And it was a *mistake*. I told you that already, and I meant it. I've never lied to you. My God, can't you tell the difference between a gravestone and a person you love? Can't you tell which one matters?"

But if I had to point to the real problem in my life, it's that I've never known the difference between a gravestone and a person I love. I have never known which is which until it's too late.

"All's fair in love and war," I reminded him, aiming for Tawny's tone. But my voice came out sounding just like me.

"Oh, yeah? And which is this?" he asked. "Love or war?"

I opened my mouth to answer, but he was already turning away in disgust, walking down the stairs, down the driveway, leaving me.

"Who was that?"

I turned to see my mother standing in the doorway behind me. Her expression was calm; she hadn't heard anything.

"Just my . . . nobody." I rubbed the bridge of my nose, trying to press back tears.

"Just your nobody?" Mom teased.

I leaned against the front door frame. "He was my friend. He's nobody now."

"You could have invited him in for tea," Mom said gently. "I made a whole pot of it."

"Thanks, but . . ." My whole body felt weary. My eyes. My heart. Even my hair. "He doesn't like tea," I told her.

"Hey, Chelsea, we're going to Belmont's! Want to come with us?"

I looked up from Bridget Burroughs's headstone ("A true Christian, a dutiful and loving Wife") to see all four milliner girls in my graveyard. Three out of the four were smiling at me like we were the best friends in the world. But the one who actually *was* my best friend in the world was gazing pointedly into the distance.

"That's okay," I said. "I have some work to take care of around here . . ."

"*What* work?" Anne asked, which was a fair question, since we were clearly alone in the graveyard.

"Come on." Patience tugged at my arm. "Have a little fun, Chels."

I wanted to ask Patience why she assumed that going anywhere with her would be fun, but instead I kept quiet and went along. You can't beat Belmont's saltwater taffy.

From the way the milliner girls were falling all over themselves to be seen with me, you would have never known that
they weren't speaking to me four days ago. Now that I was a
War hero instead of a traitor, it was like the traitor part had
never happened.

Fiona, though, was a different story. Why couldn't my
closest friend forgive me when everyone else at Essex had?

As we walked up to Belmont's, Maggie linked arms with me
and asked, "Chelsea, will you come to my party on Saturday?"

Maggie and I had worked together at Essex for three summers now, and this was the first time she'd shown any interest in seeing me outside of the Colonial times. I guess she
preferred me as the Lieutenant who would stop at nothing
to take down the Civil War than as Ezra's ex-girlfriend.

"Um," I replied, "maybe? I think I can come?"

Of course I could come. It wasn't like I had any hot dates
this weekend.

"I probably can't make it," Fiona said—to Maggie, not to
me. "It turns out I have plans that night."

I'd had enough. I stopped on the bottom stair to Belmont's.
"What is going on here, Fiona?"

She widened her eyes. "Nothing."

"Bullshit. This is not 'nothing.' You're volunteering to
skip a party just because I might show up. Okay, yes, I
kissed a Civil Warrior. I did, it's true. But then I completely
destroyed him. I humiliated him and his family and I reduced

Reenactmentland to a total mess that no one respects any-more. Last night he told me that I am a bad person with an ugly heart. Is that good enough for you? What else do you want me to do to atone for kissing him? What do you need me to do to make this up to you, Fiona?"

Patience, Maggie, and Anne stood on Belmont's porch, watching with wide eyes. I could almost feel them holding their breaths as they filed away my every word for inclusion in later text messages, e-mails, and other recountings of this moment.

Fiona shook her head. "I don't want you to do anything to atone for kissing him," she said, her voice sad.

"Then what do you *want* from me?"

She glanced up at the milliner girls. But they had front-row seats to the best show in town; they weren't going to budge.

Fiona sighed. "We'll catch up to you guys later." And, to what I'm sure was their great disappointment, she took my arm and led me away from Belmont's and toward the Palace Green, where we could talk in private.

"I'm not mad at you for kissing a Civil Warrior," she said straight off, as soon as we'd sat down in the grass. "You idiot. You think I give a shit whether the guy you're with wears a white wig or not? I barely even know the difference between the Civil War and the Revolutionary War. Hello, do you know me at all?"

"But," I said, "you joined the Essex Cheerleaders and every-thing—"

"Because I like choreographed *dances*. The War itself is so . . ." She twirled her hands around, searching for the right word to express how vastly unimportant she found the War. "*Whatever*," she concluded.

"So if you're not mad at me for sleeping with the enemy, then *why* are you mad at me?" I asked.

"Chelsea!" Fiona shrieked. "You *slept* with him? You said that you only kissed him!"

I sighed. "I did only kiss him. 'Sleeping with the enemy' is an expression. I didn't *literally* sleep with the enemy."

"Oh. Well, that's reassuring, I guess. But I'm still mad at you."

I threw back my head and squinted up at the bright midday sun. I was so sick of living in this topsy-turvy world where the milliner girls couldn't wait to hang out with me, while Fiona and Dan—the people I actually *liked*—hated me. "Why?" I asked.

"*Because*. You're supposed to be my best friend, yet somehow you couldn't even trust me enough to tell me that you were dating someone. How do you think I felt hearing this news from *Anne*, of all people?"

Now that Fiona pointed it out, I remembered that she'd started acting distant before the milliner girls saw Dan and me together outside of Reenactmentland. Fiona had been sharp with me ever since I showed up to the War Council with an inexplicable bruise on my neck. But—

"You didn't *want* me to date him. Remember, I told you about him on the night I was kidnapped. I said that I had met a cute boy, and you said that it didn't matter, because he was a Civil Warrior, so it would make me a *traitor*. You said it would never work out."

"To be fair," Fiona replied, tucking her legs under her, "I turned out to be right. He's a Civil Warrior, and it *didn't* work out."

I didn't even crack a smile.

"Look, it doesn't matter whether I wanted you to date him or not. The point is that I want to *know*. It's a big deal in your life, so I want to be included."

"It's not a big deal," I said. "I told you, he didn't matter to me. He's cute, we hooked up a couple times, but really I was just using him. He means nothing more to me than any one of your random guys meant to you." I stared down at the patch of clover next to me.

"See, this is what I'm talking about. I'm not going to forgive you until you start telling me the truth once in a while."

"What makes you think this isn't the truth?" I asked.

"Because I know you better than that, and that is not your style." Fiona looked straight at me. "You have turned down every single guy for the past three and a half months, all because they're not Ezra Gorman. So if you wanted this guy—who's *definitely* not Ezra Gorman—then there must be something special about him. What's his name, by the way? No one seems to care what his name was."

"Dan," I answered.

"Do you even listen to yourself?" Fiona asked. "Do you even hear the way you just said his name? And you expect me to believe that *you don't care about him?*"

She waited, her eyebrows raised.

"Okay," I said finally. "Okay, yes. I liked him." I closed my eyes briefly.

"Tell me why," she pressed on.

I paused. "Because he's smart and funny and really cute. And caring and ambitious and a good listener. The more I found out about him, the more I liked. And . . . I felt like he *understood* me. I felt like I understood him. Just spending time with him made me feel . . . happy."

"Wow." Fiona shook her head. "That sounds serious."

I busied myself picking clovers. "I don't know. Maybe it could have been."

"So why couldn't you tell me any of that in the first place? Did you actually think that I was going to run off and tell Tawny? Were you honestly scared that I was going to be mad at you?"

"Yes! I knew I wasn't allowed. And I thought that if I didn't tell anyone what I was doing, then it would be . . . as if I wasn't doing it."

"Firstly," Fiona said, "I *never* would have ratted you out to Tawny. I care about you more than I care about the War, or about pretty much anything else. Okay? Can you *get* that, Chelsea? Can you remember that?"

"Yes." I looked down at the clover collection on my skirt.

"Secondly, let's get real: You *weren't* actually scared that I was going to tell everyone about you dating a Civil Warrior. What *actually* scared you was getting over Ezra."

"That's ridiculous," I said. "All I have wanted for months is to get over Ezra. You know that."

"No. All you have wanted for months is for Ezra to come back to you. That's a completely different thing. You don't want the pain of missing him, sure. But you want to get rid of that pain by getting him back, not by moving on. You've been keeping yourself as this perfect little museum of what you were, so that it will be easy for him to come back to exactly what he left behind. And you're scared to admit that you're into this new guy because then you'd really have to deal with life after Ezra."

I felt short of breath, like I'd been punched in the chest. Fiona had never been this harsh with me. But, then, Fiona had never been this mad at me. "I know it seems so silly to you," I said, my voice small and dull, "how much trouble I've had getting past Ezra. I know it's silly. But I loved him. It just destroyed me that he used to love me back, until all of a sudden he didn't.

"And I know this doesn't make sense to you, because you've never felt that way about someone. For you it's never been about one boy like this, because for you there has always been some other boy. But for me, there was no one other than Ezra. Except I felt like maybe . . . there could be Dan. Until I completely killed that one." I focused on weaving together the clovers into a chain.

"You're wrong," Fiona said. "For starters, I *have* felt that way about someone."

My fingernail slipped, ruining a clover stem. "Seriously? Who? And how am I getting blamed for keeping secrets from you, when you've never told me that you're apparently *in love* with someone?"

Fiona made a face. "I wouldn't say *in love*."

"Who is it, Fi?"

She blushed. I had never seen Fiona blush when telling me about any boy before. "Nat," she said.

"Well, of course *Nat*. That's old news. That news is literally years old."

Fiona tossed her hair, still blushing. "I just didn't think I actually, you know, cared about him."

"You could have asked me. I would have told you that you actually cared about him." In my excitement, I sat up onto my knees, knocking a bunch of my clovers to the ground. "And he obviously loves you too, so this is perfect. God, I have been waiting for this all summer. I have been waiting for this since *freshman year*."

"I don't know," Fiona said.

"What do you mean you don't *know*?"

"It just seems easier," she said, "*not* to really care about them. If your life is anything to go by, it seems to me like it gets really complicated once you start to care. No offense."

"But if you don't care, then what's the point?"

"Um, it's fun?" Fiona laughed.

"Seriously, even if it winds up with your heart getting shattered . . . or even if it winds up with you breaking someone *else's* heart . . . it's still worth it, Fi. To actually care about someone."

"Do you really believe that?"

I nodded.

"Huh." She leaned back on her hands and considered me for a moment. "I'm sorry that things with Dan didn't work out," she said finally.

A "thank you" caught in my throat. I hadn't thought about it before, but *no one* had said they were sorry that me and Dan didn't work out. Not anyone at Essex, of course—because they *weren't* sorry—but not Dan, either. Not even me.

"I feel really bad," I confided in a whisper, as if someone might overhear. "I feel horrible about what I did to him."

"If it makes it any better, the Civil Warriors did this to themselves. If it hadn't been you to figure out that they falsified those documents, it would have been someone else. They dug their own grave."

"'The truth will always out,'" I quoted the TV newscaster, hugging my knees to my chest.

"Anyway, without knowing him at all, except that he's the enemy, he sounds like a good guy. Not a complete asshole like Ezra."

"Ezra was not a complete asshole," I said.

"Are you *kidding* me?" Fiona gave a dramatic sigh. "Still?"

"Yes, he broke up with me, and that was kind of an asshole move . . . But he had his reasons. Everything else about Ezra was perfect. The only imperfect thing about him was that he didn't want to be my boyfriend."

"Oh my God, Chelsea, that is delusional. You are filled with delusions."

"You just hate him on my behalf because he broke my heart," I said. "Which is sweet of you, but you're biased. You don't know what it was really like, because he wasn't *your* boyfriend."

"I do know what it was really like," she replied, "because I was the one who spent hours every single night rubbing your back while you cried."

"That was *after* he broke up with me," I reminded her.

"Oh no, it wasn't." Fiona got to her feet and echoed my father's words from last night. "You don't remember every-thing, Chelsea. For someone who's supposed to be an expert at history, you suck at remembering what's real."

"What do you mean?" I shaded my eyes to look up at her.

"I can't keep doing this," she answered. "You can't keep doing this to yourself. Stop hanging out inside of your own head all the time and pay some attention to who Ezra actually is." She put her hands on her hips as she looked down at me. "You met another guy. You felt something for him. So now *what* are you waiting for to get over Ezra?" she asked.

But I didn't answer. Because I didn't know.

Chapter 19
THE TRUTH

*N*either my father nor I have any sense of nutrition, or food groups, or even necessarily what "tastes good." Our favorite kind of food is whatever makes us stop feeling hungry and start feeling full. (The exception, of course, being ice cream.) So with Mom out at a stalp gig on Friday night, Dad and I cooked up a box of Kraft macaroni and ate it in the living room. When we pretend to care about things like kale or tarragon, it is exclusively for Mom's benefit.

"I don't know why no one ever hires me to stalp," Dad grouched, putting his legs up on the ottoman and resting his large bowl of mac and cheese on his thigh. He doesn't care what he eats, but, whatever it is, he likes it in mass quantities.

"I can stalp with the best of them. Is it because I'm not an attractive young woman?"

"Mom isn't that young," I pointed out.

Dad narrowed his eyes at me.

Stalp gigs, otherwise known as Stand There and Look Pretty gigs, are the historical interpreter's best get-rich-quick scheme. All you have to do is dress in your fanciest Colonial garb and mill around a corporate function or themed wedding party and let drunk guests take endless photos with you. At the end of the night, you can emerge with hundreds of dollars, not to mention take-home bags of leftovers. There's probably not a big market for stalping in, like, Iowa. But here in Virginia, event planners can't get enough of it.

The only thing about stalp gigs is that, in order to Stand There and Look Pretty, you have to be at least base-level pretty. Which may explain why my heavyset, balding father was not in high stalp demand.

I pushed my mac and cheese around in circles while Dad wolfed his down. These days it felt like there was constantly a rock in my stomach. I was never full, but I was never really hungry, either.

"I wish I could just leave," I muttered.

"Leave what?" Dad didn't pause in his steady noodle inhalation.

But I didn't answer because I didn't even know what I wanted to leave at this point. This house. This town. This state. I wished I could leave myself behind and start over again, brand-new, the girl with no history who is free to invent herself.

"Do you ever wish you could go back to the Colonial times for real?" I asked Dad. "Just ditch the twenty-first century?"

"Absolutely not," he said. "They played a mighty poor excuse for baseball in the eighteenth century. I would find it very depressing." This cracked him up. Let us all take a moment to be thankful that my father became a silversmith instead of pursuing a career as a stand-up comedian.

"That being said," he went on once he'd finished *ho-ho-ho*ing, "I can think of nothing I would love more than going to visit the Colonial times. Not forever, but there are so many questions that we can't answer without going and seeing for ourselves. It can be frustrating to spend your whole life study-ing a society that you will never get to see. Of course, it's no different from a paleontologist, who will never see dinosaurs. Or a physicist, who will never see electrons. We just have to trust that these things exist."

"But it's not just *trusting* that they exist," I protested. "We know that Essex is real."

"Do we?" Dad asked in his most infuriating PhD voice. He set aside his scraped-clean bowl and leaned back in his chair. "How do we know that? Were you there, Chelsea?"

"No, but we don't have to *be* somewhere to know that it exists. I mean, what, are you claiming that none of it really happened?" I asked. "That the whole Revolutionary War is just a figment of our national imagination, and Essex was built last week?"

"That's not what I mean." Dad shook his head, like he thought I was being purposefully recalcitrant. "Of course the Revolutionary War really happened. We have letters and diaries and gravestones and bayonets—all these primary sources so we'll never doubt that it happened. We have the outcome itself, which may be the most powerful proof of all: America is a sovereign nation, a free democracy.

"Unquestionably, the Revolutionary War *happened*. This is why Holocaust deniers are so infuriating and upsetting. Because it takes an insane amount of dissociation from reality to be able to look at all the primary sources, and to look at the outcomes, and still to conclude that a historical event *didn't happen*. This is why it's unacceptable to invent paperwork, as Reenactmentland did. There's a difference between reimagining and lying."

"Okay, but that's what I was saying in the first place. So what's your point?"

Dad loves to be asked what his point is. There is literally nothing he would rather do, in life, than explain what his point is. He said, "My point is that, although things actually happen, we don't remember them the way they actually were.

"History doesn't intend to have some particular emotional

value, or any particular moral. History doesn't have any intentions at all. It's just a never-ending web of events that can have pretty much any meaning at all.

"But *we*, in retrospect, make this web into a story that makes sense. We superimpose onto it a beginning, middle, and end. We decide who the main characters are, the good guys and the bad guys. We decide what the moral of the story is, and how everyone is supposed to feel about it."

"But history is facts," I said. "It's not a matter of opinion."

"To a certain extent," Dad granted. "The facts matter, to a certain extent. You can't create a story without some facts to base it on. But what 'really happened' doesn't matter. What matters is how we agree to remember it. Here's an example for you, Chelsea: the Boston Massacre."

"March fifth, 1770," I supplied automatically.

Dad said, "In retrospect, many historians come to describe it as the night the Revolution begins—though at the time, of course, the people don't know that they are headed toward all-out war. British soldiers stationed in Boston shoot into a crowd of Colonials and kill five. This event is reimagined almost immediately thereafter as a 'massacre,' even though five deaths is nothing of the sort. Calling it a 'massacre' is branding, it's propaganda to drum up support for secession. You have, of course, seen Paul Revere's famous political cartoon, depicting an orderly line of British troops opening fire on docile, unarmed Bostonians. Not true.

"These days most U.S. history textbooks teach how few victims there are in the Boston Massacre, how Revere's cartoon is exaggeration to make a point. But what these textbooks leave out are the exact circumstances of March fifth. What happened is this: Bostonians pour out of taverns, where they've been drinking for hours. They pelt the British troops with rocks and chunks of ice. They call them names that I'm not going to repeat in the presence of my teenage daughter. These men are not civilized, politically minded Patriots. They are drunks and thugs, and there's an argument to be made that, when the British troops open fire, they're acting in self-defense. So whose fault is the Boston Massacre: the soldiers or the colonists?

"Or, for another example, consider Thomas Jefferson," Dad went on. "What do you know about Jefferson?"

"Mike interprets him," I answered readily.

Dad sighed. "Anything else, or is that all that ten years of Essex employment and public-school education have taught you?"

"Thomas Jefferson . . . A great Patriot. Wrote the Declaration. The nation's third president. The Louisiana Purchase. Founded the University of Virginia. Come on, Dad, ask me a hard one."

"That's fine," Dad said. "But do you know that Jefferson used his presidential term to undermine Federalism as much as he possibly could? That he promoted traitorous relations with France at the same time that President Washington was trying to forge a peace treaty with England? That he owned slaves his entire life and refused to take responsibility when he fathered children by one of them? That his goal was to forcefully remove all nonassimilated Native Indians from U.S. soil? That he opposed giving women the right to vote because he believed they weren't as smart as their male counterparts?"

These, incidentally, are what are known as "rhetorical questions."

"Is that all true?" I asked.

Dad shrugged. "It's as true as the 'great Patriot' story. They're both just stories, just different lenses through which you can view the same man. We tend to choose the rose-colored lenses, because they make everything prettier. History is written by the victors, and the victors want to make themselves look good. Who could blame them?"

I thought about our War with Reenactmentland and said, "I don't blame them at all."

Dad got to his feet and picked up our bowls. He ate a forkful of the macaroni that I'd left congealing in mine. "Are you going out tonight?" he asked.

"Nope."

He frowned. Even when I'm not trying, I always somehow find a way to give my father the wrong answer.

"I'm going to a party at Maggie's tomorrow night, though," I added. "If that's okay."

"Good." He nodded. "You've spent too much time home alone lately. You should be out with your friends."

It sounded so simple, coming from his mouth. Just go out with your friends! You know, those people who you like, who like you in return!

"Hey, Dad," I said as he was about to leave the room with our bowls. "Thanks."

He paused. "Thanks for telling you that you should be out with your friends?"

That wasn't what I meant at all. What I meant was something like, *Thanks for telling me about history.* But instead I said, "Thanks for dinner."

He shook his head. "It was only macaroni, Chelsea." He went into the kitchen, and I slipped upstairs to my bedroom.

I shut the door and took out my Ezra file. Although I had kept the items inside pristine, the folder itself was beginning to show signs of wear and tear. One of its corners was creased. There were a few smudges on the outside.

I sat down on the floor, flipped open the folder, and pulled out the first artifact. The photo of us sitting together on one sled, him wearing a dumb cap topped with a pom-pom, me resting into him, our camera-ready smiles.

Leaning against my bed, I remembered the day this photo was taken. It was a Wednesday, and school was canceled. We'd gotten ten inches of snow the night before, a bigger blizzard than this part of Virginia had seen in years. It was hard to imagine it, on this hot summer night, but I tried my best: the way the tiny snowflakes stung my face, how I had to wear two jackets just to go outside.

I was going sledding with Fiona and a bunch of our friends from school, but I didn't even own a sled. I'd had to stop and buy one at the dollar store on the way to the golf course. Ezra met us there, and I still remembered the comfort of his arms around me as we catapulted down the hill, going faster and faster. I would have been scared without him there, but as it was, I just closed my eyes and let the wind whip past me because I knew, without a doubt, that in his arms I would be safe.

You don't remember everything, Fiona told me.

What 'really happened' doesn't matter, Dad said. *What matters is how we agree to remember it.*

What really happened, the day Ezra and I went sledding. What really happened was that all my friends were going to the golf course, and I was so excited because I hadn't been sledding since I was a little kid, and Ezra didn't want to go. What really happened was that we spent an hour on the phone in the morning, with me begging him to come sledding with us.

"It's cold," he said. "It's wet."

"You'll be fine. You'll dry," I said.

"Why don't you just come over to my house? We can watch a movie. We can make popcorn."

"Because I can go over to your house any day. We can

watch a movie any day. But we can only go sledding *today*, because *today* is the only day there's snow."

"Why don't you just do your stupid sledding thing," Ezra proposed, "and get wet and cold, and I'll stay home and watch a movie?"

"Because"—and for some reason I wanted to cry, as I tightened my grip on the phone and stared out my window at the snow twirling in the wind—"it's a snow day. It's special. So I want to spend it with you."

I finally bullied him into coming, but by then we had spent so long arguing on the phone that, when I got to the dollar store, they had already sold all the good snow tubes. I had to buy a crappy plastic sheet that barely counted as a sled. And, of course, I blamed Ezra for this.

He arrived at the golf course shortly after I did, and, even though everyone else took run after run, Ezra didn't want a turn. He just stood at the top of the hill, scarf pulled up past his nose, hat pulled down past his eyebrows, arms in a tight hug around his middle, shivering dramatically.

"You can go home if you want," I told him. "If you're not going to sled at all, you should just go home."

But he shook his head and said, "No. You said I had to be here. So I'm here."

This was in January, when Fiona was in the middle of her two-week relationship with Reginald Ellis, who was at our school only for the second half of his senior year because his father had been transferred from London. Fiona and Reginald went flying past us on her sled, her giggling, him hollering "Bollocks!" as they hit a bump.

I remembered this made me feel so desperate, that Fiona should be having this romantic interlude with a guy whom she'd first met literally one week ago, whereas my boyfriend and I couldn't muster up one single romantic moment, not even in this incredibly romantic winter wonderland.

"Please," I pleaded with Ezra, almost in tears. "Please let's just sled down the hill together once. Then we can leave."

So we sat down together on the sled, and that was when one of my friends snapped the photograph that I now, nearly seven months later, held in my hands. If I looked hard, I could see my eyes in this photo sparkling, though I couldn't say whether it was with happiness or snow or tears.

After the camera shutter clicked, we were off, down the hill. And it was perfect, for a moment. For a moment, we were perfect. I hadn't made up any of that memory. His arms really had wrapped around me, I really was pressed back against his chest, the wind really did feel so clean and pure.

When we hit the bump at the bottom of the hill, we fell off the sled together and tumbled into the snow, landing softly with his body on top of mine, pinning me down. I was laughing and gasping for air, and he said, "That is possibly the shittiest sled a person could own."

Maybe he meant it as a joke or maybe he meant it as a

criticism, but, either way, the smile cracked off my face like an icicle. I said, "I would have been able to get a better sled if I hadn't had to spend all morning on the phone with you."

"You wouldn't have had to spend all morning on the phone with me if you hadn't made such a big deal out of us going sledding together," he replied.

And then it wasn't perfect anymore. We were happy for a few minutes, we really, honestly were. And then we stopped being happy.

Now, I set the sledding photo carefully to one side, to uncover the next item in the Ezra file: ticket stubs from a midnight showing of *Bottle Rocket* at the Plainville Cinema.

Somehow I had gotten permission from my parents to stay out extra late, just to see the movie. It was early March but it already felt like springtime; for the first time in months I was wearing ballet flats and a skirt without tights underneath. I had straightened my hair and stuck a new headband in it. I remembered Ezra acting kind of flustered as he drove us to the movie theater. The whole car smelled like him, like aftershave or cologne or one of those other boy things.

"Is everything okay?" I asked, after he trailed off in the middle of a sentence for the third time.

"Yeah, fine. I just . . ." He shook his head and said in a quiet voice, "You're just really pretty."

This was one of my favorite Ezra moments, out of all of them. I never tired of replaying that moment.

We got to the cinema and he bought Sno-Caps for me and Sour Patch Kids for himself. The movie was laugh-out-loud funny, and then after it was over, but before he dropped me off at home, Ezra pulled his car onto a side street and we just went at it, our hands and mouths all over each other, fogging up the windows of his car. It was three a.m. by the time I walked in my front door, and I was prepared to tell my parents that the movie really was that long, if they asked, which they never did.

For someone who's supposed to be an expert at history, you just suck at remembering what's real, Fiona said.

Although things actually happen, we don't remember them the way they actually were, Dad said.

The way things actually were. The way things actually were is that all of that was true. Also true was that, when we got to the movie theater, we ran into a girl named Kimberly, who was on the school paper with Ezra. She was out with a group of her girl friends. When Ezra bought me Sno-Caps, he also bought a box of Junior Mints for Kimberly. He wanted to sit right behind her, so they could spend the time before the movie gossiping about other editors at the paper. I barely knew the people they were talking about, so there was nothing I could say. Kimberly tried to include me in their conversation, a little. Ezra didn't try at all.

During the movie, I put my hand on Ezra's knee, and he didn't pull away, but he didn't respond, either. He just sat there, staring at the screen, like we were two strangers who happened to be sitting next to each other, and for some reason one stranger decided it was socially acceptable to rest her hand on the other stranger's knee. During the scene where the characters rob a cold storage facility, Ezra leaned forward and whispered a comment in Kimberly's ear, and she laughed and laughed. After the movie was over, he insisted that we walk Kimberly to her car before we left.

I didn't say anything to Ezra about any of this, because what could I have said? He had told me I was pretty, he had taken me to the movies, he wanted to make out with me, and yet for some reason I was jealous of Kimberly. I couldn't tell him that. It wouldn't have made any sense.

That's what really happened. It was all true, the good and the bad, both at once. All of time happens in one moment: 1774 and 1863 and last winter and this summer. And all of a relationship is true in one moment, too. All these things exist and coexist and re-exist.

I closed the Ezra file and set it down on the floor. I climbed into bed with my clothes still on, crawled under the sheet, and remembered April 17th, the day Ezra officially broke up with me. What really happened.

I wouldn't say I was surprised when he ended things. In fact, I was the opposite of surprised. Within the course of a few weeks, we went from talking on the phone every day to almost never. He stopped texting me every time something reminded him of me, and when I texted him, he wouldn't respond for hours, or sometimes not at all. He stopped making plans with me; on Friday, I would corner him in Latin class and ask about his weekend, and he would rattle off a series of activities, none of which included me. He chatted with me online still, but less and less, and he kissed me still, but distractedly, as if he was doing me a favor. But still he didn't break up with me.

I was miserable. I checked my phone and e-mail frantically, reasoning that any communication from him would mean he still cared about me. Fiona was horrified, though I couldn't tell whether she was more bothered by the way Ezra was treating me, or by the way I was reacting. "In what way, exactly, are you two still together?" she asked me.

"In the way where he hasn't broken up with me yet."

"So why don't you break up with him? You know you're allowed to do that. He's treating you like shit."

"I don't *want* to break up with him."

We were having this conversation during lunchtime. Instead of eating in the cafeteria, I was with Fiona in the filthy first-floor bathroom at school, crying because I had just seen Ezra flirting with Kimberly in the lunch line.

"So you don't want to break up with him, what, because he makes you so happy?" Fiona asked as I splashed cool water on my eyes.

"Right."

"Okay, sure. That makes sense."

"He's really busy," I defended him. "He has a huge math test coming up, and you know he's bad at math. And he's writing the lead feature for the paper next week. And—"

"*I'm* really busy," Fiona exploded. "I have rehearsal for like four hours every day after school, but *I* still have time to see you. And do you know why that is, Chelsea?"

I didn't say anything.

"It's because I *make* time to see you. Because I actually *want* to see you. Listen to me: Nobody is so busy that they can't make time for the people they really care about. Nobody, and especially not Ezra Gorman."

The situation probably could have gone on like that for weeks longer if Fiona hadn't taken matters into her own hands. She told me that she instant messaged Ezra one night and said something along the lines of: "Look, if you don't want to be Chelsea's boyfriend anymore, that's fine—even though I think you're an idiot because Chelsea is amazing and who wouldn't want to be her boyfriend? But if you really don't, then no protest here, but *for the love of God*, will you please actually break up with her so she can start getting over you, because *I cannot go on like this*."

The next day, Ezra was waiting for me when I got out of my last-period class. "Can I walk you home?" he asked.

"Sure," I said, like a cow to slaughter. "Let's do this."

We spent most of our walk talking about normal things:

school and the weather and movies and nothing. When we were a block from my house, Ezra said, "Look, Chelsea, I think you're great and all, but I don't . . . want to be your boyfriend anymore."

"Yeah, I've been getting that vibe from you."

"I was hoping we could just take what we had and tone it down, turn it into a friendship, but, I don't know, Fiona told me I was supposed to actually break up with you."

"Sure," I said.

"I'm serious about us staying friends, though. I don't want to lose you as a friend, Chelsea. I still care about you."

"Clearly," I said. "Clearly you care about me. And my feelings. And all that stuff."

We had reached my front stairs. "You're not mad at me, are you?" he asked. "Just because I don't think we should date anymore?"

I had a million things I wanted to say, so many that I couldn't say any of them. I wanted to say, *No, I'm not mad at you because you don't think we should date anymore, but I am mad at you for not asking what I think, because it doesn't matter to you, or to anyone, what I think. I'm mad that you figured you didn't even have to tell me this, that you could just start ignoring me and that I would get the picture. I'm mad that you would tell me all of this in the same breath as telling me, with a straight face, that you still care about me. And, actually, I take it back—I am mad that you don't want to date me anymore. And I'm offended, and I love you.*

I didn't say that. I said, "Well, that's that, then."

"Give me a hug," he said, and pulled me in close. I held on to him like I was drowning.

That's true. That's what really happened.

History is written by the victors, Dad said. But who was the victor in Ezra's and my story, and who was the victim?

I fell asleep there, still trying to answer this question. I didn't even wake up to change into pajamas or turn out the light.

Chapter 20
THE PARTY

Maggie's family turned out to be—and I do not use this term lightly—filthy rich. They lived in an old plantation house set back from the street, with a wide walkway leading up through the field that I guess counted as their front yard. Enormous, lush trees flanked the porch, which was supported by Georgian columns. The steel frame of an old wagon sat outside, as if to suggest that at any moment someone might start carting around tobacco plants.

"This place puts even your old house to shame," I commented, as Fiona drove us up the driveway for Maggie's party.

"I know it." She parked the convertible, then flipped down the rearview mirror so she could apply more plum-colored lipstick. "I'd be jealous if I didn't think big houses were tacky."

"You think big houses are tacky?"

She puckered her lips at the mirror. "No. But I thought it sounded good when I said it. Like maybe I'm not as materialistic as I seem. Did it work?"

"Oh. No. Maybe try saying it to a stranger, though. I probably know you too well for that."

Fiona shrugged, then opened her car door and swiveled both her legs around in unison so she could get out without flashing her underwear.

"Fi, did your legs get longer this summer, or did that jean skirt shrink?" I asked.

"Neither. I just went to the mall and bought a shorter skirt."

I rolled my eyes and crouched on my seat, grabbed on to the top of the car door, and vaulted over it to land on the driveway. I stuck my arms in the air, the world's least talented gymnast.

"You do know that door opens, right?" Fiona asked. "Since it's a car, and all?"

"What's the point of arriving at a party in a convertible if you can't make an entrance?" I countered.

"No one's watching us make our entrance, though."

"So?"

"Good point," Fiona conceded.

We followed the sounds of music and laughter around to

the back of Maggie's house. A lot of Essex kids were hanging out on the back patio, as well as a bunch of people who I didn't recognize. There was an inground pool with big beach balls floating around in it. A hip-hop song was pumping out of speakers shaped like rocks. It was all very atmospheric, and I say this with the authority of a person whose job is to provide atmosphere.

"Hi, girls!" Maggie ran over to give me and Fiona big hugs. She was wearing—this is true—high-heeled sandals, short-shorts, and a bikini top. This girl did not need a nineteenth-century lady-of-the-night costume. She already *was* a lady of the night.

"The keg's over there," she said, pointing. "Ezra and Lenny are grilling burgers, if you're hungry. Did you bring bathing suits?"

"Where are your parents?" I asked. "Don't you have parents?"

Maggie made a *you-are-so-lame* face at me, then must have remembered that I was, after all, the greatest warrior Essex had ever seen, because she answered politely, "They're on an antiquing trip in South Carolina this week."

"An antiquing trip?" I repeated.

"Yes. It's a trip. Where you buy antiques," Maggie explained.

"Maggie's parents collect Colonial memorabilia," Fiona added.

"They have the world's largest private collection of Colonial currency, or whatever," Maggie said. "They left my brother in charge." She gestured toward a shirtless, muscular guy who couldn't have been older than nineteen. He was standing with three girls and drinking from a red plastic cup.

"Your brother's hot," Fiona noted.

"Ew," Maggie said, her tone conveying that Fiona was completely correct, but that she, Maggie, could not say so without sounding incestuous. "He's single," she added helpfully. "But just for the summer. His girlfriend's in California."

"Hmm." Fiona stared at him.

"Fi," I said, as kindly as I knew how. "Eyes on the prize, sweetie."

Fiona sighed, nodded, and turned her attention back to us.

"So did you remember your swimsuits or what?" Maggie asked.

Fiona lifted her shirt to show her bikini top.

"I didn't know you had a pool," I said.

Maggie looked confused. "Well, obviously. Otherwise, why would I be having a party?"

"Good point," I said. "Why *would* you have a party without a pool?"

"I have a bunch of extra suits on my bed upstairs," Maggie said. "You can borrow one. You probably wear a smaller top than I do, but that's okay. If you tie it really tight, I'm sure it will stay on you."

I crossed my arms over my chest.

PAST PERFECT

"Anne!" Maggie hollered.

Anne had been sitting on the edge of a lounge chair, talking to Bryan. When Maggie called, she trotted over to us.

"Show Chelsea where my room is, okay?" Maggie said. Without waiting for a response, she took Fiona's arm and led her toward the pool.

I followed Anne inside. She slid shut the glass door behind us, muffling the sounds of the party.

"Maggie's room is this way," she said and led me through the kitchen, its walls decorated with large copper pots; into the high-ceilinged front foyer, home to two Windsor chairs; and up the staircase, which was lined with paintings of various regiments crossing various rivers. I was impressed. Collecting antiques is basically what rich people do instead of going to junk shops, and, lord knows, I love junk shops. I don't know who decides, though, when something is old, whether it becomes a valuable antique or just worthless crap.

"Do you think Bryan is looking kind of cute tonight?" Anne asked.

"No," I answered.

"Oh."

"Or was that a rhetorical question?" I asked.

Anne paused on the top step, considering my words. "I don't know what that means," she eventually concluded.

We went into Maggie's bedroom, which, instead of feeling

like a high-class Colonial gallery, looked like a normal, modern place for a normal, modern girl to live. I sifted through the mess of bikinis on Maggie's queen-size bed.

"Why is Bryan even here?" I asked. I felt kind of snubbed that it had taken three years before Maggie had ever included me in a party, and then only because I was the War's MVP. Meanwhile, Bryan just scored an invitation, no big deal? *Bryan?*

"I invited him?" Anne said.

"Huh." I looked for the top to match the polka-dotted bikini bottom in my hand. "Weird."

"I'm glad you and Fiona finally showed up," Anne said. "Nat has been asking about her all night."

"Of course he has been," I said. "Has anyone been asking about me?"

"No," Anne answered. Anne is, above all else, a very honest person. "Why don't they just go out? Does she think she's too good for him? I don't get it."

"I think she's scared," I answered, trying to change from clothes into bathing suit without exposing Anne to an unintentional strip show.

"Scared of Nat?" Anne asked dubiously.

"Scared of commitment, I guess. Scared of love."

"Huh." Anne looked into the distance, pondering this for a moment, which I used as an opportunity to whip off my underpants and quickly slip into the bikini bottoms. "Have you ever been in love?" she asked me.

"Yes." I paused. "I thought I was in love, anyway. So I guess I really was, since I thought it, at the time."

"And was it scary?" Anne asked.

"Absolutely. Someone can wind up getting hurt. That's scary." I tried to adjust the shoulder straps. "A boy once told me that love without heartbreak is just a pretty myth."

"Did your Civil War boyfriend say that?"

I looked up at her sharply. "What makes you think that?"

"I don't know. I figured it was either him or Ezra, so . . ."

"Ezra and him aren't the only guys I've ever hooked up with, you know," I said.

Anne shrugged. "Okay."

"I've had *lots* of boyfriends before."

"Cool." She looked wholly unimpressed.

"I mean, not a slutty number of boyfriends. But not just Ezra and a Civil Warrior, either. Basically, what I'm saying is that I've had a normal number of boyfriends."

"Fine. Are you done changing yet?"

I put my clothes back on over the swimsuit. "But anyway," I said. "Yes, it just so happens that the one of my many boyfriends who said 'love without heartbreak is a pretty myth' was the Civil Warrior."

"Was he right?" Anne asked.

"I don't know," I said. "He might be. But even if he was right, it's still worth it. Because before the time when you're heartbroken, you get to be in love, and that's worth it."

We went back downstairs. We had been away from the party for maybe fifteen minutes, but somehow, when we came back, we found Maggie sobbing on a lawn chair with Patience hovering around her, petting her hair and dabbing at her face with tissues.

Anne immediately abandoned me to run over to her friends. I might offer nuanced perspectives on love, but let's be honest, that could never compete with the excitement of a weeping hostess.

Fiona and Nat were side by side, dangling their legs in the pool. I sat down next to them. "What did I miss?" I asked, gesturing at the huddle of distraught milliner girls.

"Ezra and Maggie had some big fight," Fiona said. "Surprise."

"Drama," Nat drawled, rolling his eyes, like he was just so over drama.

"Is everything all right?" I watched Patience and Anne support Maggie as she hobbled into her house like she had argued with Ezra, and then somehow broken her leg. Her brother stayed outside, setting up some complicated-looking drinking game. Fiona was doing a masterful job of not looking at him.

"Who knows." Nat kicked the water with his feet. "They're both a couple beers in. This might not even be a *real* fight."

"Either way," I said, "it's kind of shitty to fight with your girlfriend at her own party."

"Hold up." Fiona put up her hands. "Ezra did something kind of shitty? This is truly blowing my mind."

Nat laughed and playfully splashed her legs. I suddenly noticed something so obvious, I couldn't believe I had missed it for even an instant. "Nat, your hair!" I gasped.

His ponytail was gone. It was still longer than Ezra's or Dan's hair—still longer than a guy's hair is *supposed to be*—but for Nat, it was downright short.

"I know." He touched the ends of it. "I'm getting used to it."

"You cut it off?" I asked, impressed by Nat's sudden understanding of twenty-first-century fashion.

"Hell, no!" He looked offended. "Those farbs across the street did it. They caught me coming out of work yesterday. Two of them grabbed me. Big guys. I eventually got away, but not before one of them had chopped off most of my ponytail."

"It's horrible," Fiona murmured. "That's so traumatic."

"They're monsters," Nat declared. "The only thing that makes it even slightly okay is that I know they're being stripped of their Barnes Prize. So let them pull their stupid pranks, let them cut off my hair, which I've been growing out for *four years*"—Fiona shook her head sadly—"but it's okay, because we already won this War." Nat nodded at me. "Thank you for giving me that, Chelsea."

I didn't want to be thanked for hurting Dan. I didn't say anything.

"I think it looks just as adorable as it did before," Fiona told him, running her hand through his hair.

This was serious. If Fiona liked Nat even without his revolting, scraggly long hair, then she was going to like him no matter what.

I decided to give them some alone time. "I'm going to get some food," I said, standing up and shooting Fiona a meaningful glance. At least, I hoped it was meaningful. The meaning I was trying to convey was, *Make this happen, Fiona, for the love of God.*

Ezra stood alone by the grill, wearing swim trunks and a crew-neck T-shirt. His hair was damp, like he'd already been in the pool, and he was prodding at the burgers with a spatula.

"Got one for me?" I asked.

"Chelsea!" His eyes lit up when he saw me. Or maybe I just thought they did. It was dark outside, and who could say.

"Hey. Um, is everything okay?" It was none of my business, of course, what happened between him and his girlfriend. But if it was the talk of the party, well, I was curious.

"Yeah. Well, not really, no. This thing with Maggie isn't really . . . working." He shrugged. "Sometimes I just don't know what she wants from me. Everything seems fine, and then she freaks out at me over nothing. Literally, nothing. It's like she wants something really specific, but she doesn't tell me what it is, and then when I don't magically figure it out on my own, she flips her shit. I don't get it."

I wondered, suddenly, whether Ezra would ever be able to maintain a happy relationship with any girl at all.

Rosaline came over, looking for a burger, and after she had slathered it in ketchup and left, Ezra said to me, "Hey, do you want to go for a walk?"

"Who will man the burgers?" I asked.

He set down the spatula. "The burgers can man themselves."

So we headed off together, leaving behind the sounds and lights of the party. Maggie's property was enormous and bordered by woods; within a few minutes, we couldn't see the party at all, or even the house itself.

"Do you remember that time we went to D.C.?" Ezra asked me abruptly.

"Sure." We'd had the day off from school for President's Day, and I had told Ezra that I wanted an adventure. He picked me up in his car, and we didn't even know where we were going. He just started driving, and the next thing we knew, we were on the road to Washington.

"You had made those banana muffins," Ezra reminisced.

"Right. Because we were on an all-day interstate exploration, and I was worried that we might starve."

"And we were singing along to Elvis the whole way there."

I smiled. Neither Ezra nor I can sing. We sing *loudly*, but we can't sing.

"Wise men say," Ezra began in his horrible, faux–Elvis Presley baritone, "only fools rush in . . ."

". . . but I can't help," I joined in, "falling in love you."

We stopped singing. For a second, all I could hear were the cicadas. "It doesn't seem like that long ago," Ezra said.

"Sometimes," I said. "But sometimes it feels like forever."

He stopped walking and cleared his throat. When he spoke, his voice came out unsteady. "I miss you, Chelsea."

"I miss you, too," I said.

And as soon as the words had left my lips, he leaned in and kissed me.

For close to four months now, I had been remembering Ezra's kisses. How they were amazing, fulfilling, like fireworks. For months, I had been remembering how they made me feel. Like I was the most special girl in the world, like I could never want anything more than just this. For months, I had been unable to confront head-on the reality that Ezra would never kiss me again, and I would never feel that way again, that it was really and forever *over*.

Now it wasn't really and forever over. He was kissing me again. I was kissing him back.

And the thing about it was this: it was good. It wasn't perfect. I didn't feel like fainting or crying or throwing him to the ground in these woods and stripping off all his clothes. It was a good kiss, because he's a good kisser, and I liked it, but that was all.

I stayed there for a moment. I knew this was the last time I would ever kiss him, and I wanted to hold on to it for as long as I could. Then I pulled back.

"What about Maggie?" I asked.

He shook his head and touched my hair. "Maggie and I are over. It wasn't working. It wasn't going to work."

"It's funny," I said quietly. "You and Maggie looked so happy together."

He seemed to think about this for a moment. "Did we?"

"Mm-hmm." I sighed. "But I guess you and I must have looked so happy together too."

"Chelsea," Ezra said, cupping my face in his hands and looking into my eyes. "Let's get back together. This isn't about Maggie, this isn't about anyone else but you. I miss you, you miss me. Let's get back together, and we can spend every weekend exploring the world and doing a terrible job of singing Elvis songs to each other. Please."

I looked into his gray-blue eyes, and what came into my mind was not a chorus of hallelujahs. What came to mind was the line Mr. Zelinsky repeated every summer orientation. *Those who do not learn from the past are doomed to repeat it.*

I didn't want to be doomed to repeat the past anymore.

And I thought how funny it was. Funny and sad, at the same time. Sometimes you get everything you ever wanted, only it doesn't look like what you wanted anymore.

"No," I said to Ezra. "Thank you. But no."

His face twisted. "Is this because of your Civil War *boyfriend*? I didn't realize you were still with that farb."

"Not that it's any of your business," I snapped, "but I'm not.

We stopped seeing each other after you told Tawny everything about his dad. So, you know, thanks for ruining that, too."

"I told Tawny all of that to *help* you," Ezra protested. "No one was speaking to you. You were miserable. Now everyone at Essex adores you again. I did that for *you*, Chelsea."

And I guessed it was true, that there's a version of that story in which Ezra told Tawny because he was trying to help me. And then there's a version of that story in which Ezra told Tawny because he was using me. History is written by the victors, but I could be the victor here. I could believe whichever version of the story that I wanted.

"Either way, I'm not going to thank you," I said. "Dan might never take me back after what I did to him and his family. But that's not what matters here. Even if he never speaks to me again, I would rather be alone than be with you."

Ezra just blinked at me, like he didn't understand.

"Why now?" I asked. "Why have you decided that you want to get back together *now*? After all these months, you were just like, 'Oh, hey, it's August seventh, how about I take Chelsea back'? Wait—is it actually August seventh?"

I double-checked the date on my phone. It was.

Goddamn, that Fiona Warren was a genius.

Ezra looked confused and a little annoyed, like he hadn't expected to be put through all this rigmarole just to win me back. "I don't know," he answered. "I've been waiting to ask you out for a while, but I was with Maggie, and you were with what's-his-name, and you seemed so mad at me all the time . . . But then tonight you showed up looking so pretty, so I just . . . did it."

Although this wasn't a good answer, I believed that it was true: He probably *didn't* know why he wanted to win me back now. That wasn't how Ezra's mind worked. He felt that he wanted to date me again, so, boom, he asked me out. Just like when he felt that he didn't want to be with me, he just stopped talking to me.

Maybe it was because he and Maggie were falling apart, and he wanted reassurance that some other girl out there was still crazy about him. Maybe when he found out I was seeing someone else, it made him jealous, and it made him realize that I must have something to offer if another guy wanted me. Maybe he was impressed by how far I was willing to go to help Essex in the War, and that made him fall in love with me all over again. Maybe he had been carrying a torch for me ever since breaking up with me, and all he had thought about every minute since then was how to win back my heart. Maybe anything.

"Ezra," I said, not wanting to be cruel, but just wanting him to *know*, "you broke my heart. I couldn't stop crying. I couldn't eat. I couldn't sleep. And when I slept, I couldn't wake up in the morning because that's how much I couldn't face the day."

I'd expected Ezra to be at least a little horrified or

apologetic about this, but, once again, I had expected too much from him. However little I expected from him, he always managed to give me less.

"A person is allowed to break up with his girlfriend," he said. "It wasn't like we were *married*, okay? We went out for a few months, and then we stopped going out, and sometime thereafter, I started going out with someone else. This happens to people all the time. You can't hold it against me that *you* couldn't handle it. It wasn't my fault that you cried and stopped eating and all that stuff you said."

"But I didn't feel that way only after you broke up with me," I told him. "That was how I felt for ages before you broke up with me too, because that's what it was like to date you. That's how you made me feel. When I was with you, when you were my *boyfriend*, I worried about every step I took, because I might step wrong. I felt like I always had to be the most interesting girl in the world for you, or else you would immediately get bored of me. I never stopped being nervous around you, not in all the time we were together."

His expression was concerned, and he tried to grab hold of my arm. "It wouldn't be like that this time, Chelsea. I promise."

I wanted to believe him, but there wasn't anything believable about this. "You can't make any of that un-happen," I said. "Us getting back together wouldn't un-break my heart.

"You talk about driving to D.C., but you know what really happened that day? What really happened is that we drove there and listened to good music and ate banana muffins and kissed at stoplights and had an amazing time. All those good things *were* true, but they *weren't* enough. Because then what really happened is that we got lost on the drive home, and you blamed me because I was the one navigating, and we drove for hours, and we had to refill the gas tank, and we argued over whose fault it was that we used up so much gas and who should have to pay for it. What really happened is that I apologized for the first hour and a half of the drive, and then once we knew we were on the right road, I just started crying, and you just let me. Do you remember now? Are you remembering? That's what *really* happened, Ezra."

"None of that was my fault!" Ezra was looking seriously aggrieved now.

"None of it was my fault, either. *We were bad for each other.* That wasn't anybody's fault."

I stopped talking. He didn't have anything to say, either. We just kept staring each other straight in the eyes, only inches apart. The cicadas kept humming, the moon kept shining, the tall tree branches kept rustling in the breeze. It could have been the most romantic moment. But it wasn't.

"So, yes, Ezra, I do miss you," I said softly. "But no, I don't want you back."

We walked back to Maggie's party, next to each other, but not together. When we got there, it was more or less the same party we had left. The drinking games were in full swing. The milliner girls were outside again. Ezra squared his shoulders and beelined over to Maggie. Patience and Anne moved a few feet away so that they could listen in while Maggie and Ezra talked about whatever they needed to talk about.

Fiona didn't even look up when we came out of the woods. She was sitting in Nat's lap on a lounge chair, her arms wrapped around his neck, deep in conversation. I didn't bother them.

Despite Maggie's insistence that everyone wear a swimsuit, the pool was empty. I stripped down to my bikini and dove in alone. The water stung me with its coldness, and my chest felt tight. But that was okay, I could live with that. I swam along the bottom of the pool with my eyes wide open and, in the moment before I came up, gasping for air, I felt clean.

Chapter 21
THE BEGINNING

"Troops, it has been an amazing summer. A truly amazing summer. I cannot begin to express how proud of you I am, how honored I have felt to be the General of such a kick-ass army."

This was Tawny speaking, of course, addressing the rest of us from atop her rock. Such words could come from no one but Tawny Nelson.

"Our accomplishments have been extraordinary! Our ingenuity and tenacity have no rival! Whenever they hit us, we hit back harder!"

Cheers all around.

"It is my sincerest regret for this summer to come to an

end," Tawny went on. "But time stops for no man. School starts on Tuesday, no matter how much we want the War to go on and on forever."

I snorted, quietly, so only Fiona could hear. She was sitting next to me, holding Nat's hand, and she threw me a sympathetic look. If I could wish for anything, it would be that War *not* go on and on forever.

Well, no. If I could wish for anything, it would be for one particular boy, who was too good for me, who I would probably never see again.

"It's always sad to see the summer end," Tawny went on, "but this year is sadder for me than any other. Because, as you all know, I'm . . . going to college."

I was stunned to see Tawny blink hard a few times, like she was holding back tears. In the five years I had known her, I had *never* seen Tawny cry. Not from pain, not from sadness, not from joy. She was a *fighting machine*. Two summers ago, the Civil Warriors stole a necklace that had been a gift from Tawny's godmother before she died from ovarian cancer. Tawny didn't even *think* about crying. Instead, she led a raid on Reenactmentland that liberated not only her necklace, but also one of the Civil War's cannons in the process. Crying was not in Tawny's repertoire.

Yet here she was, standing on the tip of her rock, her voice wavering with emotion. "This place . . . and you all . . . mean so much to me. I look forward to the War all year round. But this is . . . This is it for me. I'm too old to fight anymore." She sniffled, and I saw a few other girls dabbing at their eyes too.

"I'm just glad I got to go out with a bang," Tawny said, her voice barely louder than a whisper.

So that's it, then. Tawny Nelson *does* have real, human feelings. They're caused by weird things. But they are, nonetheless, real. That may have been the biggest surprise of this entire summer.

"As of next week, you will no longer be able to count me among these ranks," Tawny went on, louder now. "Which means that it's time to elect a new General. Nominations are now open. Who among you do you want to be your leader?"

Bryan's hand immediately shot up. "I nominate Bryan Denton," he said. "I think he's been really dedicated to the War effort for many years now, and this summer, in particular, he has come into his own, especially during the Undercover Operation, which he pulled off masterfully."

"He's talking about himself in the third person, right?" I muttered to Fiona. "Is that actually what's happening here?"

She looked pained. "It's all so unclear."

Nat raised his hand too—his right hand, the one not holding Fiona's. "I nominate Chelsea Glaser," he said.

A smattering of applause.

"This has been a rough season, but Chelsea contributed more than the rest of us combined. The intel she scoped out has put us in a position of power for years to come.

Reenactmentland won't recover easily from losing their Barnes Prize, and that's all thanks to Chelsea. She's shown herself willing to take unpopular stances, if it's for the overall benefit of Essex. And from serving as Lieutenant to Tawny's General, she already has experience leading our troops. So that's my vote, and I hope it's yours, as well. Chelsea Glaser for General!"

Nearly everyone, even Tawny, burst into applause. I didn't do or say anything for a minute. I was flattered, of course, just as I'd been flattered two months ago, when they'd asked me to be Lieutenant. But being flattered wasn't reason enough. And Nat's understanding of what I'd done for the War this summer, and why I'd done it, was just so far from my reality, it was hard even to believe that he was talking about me.

Some people started chanting my name—"Chel-sea! Chel-sea!"—and it was like that first War meeting of the summer all over again. Only this time, it wasn't going to end with Dan kidnapping me, because I hadn't heard from him since the evening he showed up at my house and told me I was a bad person. I had called and texted him countless times since, trying to explain, begging him to forgive me. But for all the response I got, I might as well have been apologizing to myself.

So this meeting wasn't going to end with Dan showing up. But it wasn't going to end with me becoming General, either. That was one thing I could control.

I stood up before the cheering got too out of hand and said, "Essex!"

Everyone quieted down right away.

"Essex, I appreciate your confidence in me. But I'm going to have to say no. No, I don't want it."

Silence. Confused looks from my compatriots.

"I don't want to be always at War," I explained. "That's not me. And whatever I've done for our War efforts this summer, I promise you, most of it was unintentional. What I really want is to be at peace."

Still more confusion. If there's one thing drama kids don't really want, it's to be at peace.

I figured, *Oh, what the hell*, and continued, "But there is someone among our ranks who would rise to fill the role of General. Someone who is more dedicated to the cause of Essex than I am. Someone who will never let you down. I think we all know who that someone is."

Nope. Everyone was coming up blank.

"Bryan Denton," I said. "For next summer's General, I'm endorsing Bryan Denton."

I sat down. There was a moment of silence, then a voice slowly started chanting, "Bry-an, Bry-an." And it wasn't even Bryan who started the chant. It was *someone else*. It spread through the rest of the Colonials. Soon everyone was cheering "Bry-an! Bry-an!"—myself loudest of all.

"Bryan, do you accept this honor?" Tawny shouted over the roar of the crowd.

"Yes! Yes!" He shot to his feet and started jumping all over the place, nearly landing on Patience. He kept pumping his fists in the air and waggling his head about.

"You just couldn't help yourself, could you." Fiona sighed.

"Nope." I smiled, at peace. "I for sure could not."

"Bryan, come on up here!" Tawny hollered.

But before he got the chance, Anne, apparently overcome, darted over to him, whirled him around, and planted a big wet one right on his mouth. He kissed her back valiantly, enthusiastically, his tongue flailing.

All the other Colonials hooted and hollered. "All right, man!" Nat shouted.

Fiona and I just stared at each other. "Anne has a thing for men with power?" Fiona suggested.

"Anne has a thing for amphibians?" I guessed.

Fiona shook her head. "We may never know."

Anne sat down on my other side as Bryan ascended to the rock of power. "Thank you so much for endorsing him," she whispered to me, her eyes shining, cheeks flushed. "I just know he's going to be great at it."

"I'm sure," I agreed. And then—I mean, far be it from me to say anything derogatory about someone else's love interest, since it's not like I have such foolproof taste, but the words just slipped out. "You do know he's like a toad, right?"

"Yeah." Anne shrugged, her adoring gaze still fixed on Bryan. "I don't really mind that."

Bryan went on for a while, spittle flying out of his mouth,

about all the brilliant historical plans he had for next year. I mostly tuned him out. I wasn't sure if I would be back here next summer. And even if I worked at Essex again, I didn't want anything to do with the War.

Anyway, this year wasn't over just yet. We still had one last week to get through.

So instead of listening to Bryan, I looked around at all the other Colonials in this grove of trees with me. Fiona was resting her head on Nat's shoulder. They had been almost inseparable since Maggie's party, nearly three weeks ago. I had even heard Fiona call him her *boyfriend*, though she quickly explained that she was just using the word as shorthand.

Ezra and Maggie were sitting together a ways behind me. I had to twist around to look at them properly, so I didn't look for long. They had gotten back together the day after Maggie's party. Maybe they would work out this time around. Maybe he would finally get it together, and she would get it together, and they would make each other as happy as Ezra and I had never been.

I didn't think Ezra had told Maggie that, during the twelve hours they were broken up, he had kissed me. I didn't think anyone knew about our kiss in the woods that night except for me and him. And Fiona, obviously, because I told her.

Seeing Ezra and Maggie together, like they were now, still

made me feel a little jealous, a little hurt. I guessed that I would always feel that way. I didn't want what they had. But I wanted *something*.

There was less than a week left to summer, but that didn't stop the moderners from visiting Essex. If anything, there were more of them, and they were more high-strung, anxious to squeeze in the last bit of their children's summer enrichment before the school year began. I spent my third-to-last day of work running all over the graveyard, talking constantly, without a moment of downtime. I must have given two dozen families directions to the bathroom.

All three of the felled headstones had been put back up last week, and they looked as good as new. Or as good as old, I guess. None of the moderners gave them a second glance. The only way I could tell that they had been knocked over at all was because I remembered it.

Shortly before my lunch break, things calmed down a little. Moderners get hungry too. In fact, moderners get hungry way more than I do. It's because they're on vacation.

"What a day," Linda said to me. She sounded potentially depressed by the day we were having. But, then again, it was so hard to say.

"Seriously," I said, like I shared her emotion, whatever it was. "It's been crazy. I must have talked about the dead baby hill fifteen times."

Linda replied with her version of a smile. "You know, there might not actually be hundreds of dead babies buried there."

"What?" I exclaimed. "You're kidding me."

"At the Granary Burying Ground in Boston, there's a hill that resembles this one, where we're pretty certain the Colonials buried a large number of unbaptized infants. So we believe that this hill served the same purpose. But no one's ever dug it up to check, and the Colonials had no reason to keep careful records of the deaths of such young children. So . . ." She put out her hands and shrugged.

"But I've been telling people about those dead babies all summer long!" I felt betrayed.

"Me too." Linda looked unconcerned. "Hey, it's a great story either way."

She was right: It was a great story, true or false. It said what we wanted it to say. Tourists liked to hear about it. I liked to hear about it too. So it shouldn't have mattered to me that it might be a fiction, an accidental or purposeful misrecollection, yet somehow it did.

In my life, I wanted just one thing that wasn't a story. I didn't want to be far from authentic. I wanted one thing that I knew was true.

"I'm going on lunch now," I announced, and I didn't stick around to hear whether Linda said that was okay or not. I gathered up my petticoats and walked as fast as I could out of the graveyard, down the main road. I didn't stop for moderners requesting directions, I didn't stop by the milliner's to chat with Fiona, and I didn't stop at the silversmith's to get my sandwich. I just kept walking straight out of Essex, and, as soon as I hit the other side of the main gates, I broke into a run.

I ran across the street as fast as my Colonial shoes would let me. I ran up the main drive to Reenactmentland, I kept running . . . until I saw the ticket booth.

I had forgotten that it cost money to get into Reenactmentland. And honestly I would have paid the entry fee. I would have forked over my entire salary right then and there, just to get inside, to find Dan before the summer was over, before he went back to his modern world and disappeared from mine forever.

But Colonial women aren't allowed to carry money on them, because they are the property of their fathers or spouses, and property isn't allowed to own property.

I didn't have the time to return to Essex, go to the break room above the silversmith's, get my wallet, talk to my parents . . . More than not having the time, I just couldn't wait. I needed to do this *now*.

So I straightened my mobcap, dropped my petticoats, and strode slowly, sedately, straight past the ticket booth.

To anyone who knows anything, Colonial clothing has no resemblance to Civil War–era clothing. This would be like if someone walked into a twenty-first-century mall wearing a dress from 1925. Everyone would notice.

But apparently, to the ticket sellers at Reenactmentland, historical dress looks like historical dress, because they didn't bat an eye at me. I walked straight through like I belonged there.

Someone should tell the rest of the Colonials that sneaking into Reenactmentland didn't require as much sneakiness as we'd always thought. Someone should absolutely tell them, but it wasn't going to be me. After today, I was getting out of the War business once and for all.

Reenactmentland was quieter than when I'd been there earlier in the summer, quieter than Essex was today. The scarcity of moderners was no doubt due to the Barnes Prize scandal. We had won the War this year, anyone could see it. Our victory was thanks to the Civil Warriors who had decided to cheat in the first place, and thanks to me.

But unlike Ezra, I didn't care about winning.

This time, I knew where I was going. Purposefully, calmly, I walked to the big field filled with tents. The tent selling gentlemen's clothes, the tent selling weapons, the tent selling books. The tent where Dan and his family worked. I walked to the middle of the field, and then I stopped.

I waited. I didn't have to wait long.

The short girl, the Civil War General, came out of a tent and marched up to me. "What are you doing here?" she hissed, getting up in my face.

"I came to apologize."

She took a step back, seeming thrown by my answer. "This is *War*," she said, looking at me like she couldn't tell if I was kidding or stupid or what. "You don't apologize in War."

"Maybe you don't, but I do. I am."

She didn't reply for a moment, just sized me up, and I could tell she was thinking it over, getting ready to say, "Okay, we forgive you. Okay, we welcome you."

What she actually said was, "I'm going to give you to the count of ten to get the hell out of Reenactmentland. Start running."

Sometimes what I think is going on in people's heads is not, in fact, what is actually going on in people's heads.

"One . . . two . . . three . . ."

I didn't move. I didn't know what would happen when she reached ten, but whatever it was, I would take it.

Here is what happened when she got to ten: In the absolute farbiest move I have ever seen in all my years of reenacting, she pulled a cell phone out of her shirt and typed in a text message.

I opened my mouth to say *So what wireless carrier did the Confederate Army use?* before reminding myself that I was supposed to be here on a *peace mission*.

Moments after she sent the text message, other Civil Warriors started emerging from their tents. They walked straight over to us, forming a tight huddle around me, so no one could see in, and I couldn't get out.

"What is she doing here?"

"Who let her in?"

"The better question," said their General, "is, what are we going to do with her now that she's here?"

They closed in tighter around me. Someone behind me shoved my back, hard. I went falling forward into another Civil Warrior's hands. He threw me to the ground, and the back of my skull knocked into someone's knee. I tried to stand up, but they immediately shoved me back down.

The name-calling started.

"Farb," one of them hissed.

"Cheater."

"Liar."

"Bitch."

Someone spat on me, and I realized that, just because there were moderners and adults around somewhere, that didn't mean this couldn't get out of control. That didn't mean I couldn't get seriously hurt. These Civil Warriors weren't playing. They were *angry*.

"What the hell is going on here?" a familiar voice demanded.

I looked up to see Dan shoving his way through the crowd. The Civil Warriors stopped and just watched him, waiting to see what he would do.

"Hey," I said, and tried to smile, but I hurt all over.

He stared at me in silence for a moment, then around the circle at his friends, like he didn't know where to begin.

It occurred to me then that he could just walk away. He could tell them, "Do what you want with her, I don't care," and walk away.

If he did that, then it would be really, truly over. If he left me here, then I would know for sure that we were never going to be together. And I would get over him, I knew—Fiona would make up another arbitrary time constraint for me, and I would erase the few precious text messages he had sent me, and I would work really hard, and I would get over him. I'd done it before, and I could do it again. If he walked away.

He looked at the other Civil Warriors, and he ordered, "Get your hands off of her."

Everyone backed up slightly, giving me a little room to breathe.

"Dan, all of this is her fault," the General said.

"Yeah, I'm *aware* of that," he snapped.

"So we thought you'd want us to . . ." One of the guys gestured toward me.

"Then you thought wrong," Dan said.

"Christ, could you *be* a bigger pussy?" another guy asked him. "Okay, so you think she's hot. So what, man? She's still a backstabbing bitch, in case you hadn't noticed."

"I'd noticed," Dan replied, killing any hope I might have had that he rescued me because he still liked me. He went on, "Haven't enough people already gotten hurt in this War? How many more people have to suffer before you can all be happy?

"And you." He turned his gaze on me. "What are you doing here, Elizabeth Connelly? Didn't you even *consider* that if you came over here in the middle of the day, sashaying around in your Colonial dress, that you'd be in danger? I guess you just never have *any clue* what impact your actions might have, but it doesn't take a genius to figure this one out."

What hurt me most wasn't his tone or his criticism. It was that he called me by my Colonial name. Like he'd stopped caring who I really was. It was only our roles that mattered.

"Well?" he said, staring at me.

"Well?" I repeated blankly.

"Well, what the *hell* was going through your mind?"

"Oh. I thought that was a rhetorical question."

Dan looked furious. "No, when I ask you what you're thinking, it's because I want to *know what you're thinking.*"

And with that sentence, I loved him. I sat on the ground, bruised and muddy and spat-upon, and I just loved him. In a weird way, that was one of the nicest things that anyone had ever said to me.

"Yes," I said, starting to smile. "I knew this was going to happen."

"But you came over here anyway," Dan said.

"Yes. I wanted this to happen."

"Freak," one of the Civil Warriors coughed loudly. Neither Dan nor I glanced at him.

"I wanted this to happen because I wanted to try to make

things even between us," I said. "I'm sorry, Dan. I needed to tell you that before the summer ended. I betrayed your trust and damaged your whole family. I used you to try to win back people who weren't worth winning. I was trying to win an unwinnable war. I'm sorry. And I wanted to give you a chance to hurt me as much as I hurt you."

"Stop it." Dan exhaled a long sigh. "Just stop. I don't *want* to hurt you as much as you hurt me."

"Now that," commented the Civil War General, "is actually real sweet. Why weren't you that sweet to me when *we* were together, Dan?"

"You guys used to go out?" I blurted out, looking up at her.

"When we were *twelve*," Dan said.

"I broke his heart," the General added smugly.

A voice came from behind her. "Excuse me! Yoo-hoo! Civil War people!"

The circle around me opened up to reveal a family of moderners. A mom, a dad, and four scowling little blond boys in matching cowboy hats.

"Can we get a photo with all of you?" the mother asked. "Y'all look so fabulous in your costumes!"

"Of course," we chorused. Even me. If there's one rule that every reenactor knows, it's that you always say yes to a photograph, War or no War, heartbreak or no heartbreak.

The modern woman stared down at me. "You okay there, hon?" she asked.

"Yes," all the Civil Warriors and I said together.

"I fell," I explained, wincing as I stood up and tried to brush some dirt off my gown.

"She fell," the Civil War General agreed.

"Well, hop to. It's photo time!"

The modern woman proceeded to arrange everyone exactly how she wanted us. "Caleb, honey, you kneel here, in front of this lady. That's right. Now, you two, pretend like you're carrying that basket. Ooh, I love that!"

"Do you actually want me in this photo?" I asked the moderner. For one thing, I'd just been beat up, and I looked it. For another, I came from an entirely different century.

She looked puzzled and said, "Of course. Get on in there! Say cheese!"

I wound up placed next to Dan. "I assume this is what it's like to work with Ansel Adams," I muttered. The corner of his mouth twitched in what might have been a smile.

After the moderner had snapped a dozen photos of us and her ferocious-looking towheaded offspring, they left us alone, the children running ahead of their parents and aiming toy guns at one another. I could hear them screeching "Pow-pow! Pow-pow!" even after they'd disappeared from my view.

"I'm going to escort Chelsea out," Dan said. "And she won't come back. Will you?"

"No way," I said. "I'm done here."

We left behind the other Civil Warriors in their field and

headed toward the exit. We must have looked so mismatched together: him in a Civil War costume, me in a Colonial costume, walking side by side.

"There's blood on your gown," he said, staring straight ahead.

I glanced down. He was right. "The summer's practically over," I said. "So, unless I do this next year, I won't even have to wash it off."

His mouth curved a little again, like he was trying not to laugh.

"I'm going to tell you a story," I said. "I'm going to tell you a story that is one-hundred-percent true. Do you remember how I mentioned my ex-boyfriend, Ezra?"

"Sure. The one who sucks."

"He doesn't suck," I said automatically. And then I added, "He's incredibly misguided and careless with other people's feelings, and he has the emotional maturity of a toddler, but *sucks* is such a vulgar word. Anyway, he wanted to get back together with me a couple weeks ago."

Dan shrugged as if to say, *that has nothing to do with me.*

"And I told him no," I went on.

Dan glanced at me.

"I told him no because he hadn't changed at all since we broke up, and I hadn't changed at all, either. Neither of us had changed, either by accident or on purpose, either because we didn't know how, or because we didn't want to, or because we didn't know that we should. So if he and I got back together, then our relationship would have been exactly the same as it was before. And, as it turned out, our relationship wasn't very good."

Dan didn't say anything, but I could tell he was listening.

I took a deep breath. "I know that the things I did to you are as cruel as the things Ezra did to me. What I did was probably worse. But I want you to give me another chance. I'm asking you to give me another chance, because I *have* changed. I am trying to change. I want to do it right this time."

We walked past the ticket booths and stopped at the front gate of Reenactmentland. Dan said, "What about the thing where all of time is happening simultaneously, and all of history is actually one moment, so you can't ever move beyond it? Or did you forget about all of that?"

"No, I still believe that," I said. "I believe that history is always here, and we can't ignore it, and we can't escape it. But people aren't history. Ezra used to love me, that was true, he meant it when he said it. And then he stopped loving me, and that's also true—but that doesn't mean that he *never* loved me. Just like how I used to love him. And now . . . now I don't, anymore. So that's how I know that people can change, if they want to. And I want to."

Dan looked at me for a while, like he was memorizing me.

I cleared my throat. "Anyway, that's all I've got. Also, I'm sorry, if I didn't remember to say that."

"You might have mentioned it once or twice," he said.

"Great. I'm going to go back to work, and then I'm going to put ice on these bruises, and then—well, I'm not sure what comes next, but, whatever it is, I'm going to do it. I am *all about* doing whatever comes next."

"School starts next week," Dan stated.

"I know."

"And then you won't work at Essex anymore."

"Until next summer, maybe," I said.

"And I won't work at Reenactmentland anymore."

"Until next summer, maybe."

He shook his head forcefully. *"Ever."*

"Okay, ever. So we'll never be enemies again."

Dan took my hand. "That's a lot to look forward to." He kissed me on the cheek, lingering there for a moment before pulling back. "I'll see you soon, Chelsea Glaser."

Then he turned to walk back into Reenactmentland, and I turned to walk back to Essex. We kept holding on to each other's hands for as long as we could.

Labor Day weekend means many things: the last days of freedom before school starts. The last days that my friends and I work at Essex. The last days that Dan and his friends work at Reenactmentland. And the first days of the Virginia Renaissance Faire, which runs from Labor Day through Halloween. This year, for the first time ever, the Ren Faire wasn't taking place at the fairgrounds in Richmond. Instead, it was going to be set less than a mile down the road from Essex, and from Reenactmentland.

There is nobody farbier than these Ren Faire interpreters. I don't have to know anything about sixteenth-century history to know how badly they're misrepresenting it. The women there blatantly wear modern makeup. Their costumes are made out of polyester and cotton. There are visible speakers all around the fairegrounds, piping in horrifying chamber music.

My parents took me to the Ren Faire one weekend when I was little, because they thought it would be a fun family outing. When we saw the stage of half-naked dancers, we immediately turned around and left. Not because my parents thought it was inappropriate for their child to see barely dressed women. Just because they thought it was inappropriate for their child to see such offensive historical inaccuracies.

And now the Ren Fairies were here, infiltrating Essex. Practically in our backyards.

So Labor Day also marked the second War Council of the season. Once again, the top Civil Warriors met with the top Colonials at the ice cream shop. But this time, the issue on the table was, How can we combine our powers to take down the Ren Faire?

"A jousting match," the Civil War General was saying with conviction. "We sneak in one of our people, enter him into the jousting competition, and then, *boom*! He knocks a Ren

Fairie off his horse. Maybe even stabs him through the heart with a sword."

Everyone pondered this suggestion.

"I see some issues here," I began.

"Yeah," agreed Bryan, our new man in charge. "Like, how would we convince them that our man is really a Renaissance jouster?"

"Never mind," I muttered.

"Well, how did y'all sneak in as Confederate soldiers?" the Civil War General asked, making a note on a pad of paper. "Because if we could just use that technique . . ."

"I'll *tell* you," Patience beamed.

"Also, does anyone here know how to fence?" Ezra wondered.

Nearly everyone in the room raised their hands.

Fiona and I left them to their plotting and went up to the counter to order ice cream.

"What was that thing you said once?" I asked her. "Like, 'My enemy is actually my friend if I have another enemy who is also the enemy of my first enemy'?"

Fiona shrugged. "I might have said 'enemy' a few more times than that. But yeah, it's still true."

The ice cream scooper was the same one who had been working during the previous War Council.

"You guys came back," he noted, dipping my Moose Tracks in sprinkles. "I guess you must really like ice cream, huh?"

I glanced at Fiona.

"We do," she assured him. "We really like ice cream."

"Too bad it's almost fall," he commented as he rang us up. "This is just about the end of ice cream season."

"No," I said. "It's always ice cream season."

We took our cones to the door. Dan stood up. "Can I come with you guys?"

Fiona and I nodded. "Of course."

I pushed open the door, and the little bells on top of it tinkled. Everyone paused in their strategizing for a moment to stare at Fiona, Dan, and me.

"Aren't you going to stay and help us plan how to take down those farbs?" Bryan asked, his eyes bulging.

"No," we answered. We took our ice cream and walked outside together into the fresh air.

And that was the summer. All these moments are in the past now, but they don't disappear, and I don't forget. They are still part of me whenever I drive around with Fiona, whenever I jump on my trampoline with Dan, whenever I see Ezra and Maggie together.

Sometimes still I am bowled over by these memories. But then I pick myself up, and I keep moving forward, one foot in front of the other, relentlessly into the present.

ACKNOWLEDGMENTS

Thank you to Anica Rissi, an editor of extraordinary vision and sensitivity, and to the entire team at Simon Pulse, for everything they have done and continue to do for my writing career.

To Stephen Barbara, one of the world's great agents. I would work on *any* project with you.

To my writing partner, Rebecca Serle. I just want to say that you're beautiful; you're looking incredible; girl, you're making everybody's day.

To Kendra Levin and Emily Heddleson for their constant friendship and keen editorial guidance. You are *amazing*.

To Katie Hanson, who has been unwavering in her enthusiasm for my writing, and in her willingness to let me take over the entire living room with my notes.

To Jeremy Glaser, without whom my protagonist would have no arbitrary time constraint, and no last name.

To my history experts: Andrew and Caddie Martin, the Freedom Trail Foundation, and the Colonial Williamsburg Foundation, particularly Patti Vaticano and Kelly McEvoy. Any historical facts that I got right are thanks to these sources; any historical inaccuracies are my own inventions.

I'd like to acknowledge the influence of the writings of Benedict Anderson, Erich Auerbach, and Walter Benjamin on Chelsea's musings on history and the simultaneity of time.

And, as always, thank you to my parents and friends for their love and support.

When the pressures of prep school build up,
cracks can appear in the funniest places.

"Brilliant, poignant, and straight-up hilarious."
—LAUREN OLIVER,
bestselling author of *Before I Fall*

LEILA SALES

mostly good girls

"Pretty darn funny—and impossible to put down."
—*New York Review of Books*

From mostly good girls
by LEILA SALES

My Junior Year To-Do List,
by Violet Tunis

1. Get a perfect score on my PSATs.
2. Get A-minuses or better in all my classes.
3. Do many awesome projects with Katie.
    (Note: Projects must be awesomer than
    anything we did last year.)
4. Improve this school's literary magazine.
    At least to the point where I don't have
    to pretend like I am not really the
    editor, like the editor is someone else
    who happens to share my name
    (huge coincidence).
5. Pass my driving test.
6. Maybe become famous for something,
    so that people everywhere will know and
    respect me?
7. Make Scott Walsh fall in love with me.

Like a triple date.
Kind of.

We were late to our ice cream date with Scott. This was Katie's fault. She lives only a few blocks from Coolidge Corner, but she insisted that we leave her house nearly fifteen minutes late, because we didn't want to seem "overeager."

"If we're there right at eight o'clock, then Scott will be able to tell that we never hang out with boys," she reasoned.

"And that's a problem?" I asked. I was standing by the Putnams' front door, holding my purse and cardigan, while Katie lolled on the living room couch with Buster, rolling his ears around her fingers.

"Yeah," she said, "because then we seem like losers."

"But we *are* losers," I said.

"But we can't let him *know* that. You're supposed to lie to boys."

"Did you read that in *National Geographic* too?"

Katie wrinkled her forehead and stared up at the ceiling, like she couldn't quite recall. "Nooo," she said. "I think I just made that up."

I grabbed her arm and hauled her out the door.

"Bye, Mom!" she shouted upstairs as I pulled her away. "I'll be home in a couple hours!"

I shouted, "Unless Scott wants us to stay later, in which case we'll stay out!"

"Dumb." Katie shook her head as we headed down her block. "If Scott wants us to stay later, then we'll *definitely* have to leave. You're always supposed to keep men wanting more."

"Wow," I said. "You're just a fount of wisdom about the male psyche tonight, aren't you?" And then, "Just because you aced the PSATs doesn't actually mean you know everything about everything."

Katie slid me a sidelong glance, and I thought maybe she was going to apologize for keeping her score a secret from me, but instead all she said was, "I know."

"Were you ever planning on telling me?" I tried not to sound hurt.

Katie threw her head back, looking up at the stars. "It's just the PSATs."

Because I guess when you already have as much going for you as Katie has, the PSATs really don't matter to you. Just another astonishing feat in her string of astonishing feats. Getting a perfect score on the PSATs is only about the hundredth-most interesting thing about her. You know. Yawn.

I still felt like it mattered. But I didn't say anything else about it as we walked down the road. If I was upset about this, that was my problem. What was Katie supposed to do— apologize for being who she is? It's not her fault she's perfect and I'm not.

By the time we reached Coolidge Corner, it was already twenty minutes past eight. Because we're not overeager, see. Hilary was sitting with two boys on the hood of a parked car while Scott stood talking to them. Hilary threw us a dirty look—the sort of look you'd give your friends when they're twenty minutes late to meeting you, so you've had to make pleasant conversation with three guys all on your own.

"Hey, Katie," Scott said. "Hi, Violet."

With that one greeting from Scott, all thoughts of Katie's PSAT scores vanished from my consciousness. "Hi," I replied in a totally natural, mature way, while inside my head I was like, *Oh my God, Scott said my name. My name was said by Scott. Hmm, did anyone say my name? Oh, wait, Scott did!* Etc. I tried to archive this moment in my mind so that I could replay it for the rest of my life, like the next time Spanish class got particularly boring.

"This is Raymond," Hilary said, gesturing to the guy on her left, "and this one"—guy on right—"is Dale."

I smiled at them in a cursory way. They both looked like typical Harper Woodbane boys in their loafers, expensive jeans, polo shirts (but no ties; it's the weekend), and slightly gelled hair. Raymond's hair was shaved a little too much, so his head looked square, while Dale had some acne. I'm not claiming they were ugly or anything—I mean, they go to Harper Woodbane; you're practically not *allowed* to be ugly there. Every student at Harper Woodbane has to look clean-cut and wholesome and athletic all the time, which Raymond and Dale did. All I'm saying about them is, they were no Scott Walsh.

Scott is a solid six inches taller than me and trim without ever looking too gangly. He has dark brown hair that I have to restrain myself from tousling and a smile that could sell toothpaste by the bushel. He always stands and moves like he's perfectly at ease in his body, and also I am obsessed with the casual-preppy way he dresses. And that's just what he's like on the *outside.*

I couldn't understand why someone who looked like Scott would hang out with two normal-looking guys. For that matter, I couldn't understand why Scott would hang out with me. I'm not very skinny, and my hair is never quite curly and never quite straight, and most of the time I am wearing uncool shoes. Scott should be hanging out exclusively with supermodels. They are probably the only people he can relate to, in terms of attractiveness.

"I was just telling Hilary about drama class on Thursday," Scott said to Katie and me as we leaned against the car. "We're doing *The Tempest*, but we theorize that Mr. Moritz has never actually read it. So on Thursday we made up this word—'dink'—and then we inserted it into our lines as many times as we could. Just to see if he would notice. Like, 'We are such stuff as dreams are made on, and our little dink is rounded with a sleep.' It got to the point where everyone was saying it at least once per line, and Mr. Moritz *never noticed*, at least until Chris started laughing. And then he asked what was going on, but all Chris could say was 'dink.'"

Everyone laughed appreciatively, except for me, because I was busy searching my brain for some intelligent and witty response. I think this is how conversation usually goes—someone tells a story, and then you reply to it, and, just like that, you have a conversation. But I couldn't think of a single reply to Scott's story. I was too worried I'd say something boring. I noticed that Katie didn't say anything either, so she must have been having the same problem as me, because Katie *always* has something to say.

Fortunately, the boys didn't have this difficulty. Raymond

said, "Dink!" and Dale said, "Mr. Moritz is an idiot," and Hilary said, "Let's get ice cream," and suddenly we were all headed into the ice cream parlor, while I was still brainstorming potential clever responses to Scott's story. ("How did you come up with the word 'dink?'" Who cares. "I like *The Tempest.*" *Double* who cares. "To be or not to dink?" No, don't say that; that's not even from *The Tempest.*)

We got our ice cream and sat down at a table in the corner. Girls on one bench, boys opposite us. Katie pulled out her cell phone, typed something into it, and put it back in her purse. An instant later, my phone buzzed in my pocket. I pulled it out, and there was a text from Katie. It read, If this is a date, aren't they supposed to pay for our ice cream? I rolled my eyes at her.

"Wait a second," said Scott. "Did you"—he pointed to Katie—"just text her?"—a point to me. (*Oh my God, Scott just pointed at me! See that finger? It pointed AT ME!*)

"Uh," Katie said. "Maybe?"

"Would you care to share with the rest of the table?" Scott asked me and Katie. I shut my phone and shook my head. "Secrets, secrets are no fun," he admonished us, wagging his finger, and I giggled. "All right." Here Scott pulled his own phone out of his pocket. "Give me your number," he said to me.

"What?" I shrieked. I stared at him across my cup of mint chocolate chip. I was aware that boys sometimes ask girls for their phone numbers—I had seen this happen in television shows—but I didn't know this was the sort of thing that could actually happen to me.

"Your number," Scott repeated in a soothing tone, like I was an easily frightened feral animal. "I want to text you too."

"Oh." Right. I told him my number. He typed rapidly on his keypad. A moment later my phone vibrated again. It said, tell me what katie texted you.

I laughed. "What?" Hilary asked, trying to read over my shoulder. "What did he say?"

"Nothing." I hid my phone under the table and smiled at Scott. He smiled back at me. (*Scott Walsh smiled at me! Scott Walsh LOVES me! He obviously wants to be my BOYFRIEND!* Etc.)

I texted him back, Never. Secrets, secrets are so fun.

Scott's phone buzzed, then a minute later Hilary's phone went off, then Raymond's, then mine again, and all of a sudden we were all texting one another.

After a few minutes of texting back and forth, we turned it into a game. The goal was to send a text that would make another person at the table laugh, without laughing yourself. You got a point every time your text made someone else laugh, and lost a point every time you were the one laughing. We all sat there, staring fixedly at our cell phones, our lips pursed as we tried to hold back giggles.

Katie kept getting me because she knows exactly what I find funny. At one point she texted, Aren't you glad we didn't show up naked? and I laughed so hard Hilary suggested that I lose *two* points.

Scott was best at not laughing. It must have been all his theater experience. He looked no more amused by our texts than he would have been by reading stock reports. Somehow, this made me want to make him laugh even more, so I bombarded him with text messages.

What, you don't laugh? I texted.

Then, You have ice cream on your nose.

Still nothing. Have you ever noticed that Dale looks kind of like an elf?

Dink.

That last one made Scott crack, finally.

"Who sent it?" Hilary demanded. "Who gets the point?"

Scott pointed at me again (obviously, our relationship was progressing by leaps and bounds). "Violet," he said, still chuckling. "Funny girl."

I kicked my legs a little bit under the table, but not so hard that anyone could tell. Probably. And I sent one last text from my cell, this one to Katie: Who just called me funny? Oh, wait, Scott did! OMG. Etc.

Killing my game

It was getting late. We had finished our ice cream and were all hanging out on the hood of Scott's car again. Eventually he said, "I need to get going."

"Me too," we all chorused, like every one of us had suddenly remembered a pressing engagement at eleven o'clock on a Saturday.

"Can your mom still drive me home?" I asked Katie.

She checked the time on her phone and winced. "You might have to spend the night, Vi."

I made a face. "Really? I have to be up early tomorrow. I'm babysitting for Ronnie."

"Sounds like a way fun Sunday," Katie said, who knows that the only thing I like less than babysitting for annoying kids is waking up early to do it.

"Where are you trying to get back to?" Scott asked me.

"Arlington," I replied.

"I live in Arlington too," Scott said. "I can drive you home."

"*Really?*" I squealed. "Oh my God, that would be *amazing*!"

He laughed. "You *really* don't want to spend the night at Katie's, do you?"

Right, Vi. Maybe try for a little subtlety? "Oh, no, I do—I would—but getting a ride home—like, that's great!"

Um, that may have been subtle, but it wasn't *English*.

"I do have to stop for gas on the way home," Scott told me. "And pick up some stuff from the store."

I bobbed my head furiously. "No problem. Gas. Store. If you're giving me a ride, you know, whatever." And then we could spend even *longer* together! Time getting gas! Time at the store! Time together, just me and Scott!

"Or, if you want, I can drive you," Raymond piped up. "I live in Lexington, so your house is on my way. And I don't need to stop for gas or anything."

Before I had a chance to speak, Scott replied, "That'd be perfect. Thanks, man."

"Where in Arlington do you live?" Raymond asked me, pulling car keys out of his jeans pocket.

I stared at Raymond blankly. It had taken my brain approxi-

strict about that sort of thing. They say if they're investing this much in my education, they want me to get the most out of it. And not waste precious studying time on boys."

That sounded impressively genuine.

"Man, I'm sorry," Raymond said emotionally.

"Yeah. But if that ever changes, well, I'll give you a call. Okay, thanks again, bye!" I flung myself out of Raymond's car like I was rescuing myself from quicksand. He drove off. He wasn't even halfway down the road before I pulled out my phone and called Katie.

"Hey, lady," she answered.

"Oh my God," I said. "Raymond just asked me out."

"Damn," Katie said. *"Why?"*

"I have no idea." I explained to her the whole conversation, ending with my turning my parents into celibacy-obsessed, overcontrolling nutcases.

"Great job," Katie said. "Great escape, really, massive style there. But did it occur to you, Violet, that now every guy at Harper Woodbane will think you're not allowed to date until college?"

"Oh," I said. "Not really."

"Every guy," she repeated. "Including Scott Walsh."

I sank down onto my front stoop, frowning into the night-time. "All the more Scott Walsh for you, then, right?"

"Oh, right, I'm sure that his first move once he hears you're off the market will be to ask me out. But this was this was exactly the sort of discussion that boys used to have back in sixth grade. I was relieved to see I hadn't missed much over the years.

When we finally jerked to a stop in front of my house, I unbuckled my seat belt, stopped gripping the car door, and said, "Thanks again for the ride, Raymond."

"No problem," he said. "Hey, do you want to go out sometime?"

"Um." I was already halfway out of the vehicle. "What?"

"Go out," he said. "Sometime."

"Like on a date?"

"Sure," Raymond said. "Yeah. I guess. Like on a date."

"No," I answered quickly, because, like, *why* would I want to go on a date with Raymond? Not that there's anything obviously wrong with him, but he is just *some guy*, and merely being a) male and b) my age is not reason enough for me to date someone. What I wanted to say to him was, "Are you honestly so delusional as to believe that we have *anything* in common? Did you consider your fifteen-minute-long soliloquy about sports to be a *successful conversation*?"

But I couldn't say that aloud. Because that is mean. So instead what I said, to soften the blow of my rejection, was, "Thanks for asking, but I'm actually not allowed to date."

Total lie.

"Really?" he asked.

Absolutely not. "Absolutely." I nodded. "My parents are

Turns out Raymond is not a great driver. I wouldn't even describe him as a *good* driver. Every time there was a red light, he slammed on the brakes just before reaching it, so we came skidding to a halt, slamming me against my seat belt. I couldn't think of a tactful way to explain to him, "Look, the light turns *yellow* before it turns red, so if you see a *yellow* light, you might want to consider *slowing the hell down.*"

It did make me more hopeful for my own driving test in January, though. If Raymond could pass his, then it can't be that hard.

"How long have you had your license?" I asked, like I was making polite conversation and not just trying to figure out how likely we were to get into a car crash.

"Nearly four months," he said.

"And how long have you had your car?" I asked.

"Yeah, same. Four months. What good's a license without a car, right?"

"Totally," I said, like all our parents give us cars just because we pass the driving test.

I didn't have much to say to Raymond after that (other than "*Be careful that's a stop sign!*"). But it didn't matter, since he kept up a steady chatter about sports, including Harper Woodbane's upcoming game against Exeter, and how well he had done at fantasy baseball this year. I hadn't attended a coed school since I was twelve years old, but as I recalled,

mately one eighth of a second to construct a fantasy about Scott driving me home and gradually, over the course of the fifteen-minute trip between Brookline and Arlington, realizing that I was the only one for him. We would have stopped for gas, and he would have treated me to candy from the convenience store. He would have walked me to my front door and then kissed me under the front-porch light. Now this fantasy was suddenly not coming true, and I couldn't process it.

But there was no way out now. I couldn't say, "No, thanks, Raymond, I'll sleep over at Katie's," because I had just been going on at Scott about how *great* it was to get a ride home. And I couldn't say, "No, thanks, Raymond, I'd rather Scott drove me," because, um, then everyone would know I had a giant crush on him. And that's supposed to be a secret.

I glanced at Katie, who shrugged helplessly, and then I put on my "good sport" smile—the sort of smile I use when I get a B on a paper I worked really hard on and I want everyone to know that *it's no problem, I think a B is JUST GREAT, honestly*—and I said to Raymond, "Thank you. That is very kind of you to offer."

So everyone said good night, and Katie and Dale walked off in opposite directions toward their respective homes, and Scott and Hilary took off in their cars, and I buckled myself into the passenger seat of Raymond's Jeep.

LEILA SALES had the idea for *Past Perfect* after working as a costumed Colonial guide on Boston's Freedom Trail. Her other jobs have included camp counselor, book-seller, babysitter, and now editor and writer. Her dream job, of course, is professional ice cream connoisseur. She lives and writes in Brooklyn, New York. Visit her at leilasales.com.

pretty poorly played on your part," Katie said. "I might even call it a game killer."

"Would you?"

"Totally. Total game killer."

"Because my game was just so spot-on beforehand?"

"Oh, yeah," Katie said. "Your game was smokin'."

I groaned. "I hate everything."